"I love you, Jenny."

She snatched her hand away. "Love isn't built on deception and lies, Cage. You've been lying to me for months. What do you want me to do?"

"Love me back."

"You made a fool of me!"

"I made a woman of you!" He spun away from her, making an effort to control his temper. "If you'd stop sifting everything through your filter of propriety and conscience and guilt, you'd see things clearly. That night was the best thing that ever happened to either of us. It freed us both."

"Free?" she cried. "Free? I'll have to bear the burden of that night for the rest of my life."

A SECRET SPLENDOR

Arden Gentry was determined to find the son she'd
been forced to give away at birth. But first she
would have to introduce herself to the baby's
father—and tell him who she was.

ABOVE AND BEYOND

A terrorist bomb had left marine Trevor Rule
scarred and broken. The man he'd traded bunks
with that night hadn't been so lucky. Now Trevor
had a responsibility to his friend's lovely widow, a
woman he knew could make him whole—unless he
told her the truth. . . .

HONOR BOUND

As Aislinn Andrews opened her mouth to scream, a
hard hand clamped over her face and she found
herself face-to-face with Lucas Greywolf, a lean,
lethal-looking Navajo and escaped convict who
swore he wouldn't hurt her—*if* she helped him.

LED ASTRAY

Cage Hendren was a hell-raiser; danger followed
him like a shadow. But it was his missionary
brother who was killed, who left behind a
brokenhearted fiancée—the one woman Cage had
always wanted. . . .

Previously published under
the pseudonym Erin St. Claire.

Led Astray

Published by Silhouette Books New York
America's Publisher of Contemporary Romance

SILHOUETTE BOOKS
300 East 42nd St., New York, N.Y. 10017

LED ASTRAY

ISBN: 0-373-48256-6

Printed in the U.S.A.

Chapter 1

If they didn't stop talking about it, she was going to scream.

But they weren't going to stop talking about it. It was the one subject on everyone's mind and the chance of them switching to another was remote. The topic under discussion had carried them through the pot roast dinner. It was the type of meal usually reserved for Sundays, as though this were an occasion to be celebrated rather than lamented.

Sarah had outdone herself in preparing the food. There had even been hot, fluffy yeast rolls fresh from the oven to dip in the thick, savory beef gravy and a homemade pudding that was so rich, the calories fairly shouted.

But Jenny's tastebuds might as well have been dead for all she had enjoyed the meal. Her tongue seemed to cleave to the roof of her mouth with every bite, and her throat rebelled against swallowing.

Now, over coffee, which Sarah was pouring into the china cups with the yellow primrose pattern, they were still talking about Hal's imminent trip to Central America. The trip would encompass an unspecified period of time, virtually make him an outlaw, and probably imperil his life.

Yet everyone was excited about it, especially Hal, whose cheeks were flushed with enthusiasm. His brown eyes shone with expectation. "It's a tremendous undertaking. But if it weren't for the courage of those poor souls in Monterico, everything we've done and will do would be in vain. The honor belongs to them."

Sarah touched her younger son's cheek affectionately as she resumed her chair after refilling everyone's cup. "But you've instigated this underground railroad to help them escape. I think it's wonderful. Simply wonderful. But—" her lower lip began to tremble "—you will be careful, won't you? You won't really be in danger?"

Hal patted the soft hand that clung to his arm. "Mother, I've told you a thousand times that the political refugees will be waiting for us at the border of Monterico. We're only picking them up, escorting them through Mexico, and—"

"Illegally smuggling them into the United States," Cage supplied dryly.

Sarah glanced at Hal's older brother sourly.

Accustomed to such disdain, Cage remained unaffected by his mother's disapproving glance. He stretched his jean-clad legs far out in front of him as he slouched in his chair in a way that had always irritated Sarah. During his youth she had harped on his table posture until she was blue. Her lectures had never done any good.

He crossed one booted ankle over the other and eyed his brother from beneath a shelf of dust-colored eyebrows. "I wonder if you'll be so fired up with fanatic zeal when the Border Patrol slams your ass in jail."

"If you can't use better language than that, kindly leave the table," Reverend Bob Hendren snapped.

"Sorry, Dad." Unrepentantly Cage sipped his coffee.

"If Hal goes to jail," the pastor went on, "it will be for a good cause, something he believes in."

"That's not what you said the night you had to come bail me out," Cage reminded his father.

"You were arrested for drunkenness."

Cage grinned. "I believe in getting drunk occasionally."

"Cage, please," Sarah said with a long suffering sigh. "For once try and behave."

Jenny stared down at her hands. She hated these family scenes. Cage could be provoking, but she felt in this instance he was right to bluntly point out the risks of Hal's involvement in this venture. Besides, even she could see that Cage's derision was a response to his parents' obvious preference for Hal, who shifted uneasily in his chair. Though he basked in Bob's and Sarah's approval, their blatant favoritism made him uncomfortable as well.

Cage relented by erasing the smirk from his handsome face, but he continued arguing. "It's just that this labor of love, this mission of Hal's, seems like a good way to get killed. Why is he risking his neck in some banana republic where they shoot first and ask questions later?"

"You couldn't possibly understand Hal's motives," Bob said with a dismissive wave of his hand toward his elder son.

Cage sat up straighter and propped his arms on the table, leaning forward for emphasis. "I can understand his wanting to liberate people marked for death, yes. But I don't think this is the way to do it." Impatiently he ran a hand through his dark blond hair. "An underground railroad, escorting political refugees through Mexico, illegal entry into the United States," he said scoffingly as he enumerated the stages of Hal's mission by ticking them off his fingertips.

"And how are they going to survive once you get them here to Texas? Where will they live? What will they do? Have you thought of jobs, shelter, food, medicine, clothing? Don't be naive enough to think that everyone will welcome them with open arms just because they're from a strife-torn country. They'll be thought of as wetbacks just as all illegal aliens are. And treated as such.''

"We're trusting all that to God's will,'' Hal said a little uncertainly. His steadfastness always faltered under Cage's pragmatism. Just when Hal thought one of his convictions was unshakable, Cage shook it—to the core. Just like an earthquake, Cage's arguments opened up fissures in beliefs Hal had previously thought of as sound and indestructible. Hal prayed about it often and always came to the conclusion that God used Cage to test him. Or was Cage's astuteness a gift of the devil used to tempt him? His parents would no doubt opt for the second theory.

"Yeah, well, I hope God has more common sense than you have.''

"That's enough!'' Bob said sharply.

Cage hunched his shoulders and propping his elbows on the tabletop, carried his coffee cup to his mouth. He didn't use the tiny handle. Jenny doubted his long finger would fit in that narrow china crook. He held the cup by folding both his hands around it.

He was out of place in the parsonage kitchen. It had crispy ruffled curtains at the windows, a pastel plaid yellow vinyl floor, and a glass-fronted china cabinet that held delicate serving pieces that were treasured and used only on holidays.

Cage shrank the kitchen until its coziness became clutter. And it wasn't that he was inordinately muscular or tall. Physically Cage and Hal were much the same. From a distance and from the back, the brothers were almost indistinguishable, except that Cage was slightly more robust than his younger brother. That added brawniness was due more to the differences in their occupations than to a whim of heredity.

But there the similarity between the two ended. The main difference between them was one of attitude. Cage had a presence that made any room seem smaller when he entered it. An indefinable *something* surrounded him like an aura and was as much a part of him as his darkly tanned skin.

Indoors he was like an oversized body straining at the seams of clothing that was too small. He seemed to be squeezed into most rooms, as though what he needed around him was wide open spaces, earth, and sky. An essence of the outdoors clung to him, as if he carried the wind inside on his clothes and in his hair.

Jenny had never gotten close enough to him to find out, but she thought his skin must smell like sunshine. The ravages of long hours in the sun were evident on his face, particularly around his tawny eyes. Those web-fine lines made him appear older than he was. But then he had crammed a lot of living into his thirty-two years.

And tonight, as always wherever Cage went, there was likely to be discord if not downright warfare. Mischief and malcontent followed him like a shadow. He was a predator, stalking through the jungle, upsetting the peaceable inhabitants, raising shackles and ruffling feathers and rustling the stillness even when he wasn't looking for trouble.

"You're certain you've worked out all the rendezvous points?" Sarah asked. She was distressed that Cage had spoiled her perfect farewell dinner for Hal, but was valiantly trying to ignore her recalcitrant son and set things back on an even keel.

As Hal rehashed his travels plans for at least the hundredth time, Jenny unobtrusively began to clear the table. As she leaned over Hal's shoulder to pick up his plate, he took her hand, squeezed it, raised it to his lips, and kissed the back of it, but all without a pause in his zealous dialogue.

She longed to bend down and kiss the crown of his blond head, to clasp it to her breasts and plead with him not to go. But of course she didn't. Such an action would be outrageous and everyone at the table would think she had gone stark, staring mad.

She suppressed her emotions and finished carrying the dishes to the sink. No one offered to help. No one even took notice of her. It had been Jenny's chore to do the dinner dishes since she had come to live in the parsonage.

They were still talking fifteen minutes later when she dried her hands on the cuptowel and neatly draped it over the peg beside the sink. She slipped out the back door and went down the porch steps. She crossed the yard to the white rail fence and leaned her arms over the top.

It was a lovely night, almost windless, which was a rare blessing in West Texas. There was only a trace of dust in the air. A huge round moon looked like a shiny gummed sticker someone had pressed against a black felt sky. What stars the city lights didn't diminish were large and near.

It was a night for lovers to be clinging, snuggling close whispering outlandishly silly and romantic things to each other. It wasn't a night to be saying good-bye. Or if good-byes must be said, they should be overflowing with passion and regret, seasoned with endearments rather than the details of an itinerary.

Jenny was restless, as though she had an itch she couldn't quite locate.

The screened back door squeaked open and then closed with the soft slapping sound of old wood against old wood. Jenny turned to see Cage sauntering down the steps. She brought her head back around as he moved to stand beside her at the fence.

Without speaking, he fished in his breast pocket for a pack of cigarettes, shook it, and, closing his lips around one, drew it from the foil top. He lit it with a lighter whose flame flared briefly in front of his face. He clicked the lighter off and returned it and the cigarettes to his pocket as he drew the tobacco smoke deep into his lungs.

"Those things are killers," Jenny said, still staring straight ahead.

Cage turned his head and stared at her silently for a moment, then his body came around until he was leaning with his back against the fence. "I'm not dead yet and I started smoking when I was about eleven."

She glanced up at him, smiling, but shaking her head. "What a shame. Think what that's done to your lungs. You should quit."

"Yeah?" he said with that one-sided lazy grin that never failed to trip the hearts of women—young, old, single, or married. There wasn't a female in La Bota who could remain indifferent to Cage Hendren's smile. Some paused to consider exactly what it implied. Most knew. *I'm male, you're female, and that's all that needs to be said.*

"Yes, you should quit. But you're not going to. I've heard Sarah ask you to stop smoking for years."

"Only because she didn't like nasty ashtrays and the lingering smell of tobacco smoke. She never asked me to quit because she was worried about my health." There was the merest glimmer of bitternness in his amber eyes. Someone with less sensitivity than Jenny wouldn't have noticed it.

"*I* worry about your health," she said.

"Do you, now?"

"Yes."

"Are you asking me to quit smoking on that basis?"

She knew he was only teasing her, but she played along. Her chin lifted a notch and she said decisively, "Yes."

He tossed the cigarette into the dirt and ground it out with the toe of his boot. "Done. There. I've quit."

She laughed. Little did she know how remarkably pretty she was when she threw her head back like that and laughed. Her throat arched gracefully, showing off her honey-toned complexion. Her soft brown hair swung free and silky against her shoulders. Her green eyes sparkled. Her pert nose wrinkled delightfully. She had a whiskey-husky laugh that was flagrantly seductive, though Jenny never realized it.

But Cage did. His body responded to the sultry sound and there wasn't a damn thing he could do about it. He lowered his eyes to her petal-soft lips and glistening teeth.

"That's the first time I've seen you smile tonight," he said.

Jenny sobered instantly. "I don't feel much like smiling."

"Because Hal's leaving?"

"Of course."

"Because you've had to postpone the wedding again?"

She ducked her head and scraped the fence rail with her thumb nail. "Certainly, though that's not important."

"Why the hell not?" Cage demanded roughly. "I thought a woman's wedding was the most important day in her life. At least to a woman like you, it is."

"It is, but when measured against this mission Hal's going on—"

Cage muttered a scandalously obscene word beneath his breath which effectively silenced her speech. "What about the other times?" he asked brusquely.

"You mean the other postponements?"

"Yeah."

"Hal had to get his doctorate. It was important that he finish his dissertation before we got married and...and started a family."

As always, Cage had made her stammer like an idiot. She wanted to ask him not to stand too close, but he wasn't *that* close. He only seemed to be. He had always had this effect on her. He caused her to go breathless, to suffer a slight vertigo. She felt a need to clasp her hands tightly together, to hold herself intact as though she might fly apart if she didn't. He unsettled her. She had never found a reason why that should be so, but it was. Tonight especially, when her nerves were already ragged and her carefully maintained control was frayed, she found it difficult to meet Cage's intent stare. He saw too much.

"When did you and Hal actually start dating?" he asked abruptly.

"Dating?" Her tone implied that the word wasn't part of her vocabulary.

"Yeah, you know, going out. Holding hands. Necking at the drive-in. Dating. It must have been while I was up at Tech, because I don't remember it."

"Well, we never actually *started* dating. It just...just evolved, I guess you'd say. We were constantly together. We were considered a couple."

"Jenny Fletcher," Cage said, crossing his arms over his wide chest and staring at her incredulously, "do you mean to tell me that you've never had a date with anyone else?"

"Not because I wasn't asked!" she retorted defensively.

Cage put up his hands in surrender. "Whoa, girl. I wasn't hinting that. You could have had all the young bucks in town panting after you."

"I didn't want them panting after me. It sounds very undignified."

She blushed becomingly and Cage couldn't resist rubbing the back of his hand against her cheek. She averted her head and his hand fell to his side. "I figure a man could lose his dignity over you, Jenny," he said reflectively, then picked up in a lighter vein, "but you didn't go out with any other guys because that would have been unfaithful to Hal."

"That's right."

"Even while the two of you were at Texas Christian?"

"Yes."

"Hm." Cage automatically reached for his pack of cigarettes, remembered, and stuffed them back in his pocket. Never did his eyes leave Jenny. "When did Hal propose?"

"A few years ago. I think we were in our senior year at TCU."

"You think? You don't remember? How could you forget an earth-moving moment like that?"

"Don't tease me, Cage."

"The earth *didn't* move?"

"It isn't like it is in the movies."

"You've been seeing the wrong kind of movies." His eyebrows bobbed up and down lecherously.

"I know what kind you see," she said, slanting him an accusing glance. "The kind Sammy Mac Higgins shows in the back room of his pool hall after hours."

Cage tried to keep a straight face at her lofty tone, gave up the attempt, and let that dazzling smile break across his features. "Ladies are invited. Wanna come with me sometime?"

"No!"

"Why not?"

"Why not? I wouldn't be caught dead seeing that kind of movie. They're disgusting."

He leaned forward and taunted, "How do you know if you've never seen one?" She punched him on the shoulder and he moved back, but not without first filling his head with her fresh, flowery scent. Gradually his smile faded to a somber expression as he searched her eyes. "Jenny, when did Hal ask you to marry him?"

"I told you, it—"

"Where were you? Describe the surroundings. What happened? Did he go down on bended knee? Was it in the backseat of his car? In the daytime? At night? In bed? When?"

"Stop it! I told you I don't remember."

"Did he *ever*?" His voice was so quiet that she snapped to attention.

"What do you mean?"

"Did he ever voice the words aloud? 'Jenny, will you marry me?'"

Her eyes fell away from his. "We've always known we were going to get married."

"Who's always known? You? Hal? Mother and Dad?"

"Yes. Everybody." She turned her back on him and started back toward the house. "I've got to go in and—"

His warm, hard hand closed around her wrist and brought her up short. "Tell Hal not to go on this fool's trip."

She spun around. "What?"

"You heard me. Tell him to stay at home, where he belongs."

"I can't."

"You're the only one he might listen to. You don't want him to go, do you? Do you?" he repeated with more emphasis when she failed to answer.

"No!" she cried, wrenching her hand free of his. "But I can't stand between Hal and a mission he feels that God has called him to do."

"Does he love you?"

"Yes."

"And you love him."

"Yes."

"You want to marry him and have a house and babies and all the trimmings, right?"

"That's my business. Hal's and mine."

"Dammit, I'm not trying to interfere into your personal life. I'm trying to keep my kid brother from getting blown away. Now, whether anybody likes it or not, I'm still a member of this family and you're going to answer me."

She quelled beneath his anger, but felt ashamed, too, for shutting him out of family matters as his parents so often did. When it boiled down to it, she was the oustider, not Cage. She met his eyes levelly. "Of course that's what I want, Cage. I've waited years to get married."

"All right, then," he said more calmly, "put your foot down. Issue an ultimatum. Tell him you won't be here when he gets back. Let him know how you feel about this."

She was shaking her head. "This is something he feels led to do."

"Then lead him astray, Jenny. I'm thinking of him as much as you. Hell, if presidents and diplomats and mercenaries and God knows who else can't straighten out that mess down there in Central America, how the hell does Hal think he's going to? He's going into something he knows absolutely nothing about."

"God will protect him."

"You're only repeating what you've heard him say. I know my Bible, too, Jenny. It was drilled into me. At one time I actually studied the Hebrew war generals. Yes, they pulled off a few miraculous battles, but Hal hasn't got an army behind him. He doesn't even have the endorsement of the U.S. Government. God gave each of us a brain to reason with and what Hal's doing is unreasonable."

Jenny agreed with him wholeheartedly. But Cage was an expert at twisting words and truths to make them fit his own ends. Aligning herself with Cage's way of thinking was flirting with heresay. Besides, her loyalty had to be with Hal and the cause he had dedicated himself to.

"Good night, Cage."

"How long have you lived with us, Jenny?"

She paused again. "Since I was fourteen. Almost twelve years."

The Hendrens had taken her in when both her parents were killed. One day while she was at school, a gas heater had exploded in their house and it had burned to the ground. Later she remembered hearing the fire truck and ambulance sirens during Algebra class. She hadn't known then that it was already too late for her parents and a younger sister, who had stayed home that day with a sore throat. Her daddy had come home on his lunch hour to check on her. By nightfall, Jenny was left alone in the world, without a thing to her name except the clothes she had worn to school that day.

The Fletchers had been friendly with their pastor, Bob Hendren and his wife, Sarah. Since Jenny had no living relatives, there had been little discussion about her future.

"I remember coming home from college for Thanksgiving break and finding you here," Cage said. "Mother had converted her sewing room into a bedroom fit for a princess. She finally had the daughter she had always wanted. I was told to treat you like one of the family."

"Your parents have been very good to me," Jenny conceded in a small voice.

"Is that why you never stand up to them?"

She was offended and it showed. "I don't know what you're talking about!"

"Oh, yes, you do. It's been twelve years since you made a decision of your own. Are you afraid they'll kick you out if you disagree with them?"

"That's ridiculous," she exclaimed, flabbergasted.

"No, it isn't. It's sad," Cage said, jutting his hard, square chin into the air. "They decided who your friends could and could not be, the kind of clothes you wore, the college you went to, even who you were going to marry. And now it looks like they'll decide when the wedding will take place. Are you going to let them plan your kids, too?"

"Stop it, Cage. None of that is true and I won't listen to any more of it. Have you been drinking?"

"Unfortunately, no. But I wish to hell I had been." He moved toward her and gripped her arm. "Jenny, wake up. They're smothering you. You're a woman, a damn good-looking woman. So what if you do something they disapprove of? You're not fourteen now. They can't punish you. If they did kick you out, which they never would, so what? You could go someplace else."

"Be an independent woman, is that it?"

"I guess that capsulizes it, yeah."

"You think I should cruise the honky-tonks the way you do?"

"No. But I don't think it's healthy for you to spend ninety percent of your time cooped up in Bible study groups either."

"I like doing church work."

"At the exclusion of everything else?" Agitated, he raked his fingers through his hair. "All the work you do in the church is admirable. I'm not taking anything away from that. I just hate to see you shrivel up like an old lady long before your time. You're throwing your life away."

"I'm not. I'm going to have a life with Hal."

"Not if he goes off to Central America and gets himself killed!" He saw her face drain of color and softened his stance and his tone of voice. "Look, I'm sorry. I didn't mean to get into all that."

She accepted his apology graciously. "Hal's the real issue."

"That's right." He clasped her hands. "Talk to him, Jenny."

"I can't change his mind."

"He has to listen to you. You're the woman he's going to marry."

"Don't place so much confidence in me."

"I won't hold you responsible for his decision, if that's what you mean. Just promise you'll try to convince him not to go."

She glanced toward the kitchen. Through the windows she could see Hal and his parents still grouped around the table, deep in discussion. "I'll try."

"Good." He squeezed her hands before releasing them.

"Sarah said you're spending the night." For some reason she didn't want Cage to know it had been she who had prepared his room for the overnight stay, airing it out that afternoon and putting fresh linens on the bed. She wanted him to think his mother had gone to the trouble.

"Yeah, I promised to be here for Hal's big send-off in the morning. I hope it never materializes."

"Well, anyway, Sarah likes having you sleep at home now and then."

He smiled ruefully and touched her cheek. "Ah, Jenny. You're such a diplomat. Mother issued the invitation and then told me to clear out all the football and basketball trophies from my bedroom while I was here. She said she was tired of dusting all that junk."

Jenny swallowed a knot of emotion and her heart went out to Cage. Only a few weeks ago she and Sarah had carefully folded clean cloths around Hal's sports trophies and stored them in boxes in the attic. For twelve years it had been clear to Jenny which was the favored son. But Cage had no one to blame but himself. He had chosen a way of life his parents couldn't possibly approve of.

"Good night, Cage." Jenny suddenly wished she could hold him. He often looked like he needed to be held, which was a ridiculous notion considering his reputation as the town stud. But was that kind of loving enough, even for someone as wild as Cage?

"G'night."

Reluctantly she left him alone and entered the house by the back door. Hal raised his eyes to her and indicated with his head that she should move behind his chair. He was listening attentively to what his father was saying about collecting a state-wide offering for the support of the refugees once they arrived in Texas.

Jenny, standing behind Hal's chair, wrapped her arms around his shoulders and leaned down to tuck his head beneath her chin. "Tired?" Hal asked her when Bob stopped speaking. The Hendrens beamed on them proudly.

"A little."

"Go on up to bed. You'll have to get up early in the morning to wave me off."

She sighed and laid her forehead on top of his head, not wanting his parents to see the despair on her face. "I won't sleep."

"Take one of those sleeping pills the doctor prescribed for me," Sarah suggested. "They're so mild, one can't hurt you, and they do help me get my brain to slow down long enough to fall asleep."

"Come on," Hal said, scraping his chair back, "I'll go up with you."

"Good night, Bob, Sarah," Jenny said listlessly.

"Son, you didn't give us the name of the Mexican contact," Bob reminded Hal.

"I'm not turning in yet. I'm coming right back. I won't be a minute."

Together Jenny and Hal climbed the stairs. At the top, he paused outside his parents' bedroom. "Do you want that sleeping pill?"

"I suppose so. I know I'll toss and turn all night."

He left her and came back a few moments later with two small pink tablets lying in the palm of his hand. "The instructions on the bottle said one or two. I think you should take two."

They went into her bedroom and she turned on the bedside lamp. Cage was right. As soon as she had moved into the parsonage, this room had been outfitted to suit a princess. Unfortunately, Jenny had had little choice in the decorating.

Even a few years ago, when Sarah had suggested it was time for a change, the hated powder blue dotted swiss had been replaced with white eyelet. The room was too juvenile and frilly for Jenny's taste. But she wouldn't have hurt Sarah's feelings for the world. She only hoped that as soon as she and Hal were married, she would be allowed to decorate their bedroom suite. There had never been any mention of their moving to their own house because it was also understood that when Bob retired, Hal would assume his ministry.

"Take your pills and put on your jammies. I'll wait to tuck you in." Jenny left Hal standing in the middle of the room and slipped into the bathroom, where she did as she was told, swallowing both capsules. But she didn't put on "jammies." She put on a nightgown she had surreptitiously bought in the hope that she would have an occasion like tonight to put it to use.

She faced herself in the mirror and made up her mind to take action as Cage had dared her to. She didn't want Hal to go. It was a dangerous, fool's mission. Even if it weren't, it was stalling their marriage plans again. Should any woman have to stand for that?

Jenny had a premonition that her future hinged on tonight. She had to stop Hal from leaving or her life would be forever altered. She had to take the gamble; and the stakes were all or nothing. And she would use the oldest device known to woman to assure a victory.

God had sanctioned Ruth's night with Boaz. Maybe this was another one of those times.

But Ruth hadn't had a nightgown that slithered down her naked body, feeling sinfully slinky and sensuous against her skin. Straps as fine as violin strings held up a bodice that plunged down far between her breasts, showing the ample inner curves. The pearl-colored nightgown had a trim, body-hugging fit that didn't miss a single detail of her figure until it flared out slightly at her hips. Its fluted hem brushed her insteps.

She misted herself with a flowery, light perfume and ran a brush through her hair. For a moment after she was ready, she closed her eyes and tried with all her might to gather the courage to open the door. She groped for the lightswitch first, snapping it off before she eased the door open.

"Jenny, don't forget to..."

Whatever Hal had been about to say left his mind the instant he saw her. She was a vision, both ethereal and sensual, as she glided toward the door on bare feet and softly closed and locked it. The lamplight bathed her skin with a golden glow and cast the shadows of her legs against the sheer nightgown as she moved.

"What are you... Where'd you get that, uh, gown?" Hal stammered.

"I was saving it for a special occasion," she answered softly as she reached him. She laid her hands on his chest. "I guess this is it."

He laughed uneasily. His arms went around her waist, but lightly. "Maybe you should have saved it until after we're married."

"And when will that be?" She pressed her cheek to the open vee of his cotton shirt. He was dressed casually in jeans.

"As soon as I get back. You know that. I've promised you."

"You've promised before."

"And you've always been so understanding," he said fervently. His lips moved in her hair and his hands smoothed her back. "This time I won't break the promise. When I come back—"

"But that could take months."

"Possibly," he said grimly, tilting her head back so he could see her face. "I'm sorry."

"I don't want to wait that long, Hal."

"What do you mean?"

She took a step closer, matching her body to his in a way that made the pupils of his eyes contract as if too much light had been let in. "Love me."

"I do, Jenny."

"I mean..." She wet her lips and took the dive. "Hold me. Lie with me. Make love to me tonight."

"Jenny," he groaned. "Why are you doing this?"

"Because I'm desperate."

"Not as desperate as you're making me."

"I don't want you to go."

"I have to."

"Please stay."

"I'm committed."

"Marry me," she whispered against his throat.

"I will, when this is over."

"I need a pledge of your love."

"You've got it."

"Then show me. Love me tonight."

"I can't. It wouldn't be right."

"For me it would."

"For neither of us."

"We love each other."

"So we have to make sacrifices for each other."

"Don't you want me?"

In spite of himself, Hal pulled her closer and pressed his mouth against her neck. "Yes, yes. Sometimes I daydream about what it will be like to share a bed with you and I... Yes, I want you, Jenny."

He kissed her. His lips parted over hers as one hand slid down the curve of her hip. She responded, pressing closer, rubbing her thigh against his. His tongue barely breached the soft damp interior of her mouth before her tongue came out questing. He moaned again.

"Please love me, Hal," she said, clutching at his shirt. "I need you tonight. I need to be held and petted, reassured that what we have is real, that you're coming back."

"I am."

"But you don't know for sure. I want to love you before you go." She covered his lips and face and neck with quick, fiery kisses. He edged away from her, but she wouldn't be stopped. Finally, he gripped her upper arms and pushed her away sternly.

"Jenny, think!" She gaped at him wide-eyed as though she had been slapped. Gulping in air, she swallowed hard. "We can't. It would go against one of the principles we stand for. I'm going on a God-called mission tomorrow and I can't let you, beautiful and desirable as you are, distract

me from that. Besides, my parents are right downstairs." He
bent down and kissed her chastely on the cheek. "Now get
into bed like a good girl."

He led her to the bed and peeled back the covers. She
obediently climbed in and he pulled the sheet over her, de-
terminedly keeping his eyes off her breasts. "I'll see you
early in the morning." His mouth touched hers softly. "I *do*
love you, Jenny. That's why I won't do as you ask." He
switched out the lamp, crossed to the door, and closed it
behind him, plunging the room into total darkness.

Jenny rolled to her side and began to cry. Tears, scalding
and salty, rivered down her cheeks and into the pillowcase.
Never had she felt so forsaken, not even when she had lost
her family. She was alone, more dismally alone than she had
ever been in her life.

Even her bedroom seemed alien and unfamiliar. But
maybe that was the effect of the sleeping pills. Through the
darkness she tried to distinguish the shape of the furniture
and the outline of the windows, but everything was blurred
around the edges. Her perception was dulled by the drug she
had taken.

She had the sensation of floating and drifted toward sleep,
but a fresh batch of tears kept it at bay. How humiliating.
She had gone against her own staunch moral code. She had
offered herself to the man she loved. Hal vowed he loved
her. But he had flatly and outrightly rejected her!

Even if their love hadn't been consummated, he could
have lain with her, held her, provided her with some evidence of the passion he claimed he felt, given her a shred of
a memory to cling to while he was gone.

But his rejection had been total. How low she must be in
the order of priorities of his life. He had more important
things to do than love and comfort her.

Then the bedroom door opened.

Jenny turned toward the sound and tried to focus tear-
laden eyes on the wedge of light that was cut into the con-

suming blackness. A man was silhouetted against the sudden brightness for only a second before he stepped into the room and shut the door behind him.

Jenny sat up and stretched her hands out toward him, her heart leaping and racing with joy. "Hal!" she cried gladly.

Chapter 2

He made his way toward the bed and sank down on the edge of it. His shadow was barely discernible against the others in the room.

"You came back, you came back," Jenny repeated as she clasped his hands and raised them to her lips. She rained kisses across the ridges of his knuckles. "My heart was breaking. I need you tonight. Hold me." Her words broke into sobs and his arms encircled her with warmth. "Oh, yes, hold me tight."

"Shh, shh."

The sudden movement of sitting up, the few words she had spoken, taxed her dwindling, drug-affected coordination. Spent, she let her cheek fall into the cradle of his palm. His thumb stroked her cheekbones, sweeping off the tears. "Shh." When the tears were dried, she buried her face in the hollow between his shoulder and throat.

He bent his head down over hers. His beard was rough against her temple. With mindless curiosity her hand inched up his chest to touch his face. She gently scratched her nails over the rasping stubble on his chin, accidentally glancing his lips with her fingertips.

She heard him gasp. It seemed to come from far away, though she felt the quickening of his body. Uttering a low, rumbling sound deep in his chest, he tilted her head back and his mouth moved down to greet hers. His arms drew her possessively against his chest. Head falling back in wanton offering, Jenny surrendered her last conscious thoughts and entrusted herself only to sensual instinct.

His lips parted. This time his hesitation was short-lived. A heartbeat ticked by, possibly two, before his tongue came swirling down into the sweetest depths of her mouth, touching secret places, stroking madly.

Jenny whimpered and clung to him dizzily. Her head buzzed and she didn't know if it was the power of his kiss or the sleeping pills that made all her senses hum so deliciously. The kiss continued, gaining in fervor with each second, with each pounding heartbeat, until she thought her heart would break through her ribcage.

Had the sheet and blanket fallen away? They must have because her skin was suddenly cooled. Then warmed. As his hand... His hand? Yes. Moving over her. Touching her breasts. Caressing, kneading, finessing.

She felt her head sinking into the softness of the pillow and realized he had lowered her back onto the bed. The straps of her nightgown were lifted off her shoulders. Her moan could have been one of protest or permission. She wasn't certain. She was certain of nothing save the hands ghosting over her nakedness, acquainting themselves with her shape by touch. Fingertips grazed her nipples, again and again, plucking softly.

Then she fell victim to hot, encompassing sensations, surrounding, tugging. His mouth? Yes, yes, yes. The wet wash of his tongue flaying her gently. It caressed. Round and round. Long and slow. Quick and light.

She wanted to clasp his head and hold him against her, but couldn't. Her arms were heavy, useless, lying on the bed at her sides as though restrained by invisible bands. Her blood was pumping like molten lava through her veins, but she had neither the energy nor the will to move.

She welcomed his weight as he eased himself onto the bed and partially covered her, his tongue prowling the interior of her mouth, but softly, like a stealthy intruder. It was delicious. He was delicious. As was the whisper of cloth against her bare breasts.

Directed by his hands, she raised her hips and aided him in slipping her nightgown off. Beneath him she lay naked and vulnerable. But the hands that moved over her were kind, gentle, pleasure-giving. They touched every part of her, pausing frequently, making a gift of every caress.

The very tips of her toes were brushed by his thumb. Or was it his tongue? Her calves were gently squeezed. Her knees. Thighs. The hands lifted her, positioned her, until she felt the cool bed linens against the soles of her feet.

Mindlessly she obeyed every silent direction. To have refused, to have balked, would have been unthinkable. She was a servant of this seductive master, a priestess of sensuality, a disciple of desire.

His hair pleasantly tickled her belly as his head moved from side to side. He lightly pinched the soft flesh between his lips, laved it with his tongue, sucked at it gently.

And when he opened his hand over her mound, she bowed her head against his chest and savored the cherishing caress that revolved slowly, ground gently.

Oh, yes! her mind cried joyfully. He loved her! He wanted her! She proved her willingness by moving her body in a tempestuous ballet.

Tantalizing, investigative fingers left her flesh slippery against his. His thumb applied a massaging friction that accelerated her breathing, made a drumbeat of her pulse.

Faster. Surer. Ever whirling with a pagan beat. Until—

Her soul seemed to open up and release a flock of colorful songbirds that scattered on a flurry of wings.

It wasn't enough! *I'm still hungry*, her soul cried in protest.

His denim jeans were rough, but not unpleasantly so, against her open thighs. Buttons. Cloth. Then—

Hair. Skin. Man. Hard warmth and smooth strength. A velvety spearhead. All rubbing against her. Probing. Seeking its mate. Until they meshed the way they were intended.

The penetration was swift and sure.

She heard the sharp cry an instant after feeling the brand-hot pain shoot through her, but it didn't occur to her that she had made that surprised sound. She was too enthralled by the steely manhood imbedded tightly inside the giving folds of her body. But no sooner had she come to realize the splendor of his possession than he began to ease away.

"No, no." The words echoed through the darkened chambers of her mind, and she wondered if she had actually spoken them aloud. She was consumed with the determination that it not end yet, not quite yet.

Of their own volition, her hands slid beneath his jeans and pressed the hard, muscles of his buttocks with her palms. She felt the spasm that shuddered through his body, heard his animal groan, felt the rush of his warm breath in her ear, felt, miraculously, still more of his hardness delving into her.

Pliant, malleable, she let him gather her beneath him, positioning her for comfort and maximum sensation. Random kisses fell on her throat, her face, her breasts, leaving stinging impressions on her skin.

Her whole body responded to the myriad sensations rioting through it. She seemed trapped in the rhythm that rocked their bodies together in perfect harmony. Then the coil that had been winding tighter and tighter in her middle suddenly sprang free again. Thighs, hands, belly, breasts, replied in an ageless physical manner that milked life from him.

The body above hers tensed. Against the walls of her womb she felt each precious eruption of his love. Until there was nothing but the full pressure of him still filling her.

Replete, but selfish, her body closed around him like a silken fist. She was almost asleep when he finally left her, rolled to his side, and tucked her against him. She cuddled up to his solid frame, her fist clutching a handful of his damp shirt. She was embraced by a peace and sense of belonging she had never known before.

Still woozy, still entranced, still dazed by the experience, she was smiling when she drifted into a dreamless sleep.

She awoke early. She awoke alone. Sometime during the night Hal had left her. That was understandable and she forgave him, though it would have been wonderful to wake up in his arms. But the Hendrens would never have approved what had happened last night. Jenny, as much as Hal, wanted to protect them from finding out.

There were footsteps on the landing and whispered conversations that carried through the hallways of the old house. She could smell coffee brewing. Preparations were underway for Hal's departure. Apparently he hadn't spoken to his parents yet.

Last night had changed everything. He would be as anxious for marriage now as she. She clung to the precious memory of their lovemaking and could find no shame in it, even if she had used it to make him stay.

He belonged there with her. He would continue as associate pastor until his father retired and then take over the full ministry. She was well-trained in being a pastor's wife. Surely Hal could now see that that was what God willed for them.

But how would the Hendrens react to his change in plans?

Not wanting him to have to face the music alone, she flung the covers off, almost surprised to find herself naked. Oh, yes, he *had* removed her nightgown, hadn't he? And quite frantically, she thought with an impish smile.

She was blushing furiously as she entered the bathroom and turned on the taps in the shower. She looked no different, though upon close inspection she saw there were rosy whisker burns on her breasts.

All the same, he had left an indelible print on her. When she thought about it, she could still feel the welcome weight of his body atop hers, still feel the supple movements of his muscles beneath her hands, still hear his moans of gratification. She was both ashamed and thrilled when her body responded to the recollections.

She dressed hurriedly and sailed downstairs, eager to see Hal. By the time she reached the kitchen, her heart was pounding with expectation. Breathless, she hovered on the threshold, taking in the scene.

The Hendrens, sitting at the breakfast table, were in an attitude of prayer. Cage was there, too, reclining on his spine in the ladderback chair. His head was bowed, but he was staring broodingly into his coffee cup, which he had balanced on his belt buckle.

Where was Hal? Surely not still asleep.

Bob pronounced the amen and raised his head. He spotted Jenny. "Where's Hal?" she asked.

Silently the three of them stared back at her. She could feel a blackness closing in, like storm clouds rushing closer from a threatening horizon.

"He's already gone, Jenny," Bob said gently. He stood, scraped his chair back, and took a step toward her.

She retreated a half step as though he posed a threat to her. The encroaching blackness smothered her. She couldn't breathe. All color drained from her face. "That's impossible." The words were barely audible. "He didn't say goodbye to me."

"He didn't want to put you through another heartbreaking farewell scene," Bob said. "He thought it would be easier this way."

This wasn't happening. She had played the scene in her mind. Hal would be mesmerized by the first sight of her. She had imagined them gazing into each other's eyes, lovers sharing a marvelous knowledge that was secret from the rest of the world.

But he was gone and all that she saw were three faces gazing back at her, two with pity, Cage's with a remarkable lack of emotion.

"I don't believe you!" she cried. She dashed through the kitchen nearly falling over a chair before she pushed it aside and barreled through the back door. The yard was deserted. There were no cars on the street.

Hal was gone.

The truth hit her hard. She felt like throwing up. She felt like collapsing onto the ground and pounding her fists against the hard earth. She felt like screaming. She was swamped with disappointment.

But what had she expected? Hal was never demonstrative where his affection for her was concerned. Now, in the light of day, she realized how fanciful she had been. He hadn't made any promises not to leave. He had sealed their covenant of love with a physical expression of it. That was what she had asked of him. To have expected more was unrealistic. And it was characteristic of him to spare her the humiliation of begging him not to go. He would have wanted to avoid that for both their sakes.

Then why did she feel deserted? Bereft. Forsaken. Dejected and rejected.

And mad.

Damn good and mad. How could he leave her like this? *How?* How, when she had regretted that they couldn't even finish the night lying in each other's arms?

Jenny stood on the cracked sidewalk staring at the empty street. How could he have left her so blithely, without so much as a good-bye? Was she no more important to him than that? If he loved her—

The thought brought her mind to an abrupt standstill. *Did* he love her? Truly love her? Did she love him the way she should? Or was it as Cage had suggested last night? Had she and Hal merely drifted into the relationship everyone had expected of them, one that was convenient to her because it was safe, and convenient to him because it didn't cost him time away from his ministerial duties?

What a dismal thought.

She strove to push it aside. Why couldn't she dwell on the happiness she had basked in last night in the aftermath of their love?

But the ambiguities wouldn't be swept under the rug. They stayed there in the forefront of her mind and she realized that before Hal came home, she had to reach some conclusions. It would be foolhardy to enter into a marriage harboring the kind of doubts she had. The union of their bodies had been glorious, but she knew that wasn't the soundest foundation on which to base a marriage. And she had been dopey with the sedative. Maybe she was remembering the lovemaking as more earth shaking than it had actually been. Maybe it had all been an erotic, drug-induced dream.

Turning on her heel to return to the house, she almost collided with Cage, who had come up behind her so silently she hadn't realized he was there.

She almost jumped under the impact of his stare.

He was studying her from beneath a hood of dusty blond brows. The golden brown eyes were as unflinching and unblinking as a great cat's. He was motionless, completely motionless, until one corner of his mouth lifted involuntarily.

Jenny attributed that telltale gesture to regret and remorse. Was he feeling sorry for her because she had failed to persuade Hal to stay at home? Was that how everyone in town would see her, a pitifully forsaken lover, pining away for the man whose life's work was more important than she?

Irked by the thought, she tore her eyes from Cage's stare, straightened her shoulders, and tried to go around him. He sidestepped and blocked her path.

"Are you all right, Jenny?" His brows were pulled down into a low V over his eyes. His squint lines were pronounced. His jaw looked as hard as granite.

"Of course," she said brightly, faking a huge smile. "Why shouldn't I be?"

He shrugged. "Hal left you without saying good-bye. He's gone."

"But he'll be back. And he was right to go like that, make a clean break. I couldn't have stood to tell him a final goodbye." She wondered if her statements sounded as false to him as they did to her.

"Did you talk to him last night?"

"Yes."

"And?" he probed.

Her smile faltered and her eyes skittered away from the penetrating power of his. "*And* he made me feel much better about things. He wants to get married as soon as he gets back."

It wasn't quite a lie. It wasn't quite the truth either, and Cage's searching eyes told her he wasn't convinced. She brushed past him hurriedly. "Did you eat any breakfast? I'll fix you something. Two eggs over easy?"

He smiled, pleased. "You remember how I like them?"

"Sure." She held the screen door for him, standing straight and shrinking against the jamb as he wedged himself past her. When his body made brief contact with hers, every cell ignited. Her breasts flared to rigid points. Her thighs tingled with heat. Her heart did handstands.

Jenny was flabbergasted. She rushed to cover her agitation by hastily preparing Cage's breakfast. Her hands shook so she could barely control them, and as soon as she set the plate of food on the table in front of him, she fled to her room.

Now that her sleeping body had been awakened to sexual awareness, it seemed not to want to lie dormant again.

But, Lord, didn't it have any discernment? Any discrimination? Would it now react to every man she came in contact with?

The thought sent a surge of embarrassment through her. Nevertheless, she stripped, crawled between the covers of her bed, and pulled her knees to her chest. She let the events of last night parade through her mind again and relished the naughty sensations that still rippled through her like aftershocks.

The dark amber contents of the highball glass didn't offer any absolution for Cage's guilt, but it held his attention as though it could.

Three long-neck beer bottles were neatly lined up on the highly glossed tabletop. They were empty. He had switched to Jack Daniel's about an hour ago, but the guilt poisoning his system refused to be diluted even by near-lethal amounts of alcohol.

He had violated Jenny.

There was no sense in using euphemisms to try to blunt the edges of his guilt. He could say he had made love to her, initiated her into the rites of sexual loving, deflowered her. But no matter how his conscience juggled with semantics, he had violated her. It hadn't been a brutal rape, but she had been unwittingly in no condition to give her consent. It had been a violation of the vilest sort.

He took another swig of the stinging whiskey. It burned all the way down. He wished he could get drunk enough to vomit. Maybe that would purge him.

Who the hell was he kidding? Nothing was going to purge him of this. He hadn't felt guilty about anything in years. Now he was swamped with guilt. And what the hell could he do about it?

Tell her? Confess?

"Oh, by the way, Jenny, about the other night, you know the one, the night Hal left and you made love with him? Yeah, well, that wasn't him. It was me."

He cursed savagely and polished off the drink in one gulp. He could just imagine her face, her dear, dear face, shattering before his eyes. She would be horrified. Knowing she had been with him would probably put her in a catatonic state from which she would never recover. The most notorious skirt chaser in west Texas had taken sweet Jenny Fletcher.

No, he couldn't tell her.

He'd done bad things before, but this time he had sunk to an all-time low. He liked his reputation as a hell-raiser. He lived up to it, worked at keeping it alive, kept reminding folks of it should they think Cage Hendren was mellowing with the passing years. He'd even take credit for some things he hadn't done. He would let that slow, lazy smile answer allegations for him, and his cronies could draw their own conclusions as to whether the latest rumor was true or not.

But this...

Signaling to the bartender, Cage became aware of his surroundings. They were dismally familiar. Tobacco smoke fogged the close, stuffy, beery atmosphere of the tavern. Red-and-blue neon lights advertising various brands of beer winked from the walls like phosphorescent sprites hiding in the paneling. A sad strand of gold tinsel, left over from last Christmas, dangled from a wagon-wheel-shaped chandelier. A spider had made a home between the spokes. Waylon Jennings mourned a love gone wrong from the jukebox in the corner.

It was tawdry. It was tacky. It was home.

"Thanks, Bert," Cage said laconically as the bartender set another glass of whiskey in front of him.

"Hard day?"

Hard week, Cage thought. He'd lived with his sin for a week now, but the gnawing guilt hadn't abated. Its fangs were as sharp as ever as they ate their way into his soul. Soul? Did he even possess a soul?

Bert bent over the table and transferred the empty beer bottles to a tray. "Heard something that might interest you."

"Yeah? What about?" There was a droplet of water on the outside of the highball glass. It reminded him of Jenny's tears. He wiped it away with his thumb.

" 'Bout that parcel of land west of the *mesa*."

In spite of his black mood, Cage's interest was instantly piqued. "The old Parson's ranch?"

"Yep. Heard the kinfolks is ready to talk money to anyone interested."

Cage slipped Bert a smile worthy of a toothpaste ad, and a ten-dollar tip. "Thanks, buddy." Bert smiled back and ambled off. Cage was a favorite of his and he was glad to oblige.

Cage Hendren was indisputably one of the best wildcatters around. He could smell oil, seemed to know instinctively where it was. Oh, he'd gone to Tech and earned a degree in geology to make it all official and to inspire confidence. But he had a knack for sensing where the stuff was, a knack that couldn't be book learned. He had drilled a few dry holes, but very few. Few enough to win him the respect of men who had been in the business more years than Cage was old.

He'd been trying to lease the mineral rights on the Parson's land for years. The elderly couple had died within months of each other, but the children had held out, saying they didn't want their family's land to be desecrated by drilling rigs. That was a crock, of course, and Cage knew it.

They had been holding out while the price went up. He'd pay a call on the executor of the estate tomorrow.

"Hiya, Cage."

He had been so lost in thought that he hadn't seen the woman until she sidled up to his table, managing to nudge his shoulder with her hip as she did so. He glanced up with a notable lack of interest. "Hi, Didi. How're things?"

Without a word, she laid a single key on the polished surface of the small, round table, covered it with the pad of her index finger, and slid it toward Cage. "Sonny and I have finally called it quits."

"'S that a fact?"

Didi's marriage to Sonny had been on the rocks for months. Neither upheld their vows, especially the one promising faithfulness. She had made inviting moves toward Cage before, but he'd stayed away from her. He didn't have many scruples, but he was loyal to one; never with a married woman. Something inside him still believed in the sanctity of marriage, despite everything, and he never wanted to be responsible for helping break one up.

"Uh-huh. That's a fact all right. I'm a single woman now, Cage." Didi smiled down at him. If she had licked her lips, she would have been the perfect imitation of a well-satisfied she-cat that had just lapped up a bowl of cream. Her generous figure had been poured into a pair of jeans with a Neiman-Marcus label, and a low cut sweater. Leaning down, she gave him an unrestricted view of her deep cleavage.

Rather than inciting desire, she made him feel like he needed a bath.

Jenny. Jenny. Jenny. So clean. Her body so neatly feminine. Not overblown, not lush, not voluptuous, just womanly.

Damn!

Mentally he jerked himself erect, though he still slouched in his chair, nonchalantly twirling the bottom of his glass on the table.

Didi dragged a long fingernail down his arm. "See ya, Cage," she said with a seductive certainty as she undulated away.

One corner of his mouth twisted sardonically. Had he ever thought such a bold invitation was attractive? Didi's blatancy was almost laughable.

Jenny didn't even know she was sexy. She wore such a subtle fragrance. In comparison, Didi's heavy perfume lingered after her distastefully.

Jenny's voice was nervously breathless, a voice Cage found far sexier than Didi's affected purr. And Jenny's amateurish caresses had stirred him more than the calculated foreplay any of his former lovers had practiced.

Closing out the seamy setting before him, he let his mind wander back to that innocent bedroom that should have belonged to a child, not to a woman who wore silk nightgowns. And it *had* been silk. His touch was educated to the matchless feel of silk against a woman's body. But Jenny's skin had been almost as soft. And her hair. And—

Her virginity had been a shock. Surely, *surely* his brother wasn't that saintly. How could Hal, how could any man, have lived in the same house with Jenny all these years and not made love to her?

Were he and his brother that different? Weren't they similarly equipped? Of course they were. There was nothing wrong with Hal physically. Cage had to admire Hal's unflagging morality, though he couldn't imagine anyone imposing such a rigid code of morality on himself.

Jenny hadn't, had she?

She had been willing to give herself to Hal on the night of his departure. What a sap Hal had been not to accept that precious gift. Cage hated to think of his brother in such derisive terms, but that was how he felt about it. Hadn't Hal realized what a sacrifice Jenny had been making for him? At the moment he had encountered the frail barrier of her virginity, Cage had.

God above, had he ever known such rapture as when he was sheathed inside her? Had he ever heard any sweeter sound than the little catches in her throat when passion claimed her?

Never. It had never been so good.

But then, no other woman was Jenny. She was the unattainable one. The one forbidden and off-limits. Even beyond his far-reaching boundaries.

He had known it for years. Just as he had known that she belonged to Hal. It was understood. Years ago, Cage had had to reconcile himself to that. He could have any woman he wanted. Except the one he really wanted. Jenny.

He was rotten to the core. No good. Didn't give a damn about anyone or anything. That was what folks said about him and it was mainly true. But he had cared enough about Jenny and Hal not to ruin their lives with his interference.

He had kept his secret well. No one knew. No one would even guess. Least of all her. She had no idea that every time he was near her, he ached to touch her. Not sexually. Just touch her.

Her affection for him was purely fraternal. Yet he had always sensed that she was afraid of him, too. He made her uncomfortable and that had often broken his heart. Her fear was justified, of course. He had a scandalous reputation and any woman who valued her good name stayed away from him as though his sexuality was as contagious and dreaded as leprosy.

But he had often wondered what would have happened if Jenny had come to live with them sooner. If he hadn't been off at college, if he hadn't already been known as a hellraiser without equal, if they had had time to develop a relationship, would Jenny have turned to him instead of Hal?

It was his favorite fantasy to think so. Because he sensed that beneath Jenny's reserve, there was a free spirit longing to be released, a sensual, sexual woman trapped in an invisible cage of circumspection. If she were given her freedom, what would happen?

Maybe she wanted to be rescued. Maybe she made silent appeals to be freed that no other man had responded to. Maybe—

You're fooling yourself, man. She wouldn't want to get her life tangled up with yours under any circumstances.

He shoved his chair back and stood, angrily tossing a pile of bills onto the table. But in the process, his hand paused as a thought struck him.

Unless your life changed.

He hadn't gone into her bedroom that night with the intention of doing what he'd done. He had heard her crying and knew that her appeal to Hal had failed. She had been heartborken and it had been his intention only to comfort her.

But then she had mistaken him for Hal and, like the tide washing into shore, he had been compulsively drawn to her. He had crossed the dark room to her bed, telling himself that at any moment he was going to identify himself.

He had touched her. He had heard the desperation in her voice. He had understood the despair of craving love and not receiving it. He had answered her plea and held her. And once he had kissed her, felt the responding warmth of her body beneath his hands, there had been no turning back.

What he had done had been unforgivable. But what he was going to do was almost as bad. He was going to try to steal her from his brother.

Now that he had had her, he couldn't let her go. Not if hell opened up and swallowed him. He wouldn't let her spirit be stifled by his family any longer. Hal had been given a golden opportunity to claim her love forever, but he had rejected her. Cage wouldn't stand by and see the yearning in her face eventually become defeat, her vitality become resignation, and all her animation be smothered in a cocoon of righteousness.

He had months to win her before Hal returned, and, by God, that was what he was going to do.

"Didi." She was cuddled in a dark booth with a rough-neck who had a hand under her sweater and his tongue in her ear. Annoyed by the interruption, she disengaged herself. "You forgot something," Cage said, flipping the key toward the booth.

She missed it and it clattered noisily onto the table. Didi snatched it up and looked at Cage blankly. "What's this for?"

"I won't be using it."

"Bastard," she hissed venomously.

"Never said otherwise," Cage said breezily as he pushed open the door of the tavern.

"Hey, guy," the roughneck called after him, "you can't talk to the lady—"

"Oh, let it go, honey," Didi cooed, smoothing a hand down his shirtfront. They picked up where they had left off.

Cage stepped into the cool evening air and drew it in deeply to clear his head of alcohol fumes and the odor of the tavern. Sliding beneath the wheel of his '63 split window Corvette Stingray, he gunned the engine to a low growl and sped off into the night.

The restored classic car was the envy of every man within a hundred-mile radius of La Bota and was readily identified with Cage. It was a mean midnight black with a matching leather interior that was equally as devilish.

Sleekly it rocketed down the barren highway, then slowed to silently take the corners of the town's streets. Half a block away from the parsonage, Cage pulled it to the curb and cut the engine.

The window in Jenny's room was already dark. But he sat and stared at it for a full hour, just as he had done for the past six nights.

Chapter 3

Jenny glanced up from the altar at the front of the church when a tall silhouette loomed in the sanctuary door, dark against the bright sunlight outside. The last person she expected to see here was Cage. Yet it was he who took off a pair of aviator sunglasses and strolled inside and down the carpeted aisle of the church.

"Hi."

"Hi."

"Maybe I should increase my tithe. Can't the church afford to hire a janitor?" he said, nudging his chin toward the basket of cleaning supplies at her feet.

Self-consciously she stuck the handle of her orange feather duster into the rear pocket of her jeans, which left the plume sticking up like a tail feather. "I like doing it."

He grinned. "You seem surprised to see me."

"I am," she replied honestly. "How long has it been since you came to church?"

She had been dusting the altar in preparation for the bouquet of flowers the florist had delivered. Sunlight poured through the tall stained glass windows and made the fuzzy dancing motes look like a sprinkling of fairy dust. The light cast rainbows on Jenny's skin and her hair, which had been pinned into a haphazard knot on the top of her head. Her jeans fit snugly. The tennis shoes on her feet were appealingly well worn. Cage thought she looked as cute as a button and sexy as all get out.

"Last Easter." He dropped down onto the front pew and laid his arms along the back of it, stretching them out on either side of him. He surveyed the sanctuary and realized it had remained virtually unchanged for as far back as he could remember.

"Oh, yes," Jenny said. "We had a picnic in the park that afternoon."

"And I pushed you in the swing."

She laughed. "How could I have forgotten that? I screamed for you not to push me so high, but you kept right on."

"You loved it."

There was a trace of mischief in her eyes as she smiled down at him, the corners of her mouth turning up adorably. "How did you know?"

"Instinct."

When he sent a lazy smile in her direction, Jenny guessed that Cage had many instincts about women, none of them holy.

Cage was thinking back to the previous spring, to the Sunday they had mentioned. It had been a late Easter and the skies had been purely blue, the air warm. Jenny had worn a yellow dress, something soft and frothy that had alternately billowed around and clung to her body with each puff of south wind.

He had loved drawing her close against his chest as she sat in the swing, the old one with ropes as thick as his wrists suspending it from the giant tree. He had held her against him for an unnecessarily long time, teasing her by almost letting her go before jerking her back. It had given him the opportunity to breathe in the summery scent of her hair and enjoy the feel of her slender back against his chest.

When he did release her, she laughed with childlike glee. The sound of her laughter still rang in his ears. Each time the pendulum of the swing carried her back to him, he pushed the seat of it, almost touching her hips. Not quite, but almost.

It was true what the romantic poets penned about the fancies of young men in spring. Virile juices had pumped through his body that day, making him feel full and heady, heavy with the need to mate.

He had wanted to lie in the grass with Jenny, letting the warming rays of the sun fall on her face as gently as his lips kissed her. He had wanted to rest his head in her lap, gazing up into her face. He had wanted to make soft, unhurried, gentle love to her.

But she had been Hal's girl that day, just as always. And when Cage had taken all he could of seeing them together, he had stalked to his car to drink a cold beer from the cooler he kept there. His parents had demonstrated their extreme disapproval.

Finally, to keep from ruining everyone's good time, especially Jenny's, because Cage knew that dissonance within the family distressed her tremendously, he had bade everyone a snarling farewell and roared away from the park in his black Corvette.

Now he felt the same compulsion to touch her. Even in her mussed state, she looked so touchable and soft. He wondered if the wall of the church would cave in if he took her in his arms and kissed her the way he longed to.

"Who donated the flowers this week?" he asked before his body could betray his lusty thoughts.

Each year a calendar was circulated through the membership of the church. Families filled in a Sunday when they would provide flowers for the altar, usually in honor of a special occasion.

Jenny read the card attached to the bouquet of crimson gladiolas. "The Randalls. 'In loving memory of our son, Joe Wiley,'" she read aloud.

"Joe Wiley Randall." Cage squinted his eyes, a smile on his face.

"Did you know him?"

"Sure did. He was several classes ahead of me, but we ran around together some." He leaned his head far back and looked over his shoulder at a pew several rows behind him.

"See that fourth row there? Joe Wiley and I were sitting there one Sunday morning. When the offering plate came by, Joe Wiley stuck his chewing gum to the bottom of it. I thought that was hilarious. So did Joe Wiley. We followed the progress of that offering plate through the sanctuary, up one aisle, down another. You can imagine the expressions on people's faces when their hands got stuck in the gum."

Jenny, her eyes sparkling, sat down beside him. "What happened?"

"I got a spanking. Reckon he got one too."

"No, I mean, the card says 'in memory of.'"

"Oh. He went to Nam." He stared at the flowers for a long moment. "I don't recall seeing him after he graduated from high school." Jenny sat motionless, saying nothing, listening to the silence. "He was a helluva basketball player," Cage said reflectively. Then he hunched his shoulders and ducked his head as though God's wrath might strike him like lightning for his curse. "Ooops. Can't say that in church, can you?"

Jenny laughed. "What difference does it make? God hears you say it all the time." Suddenly she took on a serious mien and gazed at him, her eyes probing deeply into his. "You *do* believe in God, don't you Cage?"

"Yes." There was no doubt he was telling the truth. His face was rarely that somber. "And in my own way I worship Him. I know what people say about me. My own parents think I'm a heathen.''

"I'm certain they don't think that."

He looked doubtful. "What do *you* think of me?"

"That you're a stereotypical preacher's kid."

He threw back his head and laughed. "That's an oversimplification, isn't it?"

"Not at all. When you were growing up, you acted ornery to keep from being thought of as a goody-goody."

"I'm grown up, but I still don't want to be a goody-goody."

"No one would accuse you of that," she teased, poking his thigh with her index finger. She drew her hand back quickly. His thigh was hard, just like Hal's, and it reminded her too well of hard, jean-clad muscles rubbing against her naked legs.

To cover her consternation she asked, "Do you remember trying to make me laugh when I was singing in the choir?"

"Me?" he asked indignantly. "I never did any such thing."

"Oh, yes, you did. Making faces and looking cross-eyed. From way back there in the back row where you sat with one of your girls, you would—"

"With 'one of my girls'? You make it sound like I had a harem."

"Didn't you? Don't you?"

His eyes lowered significantly and took a leisurely tour of her body. "There's always room for one more. Wanna fill out an application?"

"Oh!" she cried, jumping from her seat and facing him with mock fury, fists digging into her hips. "Will you get out of here. I've got work to do."

"Yeah, so do I," he said, sighing and pulling himself to his feet. "I just signed a contract leasing a hundred acres of the old Parsons place."

"Is that good?" She knew little about his work, only that it had something to do with oil and that he was considered successful.

"Very. We're ready to start drilling."

"Congratulations."

"Save those for when the first well comes in." Playfully he yanked on an errant strand of caramel-colored hair that had escaped the knot on top of her head. Turning, he sauntered up the aisle of the church toward the door.

"Cage?" Jenny asked suddenly.

"Yeah?" He turned back around, looking rugged and handsome, windblown and sunbaked, disreputable and dangerous. His thumbs were hooked in his belt loops. The collar of his denim vest was flipped up to bracket his jaw.

"I forgot to ask you why you came by."

His shoulders bobbed in a brief shrug. "No special reason. 'Bye, Jenny."

"'Bye."

He stared at her for a moment before he put on his sunglasses and stepped through the door.

Jenny struggled to anchor the damp bedsheet to the clothesline before the strong wind ripped it from her grasp. The linens she had already hung up popped like sails and flapped around her like giant wings.

As she shoved the clothespin over the last corner and dropped her arms in exhaustion, her ears were met with a monster's roar. A threatening form reared up behind the sheet and grabbed her. It enfolded her in its massive arms as it made rapacious devouring noises.

She screamed softly, but her exclamation of fright was muffled by the smothering embrace she had been wrapped in.

"Scared you, didn't I?" the as-yet-unseen attacker growled in her ear as he pulled her close.

"Let me go."

"Say please."

"Please!"

Cage released her and peered around the sheet, laughing at her efforts to extricate herself from its folds. Miraculously it had stayed on the clothesline in spite of their tussle.

"Cage Hendren, you scared the daylights out of me!"

"Aw, come on, you knew it was me."

"Only because you've done that to me before." She made exasperated attempts to push her windblown hair out of her eyes. They were as futile as the efforts she made not to smile. Finally a grin broke through and she laughed with him. "Some day..." She let the threat dwindle, but she shook her finger at him. His hand whipped out and snatched it, entrapping it in his fist.

"What? Some day what, Jenny Fletcher?"

"Some day you're gonna get yours."

He lifted her finger to his mouth and closed his teeth around it in a playful bite, growling cannabalistically. "Don't bet on it."

Just the sight of her flesh imprisoned between his strong white teeth flustered her and she wished she could think of a way to pull her finger away from his mouth wihthout creating an awkward moment. At last he released her hand and she stepped back as though she had moved too close to a fire and hadn't realized it until the flames singed her.

She wondered why he had come to the parsonage today, though his visits weren't nearly as rare as they had been before Hal left. Since then Cage had been dropping by frequently on unimportant errands.

Ostensibly these visits were to ask if they had received news from Hal, but his excuses were so lame that Jenny wondered if he was coming around for the benefit of his parents. If so, she was touched by the gesture.

He had made several trips to the parsonage in order to empty his former bedroom of all the "junk" Sarah had asked him to remove, though it all could have been handled in one load.

Then he had come by bearing a cake he had bought at the FHA fund-raising bake sale and offered it to them, since he knew he couldn't possibly eat it all.

One evening he had stopped by to borrow an electric sander from Bob so he could polish his car with the buffer attachment. All these devices were valid enough, but Jenny still thought there was an ulterior motive behind them.

It wasn't like Cage to show such interest in the goings-on at the parsonage. His evenings were usually spent in local watering holes where he caroused with roughnecks and cowboys and businessmen—when he wasn't in the company of a woman.

And the more time she spent with him, the less Jenny liked to think about Cage and his women. The pangs of jealousy she felt were uncalled for and she couldn't imagine why they should have suddenly sprung up from nowhere.

"Is the clothes dryer broken?" Cage asked now, swinging her empty laundry basket over his shoulder and following her toward the back door.

"No, but I like the way the sheets and pillowcases smell after they've dried outside."

He smiled down at her as he held the door open. "You're a hard case, Jenny."

"I know, hopelessly old-fashioned."

"That's what I like about you."

Again she felt the need to put distance between them. When he was standing this close, looking at her in that peculiar, penetrating way of his, she couldn't breathe properly. "Would you...would you like a Coke?"

"That'd be great." He returned the basket to the laundry room, off the kitchen, while she went to the refrigerator. She plunked ice cubes into the glasses she took down from the cabinet and poured the fizzing soft drink over them.

"Where are Mother and Dad?"

"There were several people in the hospital they needed to visit."

Realizing that she and Cage were alone in the rambling old house made her unaccountably nervous. Her hand was shaking slightly when she set his drink down in front of him on the table. She didn't want to risk touching him. She had always avoided touching him if possible, but lately...

Nervously she dropped into the chair across the table from him and thirstily sipped at her cold drink. He was watching her. Though she wasn't looking directly at him, she could feel his eyes touching her. Why wasn't she wearing something beneath the old T-shirt she had on?

Then, to her mortification, as though thinking about them had coaxed forth a response, her breasts began to bead against the soft cloth.

"Jenny?"

"What?" She jumped as though she had been caught doing something dirty. She felt feverish and light-headed, much as she had the night she had made love to Hal. He had been dressed as Cage was now, in jeans and a cotton western-cut shirt.

She could almost feel the different textures of fabric against her naked skin, the cool bite of his metal buckle before he had unfastened it, the warm proof of manhood when he did. She squirmed in her chair and pressed her knees tightly together beneath the table, trying to keep her face impassive.

"Have you heard from Hal?"

She shook her head fiercely, both in answer to his question and to deny the sensations rioting inside her. "Not since that last postcard dated a month ago. Do you think we should read anything into that?"

"Yes." Her head snapped up, but Cage was smiling. "That everything is okay."

"No news is good news."

"Something like that."

"Bob and Sarah keep up a good front, but they're worried. We didn't think he'd have to go into the interior of the country, only to the border. We thought he would have been well on his way home by now."

"He might be, but just hasn't had the opportunity to notify us yet."

"Maybe." Selfishly she was hurt because the few times Hal had written, the notes had been addressed to them all. They had stressed that conditions in Monterico were bad, but that he was well and safe. He hadn't included one private word for her. His own fiancée. Was that characteristic of a man in love, especially after what had happened the night before he left?

"Do you miss him?" Cage asked her softly.

"Terribly." She raised her eyes to his, but they fell away almost immediately. One couldn't lie while staring into those tawny eyes. One couldn't even fudge on the truth. She missed Hal, but not "terribly," not like she had thought she would, not like she should. In a way, she was relieved that he wasn't constantly underfoot. And wasn't that odd?

Now that she had been to bed with him, didn't she want him anymore? What kind of depravity had she sunk into?

Oh, she longed to experience that kind of total joy again, that indescribable physical high, but she wasn't particularly anxious to see Hal. Probably because she was still angry with him for leaving without even saying good-bye to her. At least that was the answer she gave herself. It wasn't satisfying, but it was the only one she had.

"He'll be fine. Hal always comes out of scrapes smelling like a rose." Cage leaned back in his chair, balancing it on the two rear legs. "There was a family who lived through the alley there…long before you ever came to live with us. I was about twelve; Hal was eight or nine. Their poor daughter was extremely overweight. Obese. All the kids at school called her Tank, Fatso, Porky, unkind things like that. A group of bullies used to wait for her on the corner and laugh and catcall when she walked past them on her way home.''

Jenny was lulled by the tone of his voice. It was deep, a shade raspy, as though some west Texas sand had collected on his vocal cords. As he talked his fingers idly slid up and down the glass where condensation had made it slippery. The hairs on his knuckles looked very fair against his bronzed hand. Funny, she had never noticed that before. The way his fingers stroked the glass was mesmerizing and she could imagine...

"One day Hal was walking home with her and flew into the bullies when they started the name-calling. He got a bloody nose, a black eye, and a busted lip for his efforts to defend her. But that night Mother and Dad hailed him a hero for taking on a foe larger than himself. Mother gave him a double helping of dessert. Dad analogized Hal's good deed by comparing him to young David taking on Goliath.

"I thought, hell, if that's all it takes to make them happy, I can do that. I knew how to fight, and a lot better than Hal did. So the next day, I waited for those bullies behind the garage. I had two scores to settle with them. One, for beating up my kid brother. The other was for making fun of that poor girl."

"What did you do?"

"They were real proud of themselves and came chasing down the alley, laughing. I stepped from behind the garage and slammed the lid of a garbage can into one's face. Broke his nose. I buried my fist in the other's gut and knocked the wind out of him. I kicked the other one in the...where it hurts little boys."

Jenny smiled in spite of herself and ducked her head blushing. Then she lifted her eyes back to him. "What happened?"

"I was expecting the same kind of praise Hal had gotten the night before." A wry grin twisted his sensual mouth and he shook his head. "I got sent to my room with no dinner, a blistering lecture, a spanking, and a suspension in my allowance and the use of my bike for two weeks."

The front legs of the chair hit the floor with a finality compared to the way he had concluded the story. "So you see, Jenny, if I'd taken on this Central American mission, I'd have been labelled as a troublemaker and a rabble-rouser looking for a good fight. But Hal, Hal is considered a saint."

Without even thinking about it, her hand shot across the table to cover his. "I'm so sorry, Cage. I know it hurts."

His hand automatically covered the one clutching his and his eyes speared into hers. There were tears of empathy standing in the emerald depths.

"Jenny? We're home. Where are you?"

The Hendrens were coming in the front door. Cage and Jenny remained captives of each other, releasing their hands and eyes only heartbeats before his parents blustered into the kitchen.

"Oh, here you are. Hello, Cage."

Jenny jumped up, offering to get the older couple a cold drink or coffee. Cage rose to his feet, too. "I've got to be going. I just stopped by to see if you'd heard from Hal. I'll check back later. 'Bye."

There was no reason to prolong the visit. He *had* wanted to ask about Hal, but his main reason for coming to the parsonage had been to see Jenny.

He had seen her.

She had touched him.

Actually reached out and touched him.

He felt good.

Jenny bent over to place a sack of groceries in the backseat of her car. The Hendrens had given her the economical compact when she graduated from TCU. A long wolf whistle brought her around quickly, so quickly she almost bumped her head.

Cage was sitting astride a vicious-looking motorcycle wearing an expression that matched his whistle. A shiny black helmet was dangling from his hand. He had on a blue chambray shirt from which the sleeves had been ripped. Either the wind had tugged all the buttons from their holes, or he had left them carelessly undone. In either event, the only thing that saved him from indecency—and then just barely—was that the shirt was tucked into the waistband of his jeans.

There was nothing decent about them.

A faded red bandana was knotted around his neck. He looked like a bandit. Hell's Angels would have welcomed him with open arms and probably elected him their president.

Jenny was intrigued by the network of light brown hair that matted his chest. It fanned out over the upper muscles and grew inward toward that satiny ribbon of hair that bisected his stomach. She had a difficult time tearing her eyes away from the beguiling sight of all that tanned skin and the crisp carpet of masculine body hair.

"You're not very nice," Jenny chided insincerely.

"Thank you, ma'am."

She laughed.

"You're not very nice either," Cage countered.

"What did I do that wasn't nice?"

"You wore a tight pair of jeans that could inflame a man's imagination."

Glancing down at herself, she retorted, "Only some men. The ones with their minds in the gutter."

"Hm. I suppose that means me."

"If the shoe fits... No other man has whistled at me today."

"Then no other man caught you bending over."

She shot him an acid look. "Sexist."

"And proud to be one."

Placing her hands on her hips, she demanded, "What if I came up behind you and whistled like that?"

"I'd drag you into the bushes."

"You are incorrigible."

"That's what they tell me." When he smiled, his teeth shone brightly in the sunlight. Bracing his hands on the handle bars of the bike, he leaned forward slightly. The muscles in his arms bulged and Jenny could detect the strong veins beneath the taut skin. "Go for a ride with me?"

Drawing her eyes away from him, she closed the back-seat door with emphasis and opened the driver's. "A ride? You're insane." She looked askance at the cycle.

"Nope. Only incorrigible." She made a face at him and his grin broadened. "Come on, Jenny. It'll be a blast."

"No way. I'm not getting on that thing."

"Why?"

"I don't trust your driving."

He barked a short laugh. "I'm stone sober."

"For once."

It was his turn to make a face.

Jenny said, "I've ridden with you in a car before and risked life and limb every mile. Even the highway patrolmen salute you when you whiz by. They know they couldn't possibly catch you."

He shrugged, sending all sorts of muscles into play. "So I like driving fast. I'm safe."

"I'm safer. No, thank you," she said politely and slid beneath the steering wheel of her car. "Besides, the ice cream's melting," she said through the window as she started the engine.

He followed her home, weaving the cycle in and out and around her, making her stop and start lurchingly a dozen times in an effort to keep from crashing with him. Beneath the shaded visor of his helmet his grin was wide. Through her windshield she tried to look stern and disapproving, but she was laughing by the time they reached the parsonage.

"See?" He parked the motorcycle beside her car and pulled off his helmet. "Perfectly harmless. Come for a ride with me."

The sun struck his hair just right, turning it the color of ripe wheat. Through his dense, sun-tipped lashes, his eyes were compelling. Jenny hesitated, the sack of groceries growing heavier in her arms.

"When's the last time you did something spontaneous?" he asked her temptingly.

The night I seduced Hal.

But she didn't even want to think about Hal. He had been gone for ten weeks. Cage visited the parsonage often. He always popped up unexpectedly, as he had today in the grocery store parking lot. If she didn't know better, she would think he was following her.

"I can't, really," she hedged.

"Sure you can. Hurry. I'll help you put away the ice cream."

There was no arguing with him. The groceries were stashed in the pantry and refrigerator with dispatch, and since Bob and Sarah weren't at home, Jenny was fair game. Cage knew exactly how to sniff out weakened prey and bring it down.

"Pretty please," he begged, bending his knees to bring his face down on a level with hers. The lines on either side of his mouth deeped into dimples that should have been outlawed as a public menace. "With sugar on it."

"Oh, all right," Jenny surrendered with an irritated sigh. Actually her heart was pounding with anticipation.

He gripped her arm firmly and dragged her outside before she could change her mind. "I even have a helmet for you." He eased it over her head and reached beneath her chin to snap the strap closed. For an instant, only an instant, their eyes locked. He touched her cheek. But before she could determine exactly what the gleam in his eyes meant, the moment was over and he was instructing her on how to mount the motorcycle.

When she was situated on the padded seat, he swung his leg over and said, "Now put your arms around me."

She hesitated, then gingerly closed her arms around his middle. When her hands came in contact with his bare front, the fuzzy hair tickled her wrists, and she yanked her hands away. "I'm sorry," she muttered, as though she had bumped into a stranger on an elevator. Her heart was knocking painfully against her ribs.

"It's all right." He took her hands in his and folded them together just above his waist, pressing them against him. "You have to hold on tight."

Jenny's head was buzzing. Her throat had gone dry. If she hadn't been afraid of becoming dizzy and possibly falling off, she would have shut her eyes as he started the motorcycle and guided it down the street. She kept her hands perfectly still, though she had the mad urge to comb her fingers up through his chest hair and to knead the hard muscles of his chest with her fingers.

"How do you like it so far?" he shouted back at her.

Having gotten over her initial shyness, she could honestly answer, "I love it!"

The hot wind beat at them mercilessly as they left the city limits and Cage opened the cycle's motor to full throttle. They sped down the highway with the straight flying precision of a hornet. There was something wildly exciting about having only the two wheels of the cycle between her and the macadam that sped past beneath her. The motor thrummed up through her thighs, her middle, her breasts. That steady vibration was thrilling.

He turned off the highway onto a narrow blacktopped road and eventually drove through a gate. The house at the top of a gradual rise in the otherwise flat barrenness was authentically Victorian. Grass and shrubbery had been planted in the fenced yard and there was a variety of trees lending their shade. The front porch, which wrapped around three sides of the house, was shielded from the sun by the balconies of the second story. An onion-shaped cupola domed one front corner. The picture-book structure was painted the color of sand with an accent trim of rust and slate.

To one side there was a garage. Jenny noticed the Corvette parked there, along with a selection of other vehicles. Beyond the garage was a stable. Several horses grazed in the pasture behind it.

"This is my house," Cage said simply. He drew the bike to a halt and cut the engine. He let Jenny alight before he did. She stared at the house as she lifted the helmet from her head.

"This is where you live?"

"Yep. For two years now."

"I never really knew where your house was. You've never invited us out here." She turned to him. "Why, Cage?"

"I didn't want to be turned down. My folks consider this a den of iniquity, they wouldn't set foot in it. Hal probably wouldn't have come because he knew they would disapprove. It seemed simpler not to ask and just make it easier for everybody."

"What about me?"

"Would you have come?"

"I think so." But neither of them believed she would have.

"You're here now. Would you like to see it?"

He asked humbly. For all his machismo he looked extremely vulnerable. Jenny didn't hesitate this time. She very much wanted to see his house. "Please. Can we go inside?"

His mouth broke into a wide grin and he led her up the front steps. "The house was built just after the turn of the century. It went through a series of owners, each one letting it deteriorate a little more. It was truly derelict when I bought it. What I really wanted was the land that went with it, and I thought about tearing the house down and starting over with something low and sprawling and contemporary. But the house began to grow on me. It seemed to belong here, so I decided to let it stay. I've fixed it up."

That was an understatement.

"It's lovely," Jenny observed as they wandered through the tall-ceilinged, airy, sunlit rooms.

Cage had decorated simply, painting everything off-white, the walls, the shutters, the woodwork, the portiere, which separated the central hall from the parlor on one side and the rounded dining room on the other. The oaken floors had been rubbed to a soft patina. The furniture, with an emphasis on comfort, was a pleasing mixture of old and new, all tasteful and well arranged.

The kitchen was a space-age wonder, but all the modern appliances were aptly hidden behind a facade of century-old charm. The upstairs boasted three bedrooms. Only one had been fully restored.

From the doorway Jenny gazed at the room Cage slept in. Decorated in desert colors of sand and sienna, it matched his dusty-blond coloring. The massive bed was covered with an irregularly shaped, unhemmed suede spread that looked as soft as butter. Through a connecting door Jenny caught a glimpse of a lavish bathroom with a picture window immodestly placed over the enormous tub.

Cage noted the direction of her eyes. "I like to lie in the water and look over the landscape. From there the sunset is spectacular." He spoke close to her ear, close enough for his warm breath to stir her hair. "Or at night when the moon is full and the stars are out, it's a breathtaking sight."

Jenny felt herself being hynotically drawn closer to him and jerked herself erect. "The house suits you, Cage. At first, I didn't think it would, but strangely it does."

He seemed to like that. "Come see the pool."

He led her back down the stairs, through a screened "sleeping porch," and onto the limestone patio. It was a riot of color. Terra-cotta pots held clusters of blooming red geraniums. In one corner a cactus garden boasted bright yellow and pink blooms. Silvery sage bushes with their purple flowers lined the fence. The pool was as deep and blue as a sapphire. "Wow," she whispered.

"Wanna swim?"

"I don't have a suit."

"Wanna swim?"

The raspy inquiry was laden with implication, subtle and seductive, but indubitably clear.

Everything inside Jenny stilled. Her blood stopped flowing through her body because her heart ceased pumping. Her lungs shut down operation. She couldn't even blink, so captivated was she by his intent amber stare and the intoxicating huskiness of his invitation.

It was unthinkable, of course.

But she thought about it anyway.

And the thoughts, making a kaleidoscope of her mind, sent her temperature rising. She could *see* them naked, the sun beating down on their bare skin, the dry wind swirling around them. Cage naked, his toasty skin garnished with that soft golden brown body hair. And herself, shyly baring herself to the elements, to the man.

The fantasy made her mouth water.

She saw herself touching him, saw her hands gliding over those sleek bare arms, saw her fingertips tracing the veins that showed beneath the surface, saw her fingers winding through that soft pelt on his chest.

She saw him touching her, saw his strong hands reaching out gently to caress her breasts and their aching crests, to slide down her belly to her thighs, to touch—

"I need to get back." She turned and virtually ran across the patio and through the house as though the devil were after her. Cage didn't have a forked tail and horns, but the simile wasn't all that inaccurate.

He caught up with her on the porch and she waited stiffly beside him while he relocked the door of the house. When he took her arm to guide her down the steps, she flinched away from him. "Is something wrong, Jenny?"

"No, no, of course not," she said, wetting her dry lips with a nervously flicking tongue. "I like your house."

Why was she acting like this? Cage wasn't going to hurt her. She had known him for years, lived in the same house with him when he came home for summer vacations from college.

Why now did he suddenly seem like a stranger to her, yet one she knew better than any other human being on earth? She hadn't shared her heart with Cage the way she had with Hal during their quiet discussions. But she felt a kinship with this man that was beyond reason or explanation. Why?

Feelings for him churned inside her. They were all so foreign, all so sexual. But, miraculously and unnervingly, all so right.

"Okay, you've been initiated," he said, jumping onto the cycle once she had resumed her place. He revved the engine. "Hang on tight, girl."

"Cage!"

That was the last full breath she drew. He sped down the highway until the landscape was no more than a blur. Hanging on for dear life, she clung to him, no longer timorous about splaying her hands wide over his stomach and gluing her front to his back. Her thighs cradled his hips and she propped her chin on his shoulder.

When they reached the street of the parsonage, he slowed down considerably but jumped the curb and weaved in and out of the mulberry trees that some civic-minded individual had planted there decades ago. There were no pedestrians, so it was safe, but Jenny squealed, "You're crazy, Cage Hendren!"

They were gasping with laughter when he pulled into the driveway of the parsonage and killed the motor. "Want to go again tomorrow?" he asked over his shoulder.

She climbed off and her knees nearly buckled beneath her. Excitement had robbed her of equilibrium and it took her a moment to regain it while she clutched his shoulder. "No. Definitely not. That last ride was death defying."

Her cheeks were rosy and her eyes shone green. Cage had never seen her smile quite like this. Gone was the conservative mask she hid behind. Jenny had an adventurous streak to her nature and he was seeing it emerge for the first time.

He got off the bike and pulled the helmet from his head. "Pretty soon you'll get the hang of it." He helped her with her own helmet and it seemed the most natural thing in the world to comb his fingers through her matted hair. "Next time we'll break the sound barrier."

He draped his arm around her shoulders. Still weak-kneed, she slumped against his support and looped her arm around his waist. Together they staggered toward the back door.

It opened. Bob stepped out onto the steps. He looked at Cage accusingly, then at Jenny. His hard expression brought them to an abrupt halt.

"Dad?" "Bob?" they asked in unison.

But they already knew.

"My son is dead."

Chapter 4

"Jenny?" Cage's urgent whisper elicited no response. "Jenny, please don't cry. Can I have the flight attendant bring you something?"

She shook her head and lowered the damp tissue from her eyes. "No, thank you, Cage. I'm fine."

But she wasn't fine. She hadn't been since yesterday afternoon when Bob Hendren had told them that Hal had been shot by a firing squad in Monterico.

"Why the hell I let you talk me into letting you come along, I'll never know," Cage said with bitter self-reproach.

"This is something I had to do," she insisted, still blotting her puffy red eyes and dabbing at her nose.

"I'm afraid it's going to be an ordeal that will only make things more difficult for you."

"No, it won't. I couldn't just sit at home and wait. I had to come with you or go mad."

He could understand that. This was a gruesome errand, traveling to Monterico to identify Hal's body and arrange for its transport back to the United States. There would be mounds of paperwork from the U.S. State Department that must be dealt with, not to mention the tenuous negotiations with the petulant military junta in Monterico. But grappling with all that was better than staying at home and witnessing the Hendren's abject grief.

"Jenny, where have you been?" Sarah had cried. She had stretched both arms in Jenny's direction when the younger woman rushed into the living room of the parsonage after Bob had told her and Cage the news. "Your car was here...we looked everywhere... Oh, Jenny!"

Sarah had collapsed against Jenny and sobbed heart wrenchingly. Cage sat down on the sofa, spread his knees wide, bowed his head low, and stared at the floor between his booted feet. No one comforted him on the loss of his brother. He might not have been there, save for the condemning looks Bob directed toward the motorcycle helmets Cage had dropped on the hall floor as they rushed inside the house.

Jenny smoothed back Sarah's light brown hair. "I'm sorry I wasn't here. I...Cage and I went riding on his motorcycle."

"You were with Cage?" Sarah's head popped up and her eyes swung toward him. She looked as though his existence was a great surprise to her, as though she had never seen him before.

"How did you find out about Hal, Mother?" he asked quietly.

Sarah seemed to have fallen into a stupor. Her expression was blank, her skin pasty.

It was Bob who had told them what little they knew. "A representative of the State Department called about half an hour ago." The pastor seemed terribly old suddenly. His shoulders sagged, reducing his posture to that of an old man. The skin beneath his chin looked flabby and wobbly for the first time. His eyes weren't as clear and lively as usual. His voice, which sounded impressive and full of conviction from his pulpit, wavered pitifully.

"Apparently those facist hoodlums in control of the government down there didn't like Hal's interference. He and members of his group were arrested, along with some of the rebels they were going to rescue. They were all—" he cast a sympathetic glance at Sarah and amended what the government official had told him "—killed. Our government is making a formal protest."

"Our son is dead!" Sarah wailed. "What good will protests do? Nothing will bring Hal back."

Jenny had silently agreed. The two women had clung to each other for the remainder of the evening, weeping, grieving. Word had spread through the congregation of the church. Members began arriving, filling the large rooms of the parsonage with sympathy, and the kitchen with food.

The phone had rung incessantly. Once Jenny glanced up to see Cage speaking into it. At some point he had gone home and changed clothes. He was wearing a pair of tailored slacks, a sport shirt, and a jacket. As he listened to the party on the other end, he rubbed his eye sockets with his thumb and index finger. Slumped against the wall as he was, he looked tired. And bereaved.

She hadn't even taken time to go upstairs long enough to brush her hair after that madcap ride with Cage. But no one seemed to notice her dishevelment. Everyone moved about like robots, going through the motions of living with disinterest. They couldn't believe that Hal's presence in their lives had actually been snatched away in such a cruel, violent, and irreversible way.

"You look exhausted." Jenny had turned from pouring herself a cup of coffee to find Cage standing behind her. "Have you eaten anything?"

The dishes of food brought over by members of the church were lined along the countertops of the kitchen. They didn't entice Jenny, indeed, the thought of eating anything was repugnant. "No. I don't want anything. How about you?"

"I guess I'm not hungry either."

"We really should eat something," Bob had remarked as he joined them. Sarah was clinging to his arm as he eased her into a chair.

"A man named Whithers from the State Department called, Dad," Cage had informed them. "I'll go down there tomorrow and accompany Hal's body back." Sarah whimpered and crammed her fingers against her compressed lips. Cage looked down at her sadly. "This Whithers is meeting me in Mexico City. He'll go with me, and hopefully cut through some of the red tape I'm bound to run into. I'll call you as soon as I know something, so you can make funeral arrangements."

Sarah folded her arms on the table, laid her head on them, and began crying again.

"I'm going with you, Cage."

Jenny had spoken her intentions calmly. The Hendren's reaction to her announcement hadn't been so calm. But her mind was made up and they were too distraught to argue with her about it.

She and Cage had left early that morning, driving to El Paso to catch a plane to Mexico City, the same flight Hal had taken almost three months before.

Now Cage was sitting close to her. Though there was an empty seat in their row, he sat in the middle beside her, as though shielding her from the rest of the world. When her tissue began to shred, he passed her a handkerchief from the breast pocket of his sport coat.

"Thank you."

"Don't thank me, Jenny. I can't bear to see you crying."

"I feel so guilty."

"Guilty? For godsake, why?"

She waved her hands in frustration and returned her gaze to the void outside the window of the airplane. "I don't know. A million reasons. For being mad at him when he left. For feeling hurt and angry when he didn't send me a special postcard. Silly, stupid things like that.''

''Everybody feels guilty for slights like that when someone dies. It's natural.''

''Yes, but...I feel guilty for...being alive.'' She turned her head and looked at him with tear-shiny eyes. ''For having such a good time with you yesterday when Hal was already dead.''

''Jenny.'' Something hard and painful ground into Cage's chest. That same guilt had visited him, but he wouldn't tell her that.

He put his nearest arm around her and drew her against his chest. His other hand sifted comfortingly through her hair as her head rested on his shoulder. ''You mustn't feel guilty for being alive. Hal wouldn't want that. He chose to do this. He knew the risks involved. He took them.''

Cage didn't want to be consciously aware of how good it felt to hold her. But he was. He had wanted to hold her plenty of times. He hated the reason for being granted the opportunity now. On the other hand, he was human. He couldn't ignore the sheer pleasure of feeling her small, dainty body pressed against his.

Why did Hal have to die? Dammit, *why*? Cage had wanted to win Jenny in a fair fight. There was no victory in her suddenly becoming available by Hal's death. Would her own guilt be the next obstacle he must overcome?

''Why were you mad at Hal when he left?'' Had she had a change of heart and later regretted what had happened in her bed that night? Oh, please, no. He might get an answer he didn't want to hear, but he had to ask.

Jenny hesitated so long, Cage was beginning to think she wasn't going to answer. Then she said haltingly, ''Something happened the night before he left that brought us very close. I thought it had changed things. But the next morning he left without even saying good-bye as though it had never happened."

Because it hadn't happened to Hal.

"I half-way expected him to call off his trip." She sighed and Cage felt her breasts expand with the deep breath. "I felt rejected when he didn't. Deep down I really didn't believe that my feelings were more important to him than his mission, but..."

Cage had been desperate to know what she was thinking and feeling that morning. As he stared at her across the breakfast table, a thousand questions had tumbled through his mind, but he hadn't been able to ask any of them. He had been forced into silence by his own treachery.

He had wanted to say, "Are you all right?" "Did I hurt you?" "Jenny, did I imagine how wonderful it was, or was it really that good?" "Did it actually happen or was it all a fantastic dream?"

And he still didn't know the answers to those questions. But whatever her answers to them were, they belonged to Hal, not to him. She had been hurt by Hal's apparent casualness about having made love to her for the first time. She couldn't understand how he could have left the way he did if it meant something to him. Hal didn't deserve her anger. But she was innocent, too. There was only one culprit, and as usual, it was he.

Should he tell her now, explain that Hal hadn't been indifferent to their lovemaking because he hadn't experienced it? That would absolve her of the guilt she was feeling now. Should he tell her?

No. God, no. She had Hal's death to deal with. How would she cope with the knowledge that she had made love to the wrong man? How could any woman ever forgive herself for that? How could she ever forgive the man who had tricked her?

Jenny must have felt the tension in his arms, because she sat up suddenly and put space between them. "I shouldn't be bothering you with this. I'm sure my personal life is of little interest to you."

Oh, yes, it was. They had once been as personal with each other as two human beings can be. Only she didn't know it. She didn't know that he had caressed her skin until the texture of it was engraved on his palms and fingertips. He knew the shape of her breasts and how they felt against his lips and tongue. The sounds she made in the throes of passion were as familiar to him as his own voice because his mind had played them like a tape recorder over and over again when he was alone at night in his bed, thinking of her.

And he was certain no man, not even his brother, had kissed her with the same degree of intimacy he had. No one knew her taste like he did.

Abruptly his mind snapped to attention. What the hell was he doing? What kind of a sorry son of a bitch was he? His brother was dead and here he was thinking about what sex with Jenny was like.

"We'll be landing soon," he said gruffly to cover his own guilt and confusion.

"Then I'd better repair my face."

"Your face is lovely."

Her head whipped around. In spite of his disgust with himself for his previous train of thought, Cage couldn't keep himself from looking at her.

She gazed back into his eyes, realizing that no one had thanked him for all the necessary details he had attended to. He had taken on the unwelcome tasks without having even been asked to. "You've been a tremendous help through all this, Cage. With your parents. With me." She laid her hand on his arm. "I'm glad we have you."

"I'm glad you have me, too," he said with a soft smile.

He'd been right not to tell her he had been her lover that night. The old selfish Cage wouldn't have let his brother take the credit for the joy he had given Jenny that night. But this new changed Cage would continue letting her think she had been with Hal to spare her from having to heap shame onto tragedy.

The captial city of Monterico was noisy, nasty, and hot.

Concrete-and-steel skeletons were grim reminders that buildings had once stood where now there was only ruin. Piles of rubble made some streets impassable. Political slogans, painted on in blood red, screamed the grisly story of civil war from every available billboard.

Soldiers, wearing fatigue pants and combat boots and tank tops, patrolled the streets. Their expressions were surly, their attitude arrogant and rude. The civilian population was cowed, their eyes watchful and afraid, their movements furtive, as they went about their workday activities.

Jenny had never seen such a depressing place. She began to feel an empathy with Hal's cause and to experience some of his determination to correct this wrong and put an end to this suppresion of the human spirit.

Whithers, the State Department official who had met them in Mexico City, was a disappointment. Jenny had expected a Gregory Peck type whose very carriage proclaimed authority and commanded obedience. Mr. Whithers looked like he couldn't withstand a strong wind, much less adversity from a government hostile to the United States. He looked far from authoritarian and commanding in his wrinkled seersucker suit. She could visualize him being the butt of cruel jests, rather than posing any threat to a military junta.

But he had been kind and sensitive to their grief as he walked Cage and her through the crowded airport to the plane that would carry them to Monterico. He had treated her with deference.

Jenny let Cage do most of the talking. But while he took official matters into his own hands, he never let his attention slip from her. She was never far from him; he was constantly at her side, usually with a protective arm around her shoulders or a tender hand beneath her elbow.

She drew on his strength, relied on it without apology. Lord, what would she do without it? She wondered why people didn't credit Cage with having any sensitivity.

"Cage Hendren doesn't give a damn about anybody or anything."

That was how people saw him.

But they were wrong. He cared a great deal. About his brother. And he couldn't have been kinder to her.

Upon their arrival in Monterico, Jenny, Cage, and Mr. Whithers had been packed into the backseat of an aging Ford. In the front seat were a driver and a soldier with a Soviet AK-47 tucked beneath his arm. Every time Jenny looked at the automatic weapon, shivers went down her spine.

The driver and his partner represented the government currently in control of the country. They made no effort to disguise their contempt for their passengers.

After a circuitous journey through the city, they were finally deposited in front of a building that had formally housed a bank. Now it served as government headquarters. A goat was tethered to one of the columns of the building's facade. He seemed as ill tempered and hostile as the other residents of Monterico.

Inside, overhead fans vainly tried to circulate the thick, stifling air. But at least the former bank lobby provided a repose from the scorching sun. Jenny's blouse was sticking to her back. Cage had long since taken off his jacket and tie and rolled up his shirt sleeves.

They were ungraciously shown a seat by a soldier who poked his rifle toward a dilapidated couch and grunted what they assumed was an order for them to sit down. Mr. Whithers was ushered in to confer with the military commander. He was agitatedly mopping his brow with a handkerchief when he left the office a few minutes later. "Washington will hear about this," he said indignantly.

"About what?" Cage demanded.

Standing with his feet spaced widely apart, his jacket slung over his shoulder by a crooked finger, his shirt open to reveal that breath-snatching chest, and virtually growling through clenched teeth, he looked more fearsome than any of the soldiers.

Mr. Whithers explained to them that Hal's body hadn't yet reached the city. "The village where the...uh..."

"Execution," Cage provided bluntly.

"Yes, well, the village where *it* took place is sealed off by guerrilla fighting. But they expect the body to be delivered by nightfall," he rushed to add reassuringly.

"Nightfall!" Jenny exclaimed. Spending one afternoon in this war-torn place was a dismal prospect.

"I'm afraid so, Miss Fletcher." Mr. Whithers cast a nervous glance toward Cage. "It might be sooner. No one seems to know for certain."

"What are we supposed to do in the meantime?" she asked.

He cleared his throat and swallowed. "Wait."

And they did. For endless hours that ticked by with monotonous sluggishness. They weren't allowed to leave the building. When Mr. Whithers used all his diplomatic powers to get them food and drink, they were brought stale ham sandwiches and glasses of rusty tepid water.

"No doubt these are leftovers from the prison camps," Cage said and with scathing disgust tossed the offensive sandwich into the nearest overflowing trash can. Jenny couldn't eat hers either. The ham had a slightly greenish cast. But they drank the water out of fear of dehydration. They sweltered in the afternoon heat while the soldiers propped themselves and their rifles against the walls and took their *siestas*.

Cage paced, incessantly cursing and mouthing epithets about Monterico in general and their guards in particular. Jenny's light hair and green eyes were a novelty in this country, where most of the populace was of Latin descent. Cage was aware of that even if she wasn't. Every time one of the cocky soldiers cast a speculative glance in her direction, Cage's eyes narrowed dangerously.

The guards weren't aware that he was fluent in Spanish and when one guffawed a crude remark about Jenny to his buddy, Cage went storming toward the soldier, his hands balled into fists. Mr. Whithers grabbed him by the sleeve.

"For godsake, man, don't do anything stupid. Otherwise we might have three bodies to ship home to your parents."

Whithers was right, of course, and Cage belligerently returned to his seat on the couch. He clasped Jenny's hand hard. "Don't leave my sight for an instant, for any reason."

Just as the sun was sinking over the top of the dense jungle in the distance, a large military truck rumbled up the street and wheezed to a halt outside the government building. The driver and his cohorts came out of it leisurely, lighting up cigarettes, joking among themselves, stretching after what must have been a long, dusty ride. The one with the biggest belly and highest rank waddled into the commander's office.

"This must be it," Mr. Whithers said hopefully.

He was right. The commander came out of his office, waving a sheaf of papers, beckoning them to follow him outside. The canvas flaps at the back of the truck were flung aside and the commander heaved himself up. Whithers followed. Then Cage.

"No," he said to Jenny, when she placed her foot on the tailgate.

"But, Cage—"

"No," he repeated firmly.

Inside the truck there were four caskets. Hal was in the third one they opened. Jenny knew by the expression on Cage's face when the top was pried off. As though someone had stamped a new expression on his face, it changed drastically. He squeezed his eyes shut and grimaced, baring his teeth. Whithers asked him a brief question and he nodded.

When his eyes opened, they roved the interior of the truck as though he couldn't bring himself to look down at his brother again. But eventually he did. And his face softened and tears sprang into his eyes. He extended his hand and lovingly touched his brother's face.

Then the commander issued a curt order in rapid Spanish and the casket was resealed. Cage and Whithers were prodded out of the truck and four soldiers were ordered up into it to lift the coffin out.

The moment Cage jumped out of the truck, he put his arms around Jenny. Until then, she hadn't realized she was crying. "Get us out of here," he said to Whithers, who hovered nearby. "Have them take the coffin to the airport and let's leave immediately."

Whithers rushed off to do Cage's bidding. Placing a finger beneath her chin, Cage lifted Jenny's head. "Are you all right?"

"Was he...is his face...?"

"No," he said smiling gently and brushing back her hair. "He looks untouched, like he's sleeping. Incredibly young. Very peaceful."

She heaved a sob and buried her face in the collar of his shirt. He bent his head down low over hers and held her close. His hands smoothed her back. Despite her confused feelings for Hal, he was like a brother. She had lived with them long enough to feel that kind of kinship with him. Cage knew what she was suffering. He felt like a part of himself was in that casket.

Whithers cleared his throat loudly and uncomfortably. "Uh, Mr. Hendren." When Cage lifted his head and looked at him, he said hurriedly, "They're taking your brother's body to the airport now." He indicated a rickety pickup truck that was jostling its cargo as it lumbered up a hill, its gears grinding.

"Good. I want to get Jenny the hell out of here. We can be in Mexico City by—"

"There's, uh, a problem."

Cage was already in motion. He stopped and wheeled around, bringing Jenny, who he had by the arm, with him. "What kind of problem?" he asked with a glower.

Whithers shifted his weight from one foot to the other, then back again. "They won't let a plane take off after dark."

"What?!" Cage exploded. The sun had set by now. The dusk was impenetrable, the way only a tropical dusk can be.

"Security precautions," Whithers explained. "They won't turn on the landing strip lights after nightfall. If you'll recall, the runways were camouflaged when we landed today."

"Yeah, yeah, I remember," Cage said irritably, raking a hand through his hair. "When can we leave?"

"First thing in the morning."

"If we don't, I'm going to raise hell. I can fight dirty, too, by God. They've yet to meet a guerrilla fighter meaner than me." His warning carried with it jabbing thrusts of his index finger. "And if they think I'm going to subject Jenny to a night in that bank building, they're wrong!"

"No, no, that won't be necessary. They've made arrangements with a local hotel for us to spend the night."

"I'll bet they have," Cage spat. "We'll find our own hotel."

But the selection was limited and as it ended up they stayed where the government officials had assigned them in the first place. If the rooms were as sad as the lobby, Jenny thought, they were in for an uncomfortable night. The furniture was dusty and stained. The fans overhead turned desultorily. The drapes were shabby and their hems straggled to the scarred floor. A rack of magazines had been there so long the covers were faded and dust obscured the titles.

"Not exactly the Fairmont," Cage said from the side of his mouth. The lobby was patrolled not by brisk bellmen, but by sardonic soldiers carrying automatic rifles.

After a conference with the unkempt concierge, Withers handed them each a key. "We're all on the same floor," he said happily.

"Terrific. I'll have room service bring up champagne and caviar and we'll have a party."

Whithers actually looked hurt by Cage's snideness. "Miss Fletcher, you're in three nineteen."

Cage intercepted the key before it could be passed to Jenny and checked the number on his own. "Miss Fletcher is in three twenty-five with me. Come on, Jenny." Cage took her arm and led her across the lobby toward the stairs, opting to walk up rather than take the elevator. It if was in the same derelict condition as everything else in this godforsaken country, he wouldn't risk their lives by using it.

"But they were specific about the rooms," Whithers protested, trotting after them like a pesky puppy. "We were assigned rooms."

"To hell with that and them. Do you think I'm going to leave Jenny alone and at their mercy? Think again, man."

"But this is a breach of our agreement."

"I don't give a damn if this breach in your agreement brings on World War III!"

"I seriously doubt if they'd do anything to harm Miss Fletcher. After all, they're not savages."

Cage spun around and glared at the other man so hard, the state official shrank back. "She stays with me."

There was no arguing with the finality with which Cage spoke those four words.

Room three twenty-five was as hot and stuffy and dusty as all of Monterico seemed to be. Cage turned the lamp down low. He crossed to the window and checked outside. Just as he suspected, three stories below, they were being watched by two soldiers, distinguishable only by the glow of their cigarettes in the dark. He left the window open but adjusted the louvered shutters to give them a measure of privacy. Some of the cooler night air filtered in, making the hotel room at least livable.

"Whithers said they're sending up dinner."

"If it's anything like lunch, I can hardly wait," Jenny said, listlessly dropping her handbag onto the bed and flopping down on its edge. There was a definite droop to her shoulders, but Cage was glad to see she was still capable of humor.

"Take your shoes off and lie down."

"Maybe I'll just rest a minute," she said weakly and lay down. The bedspread had a red florid print that seemed to gobble her small form alive.

A half hour later a soldier knocked once on the door, then swung it open to carry in a tray. Jenny, who had been dozing jackknifed into a sitting position on the bed. Her skirt slid back to the top of her thighs. The soldier leered at her.

Cage, disregarding Whither's warning, grabbed the tray and shoved the soldier outside. He snapped closed the flimsy lock and braced a chair beneath the doorknob. Such measures wouldn't stop a round of AK-47 bullets, but it made him feel better to show even that much defiance.

"Dinner" was a dish comprised of rice, chicken, beans, and enough hot peppers to bring tears to Jenny's eyes. She didn't feel like eating anyway and after only two bites set her fork down.

"Eat," Cage commanded, pointing at her plate.

"I'm not hungry."

"Eat it anyway. Anything that doesn't move, that is."

He was unrelenting and she forced down half the portion, picking out the stringy pieces of chicken. Murky red wine accompanied the meal. Cage poured some from the foggy caraffe, tested it, and made a face. "I think they clean commodes with this."

"Is this the lush of La Bota County speaking?"

"Is that what they call me?" he asked, arching one brow.

"Sometimes."

He poured her a glass of the wine. She took it but looked at him as if to say, "What am I supposed to do with this?"

"Drink it," he said, answering her unspoken question. "I don't trust the water, and believe me, no germ could live long in that brew," he said of the wine.

She sipped, made a face that he laughed at, and sipped again. She managed only five swallows. "That's all I can take," she said, shuddering at the bitter aftertaste.

Cage placed the tray with their dirty dishes on the floor near the door. He listened there for a long moment, but he didn't think anyone was monitoring them. At least not just outside the door. But he knew that sentinels must have been posted near the elevator and stairs.

"Do you suppose the shower works?" Jenny asked, venturing into the bathroom.

"Try it out."

"Do you think I'll catch an infection?"

He laughed. "At this point, we'll have to chance it." He lifted his soiled shirt away from his chest. "I have no choice."

"I guess I don't either," she said, glancing at her reflection in the wavy mirror.

Closing the door between them, she peeled off her clothes and stepped into the shower stall. Ordinarily she wouldn't have considered setting her bare foot in such a mildew-ridden cubicle, but as Cage had said, she didn't have much choice. It was either use the shower or live with herself grimy and dusty.

Surprisingly the water that rained down on her was hot, and the soap was a United States export. She even used it to wash her hair in lieu of shampoo.

After she had dried herself off, she was in a dilemna as to what to put on. She had to rinse out her underclothes and blouse or she wouldn't be able to force herself to put them on again in the morning. She settled on wearing her full slip to sleep in and put her suit jacket over it for modesty's sake. It was a ridiculous looking outfit, but it would have to do.

She hand-laundered her lingerie in the sink and hung the panties, stockings, brassiere and blouse on the only towel rack available. Switching off the light, she opened the door.

Her hesitant eyes met Cage's curious ones across the room. Self-consciously she fingered the buttons on her jacket as she kept it pulled over her breasts. Her bare toes bashfully curled downward. Had Cage ever seen her with wet hair? "I, uh...there was only one towel. I'm sorry."

"I'll air dry." He smiled and made his voice sound flippant and light, but his eyes were on the deep lace border of her slip just above her knees.

She moved toward the bed and he brushed past her on his way into the bathroom. Once the door was closed behind him, she remembered her intimate apparel hanging up to dry. Scalding color rushed to her cheeks. Which was foolish. They had lived in the same house. When he was home from college, their clothes had been washed together. One couldn't go into the laundry room without seeing a garment belonging to somebody else. Cage had seen her in nighties and robes and in various stages of dishabille on numerous occasions.

But this was different. There was no use pretending that it wasn't. And the thought of Cage's eyes on her underwear made her go hot all over.

By the time he came out of the bathroom, she had taken off her jacket and was lying beneath the top sheet.

He smelled of damp male flesh and soap. He had pulled on his trousers, but that was all. His feet were bare. The hair on his chest was curly and damp. He must have rubbed his head with the towel. The dark blond strands weren't dripping, but they were still wet and tousled.

He flipped out the light and crossed to the bed, sitting down on the edge of it. "Comfy?"

"All things considered, yes."

He reached for one of the hands clutching the sheet to her chin and laced his fingers through hers. "You're something, Jenny Fletcher," he said softly. "Did you know that?"

"What do you mean?"

"You've been put through hell today, but you haven't murmured one word of complaint." With his free hand he wound a strand of her hair around his finger. "I think you're terrific."

"I think you are, too." There was a tremulous catch in her voice. "You cried for Hal."

"He was my brother. Despite our differences, I loved him."

"I keep thinking about—" She broke off and clamped her lower lip with her teeth when a tear slipped over the brim of her eyelid and rolled down her cheek.

"Don't think about it, Jenny." He smoothed her cheek with the backs of his fingers.

"I've got to!"

"No, you don't. You'll go mad if you think about that."

"You've thought about it, too, Cage. I know you have. What was it like right before he died? Was he tortured? Was he frightened? Was he—"

He laid his finger along her lips, stilling them. "Sure I've thought about it. And I think Hal must have faced it bravely. He had unshakable faith. He was doing what he felt led to do. I don't think that faith would have deserted him, no matter what."

"You admired him," she whispered with sudden insight.

He looked chagrined. "Yes, I did. Our reactions to circumstances were always different. I was violent, Hal was peaceable. Maybe it takes more courage to be meek and docile than it does to be a hell-raiser."

Without thinking, she reached up and laid her hand along his cheek. "He admired you, too."

"Me?" he asked incredulously.

"For your defiance, grit, whatever you want to call it."

"Maybe," Cage said pensively. "I'd like to think so." He replaced the sheet over her shoulders and patted it into place.

"Get some sleep." He turned off the lamp and hesitated only a moment before bending down and pecking a brotherly kiss on her forehead.

He moved the only moderately comfortable chair in the room to the window and settled into it. The day had taken its toll. In minutes both of them were asleep.

"What was that?" Jenny bolted upright in the bed. The room was dark, but bright light flashed periodically at the unfamiliar window.

Cage whirled around at her fearful exclamation and crossed to the bed quickly. "It's all right, Jenny." He sat down and tried to ease her back onto the pillows, but she was rigid. "It's several miles away. It's been going on for about half an hour. I'm sorry it woke you."

"It's not thunder," she said hoarsely.

He paused before saying, "No."

"It's fighting."

"Yes."

"Oh, Lord." She covered her face with her hands and fell back against the pillows. "I hate this place. It's dirty and hot and they kill people here. Good people, beautiful people like Hal. I want to go home," she cried. "I'm scared and I hate myself for being scared. But I can't help it."

"Ah, Jenny."

Cage lay down beside her and rolled her against him, holding her close. "The fighting is far away. Tomorrow morning we'll leave and you won't ever have to think about Monterico again. In the meantime, I'm here with you."

His fingers combed through her hair to massage her scalp, as though to press the reassuring words into her brain. He rubbed his chin on the top of her head and planted a fervent kiss there. "I won't let anything hurt you. God, as long as I'm alive, nothing will hurt you."

She took comfort from his words and the husky, soothing voice that kept repeating them. His physical strength was like a lifeline that she clung to. When he propped his back against the headboard and pulled her across his chest, she didn't resist but curled up against him, instinctively craving contact with another being who was larger and stronger.

Her fingers wove through the thick mat of hair on his chest and she pressed her cheek against the muscled wall. Her other arm hugged his waist tight as she burrowed beneath the shelter of his securing arms.

He held her in a close embrace, whispering the promises she was desperate to hear. Cage's mind wasn't on what he said, but on the precious feel of her lying against him.

Her slip showed up smooth and pale in the dark room. The lace-trimmed silk dipped at her waist and molded over the tantalizing curve of her hip. Her breasts felt soft and feminine against his chest.

Frequently a tremor rippled through her and he would kiss her hair while his hands caressed her bare shoulders. He marvelled over the smoothness of her skin and tried to keep his touch impersonal.

Then she slept. He could tell by the even, warm breathing that sifted through his chest hair. And, when in sleep, she moved one leg to cover his shin, he ground his head against the headboard. Her thigh rested atop his, her knee almost nudging the fly of his trousers. He clenched his teeth against the desire that knifed through him. He stared at her hand where it lay in repose on his lap. His need for her to touch him was so profound, it almost killed him. Yet if she had, he probably would have died in a spasm of agony and ecstasy anyway.

He listened to the rumbling echoes of the distant battle until all was still again. He watched the dawn creep over the eastern horizon. And still he held her, Hal's fiancée.

But his love.

Chapter 5

Hal Hendren's funeral drew public attention. It was thought by all those in attendance that he had been martyred. Those who had scoffed at his fanaticism before he left, now had their heads bowed reverently at the gravesite. Television news teams from major Texas cities and several national networks crawled over the cemetery like ants, setting up their camera angles.

Jenny, sitting with Bob and Sarah beneath the temporary tent, still couldn't believe that Hal's mission had resulted in this. It still seemed impossible that he was dead. She expected any moment to wake up from a bad dream.

Since she and Cage had returned from Monterico, the parsonage had been in chaos. The telephone never stopped ringing. There was a steady stream of visitors. Government agencies sent representatives to interview Cage and her about their impressions of the Central American country. With the interference of well-meaning church members, the whole event had taken on a carnival atmosphere.

Jenny had slept very little since she had awakened in Cage's arms in the hotel room in Monterico. She had come awake slowly, and when she realized that she was sprawled across his naked torso, wearing only her slip, she shoved herself up to find his eyes open and watchful.

"Ex...excuse me," she stammered as she scrambled off the bed and retreated to the bathroom.

Tension between them crackled like a bonfire as they dressed to leave. They seemed prone to bump into each other accidentally, which required awkward mumbled apologies.

Every time she hazarded a glance in Cage's direction, his eyes had been as sharp as razors, studying and analyzing her. So she had avoided looking at him, and that had seemed to irritate him.

They had been driven to the airport in another rattletrap car and put on the aircraft bearing Hal's coffin. In Mexico City Mr. Whithers had scuttled around like a beetle, making arrangements for their flight to El Paso, where a funeral home limousine from La Bota would meet them to carry the body home.

Cage had stood at the window of the airport staring at nothing, his shoulders hunched, his face tense, chainsmoking. When he caught her eyes on him and saw the surprise on her face—she hadn't seen him smoke since that night before Hal left—he cursed under his breath and ground the cigarette into the nearest ashtray.

They had said little to each other on the flight to El Paso. The drive from there to La Bota, which had seemed interminable as they followed the white limousine with its grim cargo, had been viturally silent.

They had said little to each other ever since.

The comradeship that had developed between them in Monterico no longer existed. For reasons she couldn't even name, Jenny was even more uneasy around him than she had been. He entered a room; she left it. He looked at her;

she averted her head. She couldn't say why she took such pains to avoid him, but she knew it had something to do with that night in the Monterico hotel room.

So he had held her. So?

So he had held her against him on a bed while they slept. So?

So he had held her against him on a bed while they slept, while she had been wearing nothing but a slip and he only a pair of slacks. So?

They had been surrounded by danger. They were friendless aliens in a foreign land. People did things in situations like that they wouldn't ordinarily do. One couldn't be held accountable for uncharacteristic behavior.

And it was probably insignificant that when she was first roused from sleep, one of his hands had been splayed wide on her derriere, the other closed loosely, but possessively, around her neck, and that her fingers had been entwined in his chest hair, her lips alarmingly near the flat disk of his nipple.

Now Jenny stared straight ahead at the flower bedecked coffin and willed away the memories of that morning. She didn't want to recall that infinitesimal span of time just after waking when she had felt warm and safe and serene, before she came to the jolting realization of just how wrong that serenity was.

She wouldn't risk getting close to Cage again. His strength and endurance were like a magnet that relentlessly pulled at her. She might even be tempted to look to him for support now if he weren't sitting on Bob's far side, his parents between them.

The bishop concluded the gravesite service with a long prayer. In the limousine that took them home, Sarah wept softly against her husband's shoulder. Cage stared moodily out the window. He had loosened his tie and unbuttoned his collar button. Jenny twisted her handkerchief and said nothing.

Several ladies from the church were already at the parsonage, brewing coffee, ladling punch, slicing cakes and pies for those who would come by to pay their respects after the funeral. And there were many. Jenny thought the parade would never stop. Weary of being consoled, she left the living room and went into the kitchen, where she insisted on washing dishes.

"Please," she said to the woman she replaced at the sink. "I need to keep busy."

"You poor dear."

"Your sweet Hal is gone."

"But you're young yet, Jenny."

"Your life must go on. It might take a while..."

"You're holding up well."

"Everybody says so."

"That trip you took to that horrid country must have been a nightmare."

"And with *Cage*."

The last speaker made a *tsking* sound with her lips and shook her head mournfully as if to say that, for a woman, traveling in Cage's company was tantamount to a fate worse than death.

Jenny wanted to lash out at them all, to tell them if it hadn't been for Cage, she probably would have fallen apart altogether. But she knew their comments were guileless and stemmed from ignorance. As they left one by one, she thanked them, forgiving them their stupidity, because their concern was sincere.

She finished the dishes that were stacked on the counter and went searching for others scattered throughout the house. When she entered the living room, she was relieved to find only the Hendrens there. Finally everyone had gone home. Gratefully Jenny sank into an easy chair and let her head flop back on the headrest.

Her eyes popped open when she heard the click of Cage's cigarette lighter. The flame burst from it to ignite the end of the cigarette he held between his lips. He returned the lighter to his pocket and drew on the cigarette.

"I've told you not to smoke in this house," Sarah snapped from her place on the sofa. Her eyes were dry but ringed with muddy shadows. She looked wrinkled and shrunken, almost skeletal. Her expression was so bitter, it bordered on meanness.

"I'm sorry," Cage said with genuine apology. He went to the front door and flicked the cigarette into the night, which had fallen without anyone noticing. "Habit."

"Must you bring your nasty habits into this house? Don't you have any respect for your mother?" Bob asked.

Cage halted on his way back to his chair, stunned by Bob's harsh and condemning tone. "I respect both of you," he replied softly, though his body strained with tension.

"You don't respect anything," Sarah said tersely. "You haven't told me once that you're sorry about your brother's death. I've gotten no sympathy from you."

"Mother, I—"

She went on as though he hadn't spoken. "But then I don't know why I expected it from you. You've done nothing but give me trouble from the day you were born. You were never considerate of me the way Hal was."

Jenny sat up straight, wanting to remind Sarah that for days Cage had been taking care of the media and relieving them of the legal details surrounding Hal's death. She didn't get a chance to say anything before Sarah continued.

"Hal would have been at my side constantly through something like this."

"I'm not Hal, Mother."

"You think you have to tell me that? You couldn't hold a candle to your brother."

"Sarah, please don't," Jenny cautioned, sliding to the edge of her chair.

"Hal was so good, so good and sweet. My baby." Sarah's shoulders began to shake and her face crumpled with another burst of tears. "If God had to take one of my sons, why did He take Hal and leave me with you?"

Jenny's hand flew to her mouth. "Oh, my God."

Bob dropped to his knees in front of his wife's chair and began to comfort her. For a long moment Cage stared down at his parents in total disbelief, then his face hardened. He spun on his heel and strode toward the door. The screen was brutally punched by the heel of his hand and went crashing against the outside wall. He bounded across the front porch and down the steps.

Without pausing to think about it, Jenny went tearing after him. She raced across the yard and caught up with him at the curb where his Corvette was parked. He was shrugging out of his dark suit coat as though it were on fire and ripping at the buttons of his vest.

"Go back where you belong," he shouted at her.

He squeezed himself into the low seat of the sports car and twisted the key in the ignition. It surprised Jenny that the key didn't break off. Stamping on the clutch, he shoved the car into first gear. She yanked open the passenger door and scrambled in just as he stamped on the accelerator.

The car shot forward like a missile. It fishtailed into the middle of the street and careened around the next corner without the benefit of brakes to slow its turn. Jenny reached for the door handle and miraculously managed to slam it closed without falling out onto the pavement or wrenching her arm from its socket.

Cage had shifted up to fourth gear by the time they reached the city limits sign. As he worked the gear stick, he ground his jaws together as though that would command better performance from the car. Jenny didn't risk looking at the speedometer. The landscape was no longer distinguishable. The headlights sliced through the endless darkness in front of them.

He reached for the knobs on the radio, controlling the car with one hand until he found the acid-rock station he wanted. He turned the volume up full blast, filling the interior of the car with the deafening clamor of metallic music.

"You made a big mistake," Cage shouted over the cacophony. "You should have stayed home tonight."

Reaching across the car and fumbling around her knees, he opened the glove compartment and took out a silver flask. Wedging it between his thighs, he unscrewed the cap, then raised it to his lips. He drank long. The face he made when he swallowed let Jenny know the liquor was potent. He drank again, and again, speeding down the center stripe of the highway with only one hand on the wheel.

The windows of the car were opened and the wind tore at her hair, tugging it free of the pins that had contained it in a neat, demure bun for the funeral. The wind sucked the breath from her nostrils. She didn't know how Cage had managed to light his cigarette, but the tip of it glowed against his dark face, illuminated only by the lights on the dashboard.

"Having fun?" He leered at her mockingly.

Seemingly unaffected by his sarcasm, she turned her head and stared out the windshield. She refused to honor him with an answer. The speeding car terrified her. She disapproved of it all, but she would remain mute if it killed her. And she thought it very well might, as he turned the car off the main highway onto a road that had no markings. How he had known it was there, Jenny was never able to figure out.

He abused the vintage Corvette by driving it over the dirt road, which was as corrugated as a washboard. Jenny's teeth slammed together and she clenched down on them to hold them intact. She gripped the cushioned seat beneath her in an effort to keep her head from bumping the ceiling as they bounced jarringly over the pock-marked road.

They were climbing. She could sense the change in altitude, though there was nothing to be seen, no relief from the darkness that surrounded them. The headlights bobbed crazily with each erratic movement of the car. Even the moon had slipped behind a cloud and lent no light, as though to say that Cage Hendren was pulling one of his wild stunts and no one should have to be witness to it.

He brought the car to an abrupt halt that almost sent Jenny through the windshield and made the tires skid fifty feet before coming to a complete standstill.

Cage cut the motor, creating a sudden silence as the blaring radio died with the engine. He propped his arm on the open windowsill, took the cigarette from his mouth, and replaced it with the spout of the flask. He drank deeply again and smacked his lips with satisfaction after he had swallowed.

He turned to Jenny, who was watching him in silent reproof. "I'm sorry. Where are my manners? Drink?" He tilted the flask toward her. She didn't move and her bland expression didn't change. "No?" he said, shrugging. "Too bad." He drank again, then offered her the pack of cigarettes. "Smoke? No, no, of course not."

He swigged more liquor. "You're the lady without blemish, aren't you? The viceless Miss Jenny Fletcher. Untainted. Untouchable. Fit only for saints like our dearly departed Hal Hendren." He dragged a goodly portion of nicotine into his lungs and released the smoke in a long gust aimed directly at her face.

Still she showed no reaction.

Then, as though her composure angered him, he threw the cigarette out the window. "Let's see, what would rattle your cage? What would get you to shriek in terror? What would provoke you into getting the hell out of my car, out of my sight, and out of my goddamned life?"

He was shouting. His breathing was labored and harsh. Jenny watched him visibly rein in his temper and control himself. When he spoke again, his voice still shook with hurt and fury, but he was calmer.

"What would disgust you enough to flee in fear for your virtue? A barrage of dirty words? Yeah, maybe. I doubt if you even know any, but we'll give that a try. Should I put them in alphabetical order or just say them as they come to my mind?"

"You can't disgust me, Cage."

"Wanna bet?"

"And nothing you say or do will make me leave you now."

"Is that right? You've set out to save me. Is that it?" He laughed mirthlessly. "Don't waste your time."

"I won't leave you," she repeated softly.

"Oh, yeah?" A sardonic curl lifted one corner of his lip. "We'll see."

He lunged across the console. One hand cupped the back of her head and hauled her against him. His lips crushed down on hers, hard and bruising. His teeth brutally ground against her tender mouth. She didn't fight him. Even when his tongue plunged between her lips to violate her mouth in the most demeaning way, she withstood its violent pillage without resistance.

The dress she had worn to Hal's funeral was a two-piece black knit. Cage fumbled at her waist, lifted her top, and plowed his hand beneath it.

"You've no doubt heard of my reputation with women," he rasped hotly against her neck. "I'm ruthless, without scruples. A despoiler of virgins, a wife-stealer, a sex machine run amok. It's said I'm so horny, it's tough for me to keep my pants zipped." He parted her knees with one of his. "Know what that means to you, Jenny? Bad news. You're in a heap of trouble, girl."

He brutalized her mouth again with another insulting kiss as his hand found her breast beneath her top. He pressed his hand over it, then dug into the fragile cup of her brassiere to lift her out. He massaged her breast roughly and rolled his thumb over its tender crest.

Despite her determination not to react, Jenny's back bowed off the seat. She drew herself up taut and tense against him. But she didn't fight or struggle. She resisted with passivity.

Her soft gasp was as effective as a siren's blast in Cage's head. He came to himself, realized what he was doing, and sagged against her like an inflatable toy someone had just punctured with a hat pin. He drew in several restorative breaths against her mouth, where his lips no longer exacted their revenge.

The oxygen served to clear the fog of alcohol and rage from his head. Contritely he withdrew his hand from her brassiere and in a pathetic attempt to make amends, tried to adjust the lace cup back over her breast. When he pulled his hand from beneath her top, he moved back to the driver's side of the car and got out.

Jenny buried her face in her hands and gulped in shuddering breaths. When she was somewhat composed, she straightened her clothing, opened her door and stepped out.

Cage was sitting on the hood of the car, staring out at nothing. She recognized their surroundings now. They were on the *mesa*, a table of land that rose above the surrounding countryside. It extended for miles. Beneath them the prairie was dark and still. The hot, dry wind plastered her clothes to her body and whipped through her hair. It whislted mournfully, nature's keening.

She moved to stand directly in front of him, blocking his view, such as it was. Their knees almost touched. He raised his head, looked at her briefly, then let his chin drop to his chest.

"I'm sorry."

"I know." She touched his hair, smoothing it back from his forehead, but the wind immediately whisked it from her fingers.

"How could I have—"

"It doesn't matter, Cage."

"It does," he insisted through gritted teeth. "It matters."

He raised his head again and reached out to gently lay his hand on the breast he had assaulted only moments before. There was nothing sexual in his touch. He could have been touching the shoulder of an injured child. "Did I hurt you?"

His hand was warm, healing, and Jenny brought her hand up and covered his where it lay. "No."

"I did."

"Not as much as they hurt you."

They stared deeply into each other's eyes. An unlabelled emotion arced between them like an electric current. Jenny dropped her hand. He lowered his just as quickly.

Jenny sat down beside him on the hood of the car. The waxed surface was hot even through their clothes, but neither of them noticed.

"Sarah didn't mean what she said, Cage."

He snorted a laugh. "Oh, yes, she did."

"She's distraught. That was grief talking, not her."

"No, Jenny." He shook his head sadly. "I know how they feel about me. They wish I'd never been born. I'm a living reminder that somehow they failed, a perpetual embarrassment to them and a constant insult to what they believe. Even if it is never spoken aloud, I know what they are thinking. It's probably what everyone is thinking. Cage Hendren deserves to die. His brother didn't."

"That's not true!"

He got up and walked to the brink of the *mesa*, sliding his hands into his pockets. His white shirt showed up starkly against the blackness. Jenny followed him.

"When did it start?"

"When Hal was born. Maybe before that. I can't remember. I just know it's always been like that. Hal was the fair-haired child, literally. I should have had black hair. Then I really would have been the black sheep."

"Don't say that about yourself."

"Well, it's true, isn't it?" he asked brusquely, turning to face her belligerently. "Look what I almost did to you. I came close to raping the woman I—" He broke off in midsentence and Jenny wondered what he had been about to say. He made a taut, thin line of his lips to seal the unsaid words inside and turned away again.

"I know why you did that to me, why you were drinking and driving fast. You were trying to make your point that they're right about you. But they're not, Cage." She moved closer to him. "You're not some bad seed that turned up as a genetic accident in an otherwise flawless family. I don't know which came first, your naughtiness, which your parents didn't handle well, or their scorn, which made you act naughty."

She caught his sleeve and forced him around to face her. "Isn't it apparent? You've been reacting to them all your life. You *work* at being bad because that's what you know people expect of you. You've made a career of being the black sheep of the minister's family. Don't you see, Cage? Even as a child you did outlandish things to get their attention because they doted on Hal. That was wrong of them. *Their* failure, not yours.

"They had two sons and each of you had a different personality. But Hal's suited them best, so he became the model child. You tried to win their approval and when that failed, you turned around and did just the opposite."

His grin was patronizing. "You've got it all figured out, I see."

"Yes, I do. Otherwise I would have been terrified by what happened tonight. Even a few months ago I would have been. But tonight I knew you wouldn't hurt me. I know you better now. I've watched you lately. I saw you cry over your brother's body. You're not nearly as 'bad' as you want people to think you are. You couldn't compete with Hal's goodness, so you made it your goal to be a champion in another arena."

She had his attention. He was listening. And as much as he wanted to dispute her, what she said made sense. He stared at his feet as the toe of his shoe stirred up clouds of dust that swirled in the wind.

"I just worry about how far you'll carry it."

His head came up. "Carry what? What do you mean?"

"You've been made to feel you have no self-worth. How far will you go to prove them right? How far will you go to prove just how unworthy you are?"

He hitched his thumbs in the waistband of his pants and tilted his head arrogantly to one side. "You've gone this far. Why don't you just come right out and say what you're skirting around? You think I'm living a death-wish."

"People who have no self-esteem do stupid things."

"Like drive fast and drink irresponsibly and live recklessly?"

"Exactly."

"Aw, hell. Ask anyone. They'll tell you about my self-esteem. They'll tell you how conceited I am."

"I'm not talking about how you *act*, but how you feel on the inside. I've seen the other side of you, Cage, the sensitive side you don't show anyone else."

"You think I'm committing a slow form of suicide?"

"I didn't say that."

"But that's what you meant," he said, shoving his hair off his forehead with aggravated fingers. "You've taken your armchair psychology a step too far, Jenny."

He was defensive enough to convince her that maybe she had. "All right, I'm sorry," she said. "But I'm only worried because I care about you, Cage."

He relaxed his stance immediately and his eyes softened. "I appreciate your concern, but you don't have to worry about me disposing of myself. I like driving fast and drinking irresponsibly and... What was the other thing?'' he asked teasingly.

But Jenny wasn't finished with being serious yet. "I think your parents care about you, too."

His humor was fleeting. With bleak amber eyes he gazed over and beyond Jenny's head, out onto the barren landscape. "Doesn't Mother realize that I wanted to hover around her, around them both? Since we heard about Hal, I've wanted to go to them and hold them." His voice dropped a decible. "I've wanted them to hold me."

"Cage." Jenny reached out to touch his arm. He yanked it away. He didn't want anyone's pity.

"I didn't go near them because I knew they didn't want me near them. So I tried to show my love and sympathy in other ways." He sighed. "Only, they didn't notice."

"I noticed. I was grateful."

"But you didn't let me come near you either, Jenny," he said abruptly, lowering his eyes to meet hers.

She looked away quickly. "I don't know what you mean."

"Like hell you don't. When we were in Monterico, you depended on me, leaned on me emotionally and physically. Since we've gotten back, I'm a leper again. It's 'hands off.' No touching. No talking. Hell, you wouldn't even look at me."

He was right, but she wouldn't admit it.

"Does your avoidance of me have anything to do with that night we shared in Monterico?"

Her head snapped up and she wet her lips, though her tongue had gone dry. "Of course not."

"Sure?"

"Yes. What difference could that have made?"

"We slept together."

"Not like that!" she exclaimed defensively.

"Exactly," he said, taking steps forward until he loomed over her. "But by the way you're acting, it could have been 'like that.' What are you feeling so guilty about?"

"I'm not feeling guilty."

"Aren't you?" he pressed. "Aren't you thinking that you had no business sleeping in my arms, wearing nothing but your slip? Don't you feel that we were somehow being disloyal to Hal while he lay dead in his coffin? Isn't that what you're thinking?"

She turned her back on him and crossed her arms over her stomach as though it pained her. Tightly she clasped her elbows with the opposite hands. "I shouldn't have been with you like that."

"Why?"

"You know better than to ask."

"Because you know what everyone thinks of a woman who spends a night on a bed with me."

She said nothing.

"What are you afraid of, Jenny?"

"Nothing."

"Are you afraid that someone will find out about that night?"

"No."

"Afraid that your name will be added to the list of Cage Hendren's has-beens?"

"No."

"Are you afraid of me?"

Even the relentless wind couldn't disguise the hesitation and heartbreak in his voice. She whirled around and saw the misery on his face. "No, Cage, no." To prove it, she stepped forward and put her arms around his waist, laying her cheek on his chest.

Instantly his arms went around her and held her close. "I wouldn't blame you if you were, especially after what happened tonight. But, God, I'd hate that. I'd hate that worse than anything else. I couldn't bear for you to be afraid that I'd hurt you."

She could have told him that she wasn't as afraid of him as she was of her own reactions to him. When he was near her, she stepped out of the shell she lived behind in the parsonage and became another woman.

He made her heartbeat escalate, her breathing accelerate, her palms grow moist. She was never herself when she was with Cage, whether it was riding a motorcycle and loving it, or sharing a bed with him. With him she forgot who she was and where she came from, living only for a moment.

It was almost as if she had been in love with Cage all these years instead of Hal. She had made love with Hal, but the night she had slept in Cage's arms had been almost as wonderful. She couldn't quite reconcile herself to that. How was it that only a week after Hal's death, she could be wondering what making love with Cage would be like?

Startled by the thought, she backed away from him. "We'd better go home. They'll be worried."

He looked disappointed but escorted her to the car without argument. Ruefully he recapped the flask and returned it to the glove compartment. He tossed the pack of cigarettes out the window.

"Litterbug," Jenny said from her side of the car.

"Women," Cage muttered in exasperation as he put the car into low gear. "They're never satisfied."

They grinned at each other. Everything was all right.

When they arrived at the parsonage after a sedate trip back into town, he came around and opened the door of the car for her. He placed his arm around her waist as he walked her toward the door, and companionably, she did the same.

"Thank you, Jenny."

"For what?"

"For being my friend."

"Lately you've been mine often enough."

"Thanks anyway." At the door they stood facing each other. He seemed reluctant to leave. "Well, good night."

"Good night."

"It may be a while before I come visiting."

"I understand."

"But I'll be calling you."

"It breaks my heart for this chasm to be between you and your parents at a time when you need each other the most."

His sigh was laden with sadness. "Yeah, well, that's the way it goes. If you need anything, *anything*, holler."

"I will."

"Promise?"

"Promise."

He squeezed her hand and bent down to press a soft kiss on her cheek. His lips lingered before he finally withdrew them. Or perhaps that was only her imagination. She hadn't quite decided as she let herself in and climbed the stairs to her room. The house was dark. The Hendrens were already in bed.

She opened the door to her room and stepped inside. She gazed around the childishly decorated bedroom. *Now what?* she thought.

What was Jenny Fletcher going to do with the rest of her life?

She pondered the question as she undressed, and for long hours after she got into bed the problem kept her awake.

By morning she had an answer. But how was she going to tell the Hendrens? As it turned out, they made it easy for her to broach the subject.

Chapter 6

Bob was making toast when Jenny entered the kitchen the following morning. She smiled at his apron as she kissed him on the cheek. After pouring herself a cup of coffee, she sat down at the table with Sarah, who was idly shifting a portion of scrambled eggs from one side of her plate to the other.

"Where did you go last night?"

No "Good morning," no "How did you sleep?" Nothing. Just that bald question.

As she asked it, Sarah's lips were pinched. There was a strained expression on her face.

"We," Jenny stressed the word, "just went for a drive."

"You came in awfully late." Bob tried to make the comment sound off-handed, but Jenny knew this conversation wasn't off-handed or spontaneous by any stretch of the imagination. There was an air of hostile suspicion among them, as though there were an enemy in the camp that had to be sniffed out.

"How do you know when I came in? You were already sleeping."

"Mrs. Hicks came by this morning. She saw...she saw you and Cage together last night."

Jenny looked from one of them to the other. She was both bewildered and angry. Mrs. Hicks was the nosiest neighbor on the block. She loved to spread rumors, especially if they were bad. "What did she say?"

"Nothing," Bob said uneasily.

"No, I want to know. What did she say? Whatever it was, it obviously upset you."

"We're not upset, Jenny," Bob said diplomatically. "It's just that we don't want people to start linking your name to Cage's."

"My name is already linked to Cage's. He's a Hendren, your son," she reminded them angrily. "I've spent the last twelve years of my life in the Hendren household. How could my name *not* be linked with his?"

"You know what we mean, dear," Sarah said. Tears were glistening in her eyes. "You're all we have left. We—"

"That's not so!" Jenny cried angrily, getting out of her chair. "You have Cage. I never thought I'd say this, but I'm ashamed of you both. Sarah, do you realize how you hurt Cage last night? You might not be pleased with everything he does, but he's still your son. You wished him dead!"

Sarah bowed her head and burst into tears. Jenny, ashamed of her outburst, sat back down. Bob patted Sarah's shoulders in a feeble attempt to comfort her.

"She was distressed last night when the two of you raced out of here," Bob explained to Jenny. "She realized what she had said and was sorry about it."

Jenny sipped her coffee until Sarah's tears subsided. Finally she set her cup in her saucer. "I've decided to leave."

As Jenny had anticipated, they were stunned. For several moments neither of them moved. They stared at her with blank, disbelieving eyes. "Leave?" Sarah wheezed at last.

"I'm going to move out of the parsonage and begin a life of my own. For years I've been living here, biding my time until Hal and I got married. Perhaps if we had married and had children..." She let that thought dwindle away. "But since we didn't, and since we never will now, there's no reason for me to stay. I have to make a future for myself."

"But you have a future with us," Bob argued.

"I'm a grown woman. I need to—"

"We need you, Jenny!" Sarah cried, clamping a damp cold hand on Jenny's arm. "You remind us of Hal. You're like our own daughter. You can't do this to us. Please. Not now. Give us time to adjust to Hal's death first. You can' go. You just can't." She broked down again, burying her face in a sodden tissue.

Jenny felt a cloak of guilt closing around her. She had a responsibility to them, didn't she? They had taken her in and given her a home when she had had nothing. Didn't she owe them something? Time? A few weeks? A few months?

The thought of it depressed her, but then duty often did feel shackling.

"All right," she conceded dispiritedly. "But I won't live under Mrs. Hicks's censorship or anyone else's. I was engaged to Hal and I loved him, but he's dead. I've got my own life to lead."

"You've always been free to come and go as you like." Bob said, happy now that talk of her leaving was over. "That's why we bought you the car."

That wasn't the kind of freedom Jenny referred to, but she didn't think they would understand if she tried to explain it to them. "My other condition is that you both apologize to Cage for what you said last night."

When they would have protested, she stared them down. Their eyes fell away from her steady gaze. "Very well, Jenny," Bob said at last. "For your sake we will."

"No, not for my sake. For his and for yours." She stood up and headed for the door. "I think Cage will forgive you because he loves you. I only hope God will."

The grocery baskets crashed together. Jenny's rattled upon impact. A box of detergent toppled over. Canned goods rolled about noisily. A roll of paper towels bounced onto the carton of eggs.

"Hi."

"You bully. You did that on purpose."

His grin was slow, lazy, and totally unrepentant. "It's a great device to meet a pretty woman on a slow afternoon. Crash into her grocery cart. Then she's flustered, sometimes angry, but always at your mercy. Ideally I try to lock up the wheels of the carts." He glanced down and frowned. "You were too quick for me."

"You're without conscience, Cage Hendren."

"Absolutely."

"Then what happens?" Jenny asked him. "I'm fascinated."

"You mean after—"

"After you've crashed into her grocery basket and gotten the wheels locked together and she's flustered, etc. What do you do then?"

"Ask her to go to bed with me."

Jenny took that piece of information like a soft cuff on the chin. "Oh." She maneuvered her basket around his, which was empty, and continued down the aisle of pet food. Since the Hendrens didn't have a pet, the attention she gave the shelves was rather ludicrous.

"Well, you said you were fascinated," Cage said defensively, pushing his cart up beside hers.

"I am, I was, but I thought you'd lead up to the seduction a little more subtly."

"Why?"

"Why?" She spun around to look up at him, letting her perusal of tender morsels and chewy bits lapse for the moment. "You mean it's that simple? Just like that?" She snapped her fingers.

He wrinkled his brown in feigned concentration. "Not always. A few times it has required more time and effort." His golden brown eyes swept over her, taking in her neat slacks and cotton knit pullover. "Now, take you for instance. I'm betting you'd be a difficult case."

"Why do you say that?"

"Will you go to bed with me?"

"No!"

"See. I'm right every time." He tapped his forehead with his index finger. "When you've been doing this sort of thing as long as I have, you learn a few things along the way. You develop a sixth sense. I could tell immediately that I would have to use the long, slow, easy approach with you. It was the way you frowned slightly when the box of Tide mashed your bag of marshmallows. A dead give-away that you weren't going to be easy."

She gazed at him in mute wonder for several seconds, then burst out laughing. "Cage, I swear, you're amoral."

"Shameless." He winked. "But I'm sincere."

She turned out of the pet food aisle into another. He barged in front of her, blocking her path. "You look terrible."

"Is that an example of the long, slow, easy approach? If so, it needs work," she said dryly.

When she tried to go around him, he adroitly turned his basket sideways to block the aisle entirely. "You know what I mean. You look tired. Way too thin. What are they doing to you over there?"

"Nothing." She avoided his eyes.

But she knew she wasn't deceiving him any more than she had been deceiving herself. The Hendrens hadn't listened well to her declaration of independence. Or else they had listened, but were ignoring what she had said. They had every day's activities outlined for her before she came down to breakfast.

First there had been all the acknowledgments to be written after Hal's funeral. She had been almost grateful for that job because it had allowed her to call Cage and ask him to pick them up and mail them. That had created an opportunity for his parents to aplogize to him.

It had been an awkward reunion. Cage had stood at the front door, looking like he feared they wouldn't invite him in. Jenny had held her breath, unable to distinguish the words he and Bob exchanged in the hallway. Then he was standing in the living room, looking at Sarah, who was huddled on the sofa. At last she raised her head.

"Hello, Cage. Thank you for coming by."

"Hello, Mother. How are you feeling?"

"Fine, fine," she said absently. She shot a questioning glance toward Jenny, who nodded her head slightly. Sarah wet her lips. "About the other night, the night of Hal's...funeral... What I said—"

"It doesn't matter," Cage had rushed to say. He crossed the room and knelt on one knee in front of his mother's chair, covering her pale, bloodless fingers with his hand. "I know you were upset."

Jenny's heart had gone out to him. He wanted so badly to believe that. But whether Sarah's apology was sincere or not, whether he believed it or not, they were at least voicing aloud the sentiments they should feel.

Jenny's chores at the parsonage seemed endless. The Hendrens had even discussed the posibility that she continue Hal's crusade to help the political refugees in Central America. Even the thought of tackling such a campaign exhausted her, and she refused to speak at rallies and such. But she had taken on the job of sending out a newsletter that detailed the problems as she had witnessed them firsthand and asked for donations to further the relief cause.

She knew her eyes were shadowed with fatigue, knew that she had lost weight due to a notable lack of appetite, knew that she was wan and pale from not spending any time outdoors.

"I'm worried about you," Cage said softly.

"I'm tired. Everyone is. Hal's death, the funeral, it's all taken its toll."

"It's been over two weeks. You spend more time in that parsonage than ever. That's unhealthy."

"But necessary."

"The church is their calling, not yours. They're going to make an old woman out of you if you let them, Jenny."

"I know," she said wearily, rubbing her brow. "Please don't badger me about it, Cage. I told them I needed to move out, but—"

"When?"

"The day after the funeral."

"Why didn't you?"

"They got so upset, I couldn't. And, really, it would have been cruel to move out right after they had lost Hal."

"So what about now?"

She smiled and shook her head. "I don't even have a job. At least not a paying one. I know I've got to make a life for myself, but I've let them manage things for so long, I don't know how to go about it."

"I've got an idea," Cage said suddenly and grabbed her arm. "Come on."

"I can't leave the groceries."

"You don't have the ice cream as an excuse this time. I caught you before you got to the freezer."

Figuratively she dug her heels in. "I can't leave a full basket of groceries in the aisle of the store."

"Oh, for heaven's sake," Cage said irritably. He spun the basket around and, taking long striding steps, pushed it to the front of the store. "Hey, Zack!" The store manager peered over the partial wall of his office. He was counting back money to someone who had cashed a check.

"Hiya, Cage."

"Miss Fletcher's leaving her groceries here," he said, parking the basket near a display of pots and pans that could be obtained with saved coupons. "We'll be back for them later."

"Sure, Cage. See ya."

Cage picked up a Milky Way bar as they passed the candy counter and saluted the manager with it before looping his arm over Jenny's shoulders and leading her from the store.

"Did you steal that?"

"Sure," Cage said, peeling the candy open and cramming half of it into his mouth. "This half's for you."

"But—" He stopped her protest by popping the remainder of the candy bar into her surprised mouth.

"You never stole a candy bar?" Jenny shook her head, shifting the huge bite of candy from one side of her mouth to the other in an effort to chew it before it choked her. "Well, it's about time you did. Now you're my partner in crime." He opened the door of his Corvette and gently, but inexorably, pushed her into the passenger's seat.

Cage drove through the busy downtown streets with only a little more discipline than he drove on the highway. He turned into a curbside parking space in front of a row of offices. When he got out, he reached beneath the seat of the car and took out a cloth bag. It was the kind the city used to cover parking meters on holidays. He slipped it over the meter in front of the Corvette and winked at Jenny before catching her elbow and ushering her to the door.

"Can you do that?" she asked, worriedly glancing at the covered meter.

"I just did."

He unlocked the office and she stepped in ahead of him.

But she came to an abrupt halt on the other side of the threshold and stared around her in dismay. The room was in semidarkness, but it only looked worse when Cage went to the window and adjusted the dusty blinds to let in more sunlight.

Jenny had never seen a room in such disorder. A sad sofa, straight out of a fifties television situation comedy, was pushed against one wall. The rose-colored upholstery, which hadn't had much going for it in the first place, was grayed with generations of dusty. The cushions were hollowed out in their centers.

Ugly metal shelves took up another wall. They were stuffed with papers and ledgers and maps, the corners of which were curled and yellowed.

Every available ashtray was full to overflowing.

The desk in the middle of the far wall should have been junked years ago. A deck of playing cards held up the corner where one caster was missing. It was piled with dated magazines, littered with empty coffee cups, and crisscrossed with scratches and scars. An egotistical vandal had carved his initials in one corner.

Jenny turned to Cage slowly. "What is this?"

"My office," he said abashedly.

Incredulity caused her jaw to drop open. "You actually run a business out of this trash heap?"

"I wouldn't go so far as to call it *that*."

"Cage, if Dante were alive, this is how he would describe Hell."

"That bad?"

"That bad." Jenny ambled toward the desk and picked up a half inch of dust on her finger when she dragged it over the marred surface. "Have you ever had this place cleaned?"

"I think so. Oh, yeah, once I hired a janitor service. The guy they sent over was a real cutup. We got to drinking and—"

"Never mind, I get the picture." She edged around an overflowing waste paper basket and went toward a door she assumed belonged to a closet.

"Uh, Jenny..." Cage lifted his hand and tried to forestall her, but it was too late.

As the door opened a giant wall calendar swung outward and tipped her on the shoulder. She jumped back, startled. But not nearly as startled as she was when the calendar seesawed back and forth until it came to rest on its nail and she saw the glossy photograph.

The pouting redhead was sporting a strategically placed shiny blue star that had "Deep in the Heart of Texas" inscribed on it. Pillow-sized breasts with nipples as large and red as strawberries took up a good portion of the picture.

Cage cleared his throat uncomfortably. "A crew of roughnecks gave me that last Christmas."

Jenny shut the closet door firmly and turned to face him. "Why did you bring me here?"

He pushed his hands into the back pockets of his jeans, withdrew them, then lightly slapped his thighs nervously. "Here, Jenny, sit down," he said, suddenly lunging forward to clear off a place on the sofa for her.

"I don't want to sit down. I want to get out of here so I can breathe some fresh air. Tell me why you brought me here."

"Well, you said you wanted a job and I was thinking—"

"You can't be serious," she interrupted him, gleaning his thought.

"Now, Jenny, hear me out. I need someone to—"

"You need a demolition squad, then a bulldozer. After they're done, I suggest you start from scratch." She headed toward the door.

He blocked her escape and clasped her shoulders. "I'm not talking about someone to clean it up. I'll get it straightened up. I thought you could answer the telephone, do general office work, you know."

"You've survived without someone all these years. Who's been taking your calls?"

"An answering service."

"Why change now?"

"It's damned inconvenient to check in every hour."

"Wear a beeper."

"I tried that."

"And?"

"I had it hooked to my belt, but I, uh, lost it."

Her eyes flew up to his. He looked away guiltily. "Hm, I can see how having it hooked to your belt could get inconvenient." She tried to move around him again. He held her forcibly.

"Jenny, please, listen. You need and want a job. I'm offering you one."

"A chimpanzee could be trained to sit and answer a telephone. Besides, you said you have an answering service."

"But how do I know they get all the calls? Besides, there are other things to be done."

"Such as?"

"Correspondence. You'd be surprised how much."

"Who's doing it now? You?"

"No, a friend of mine."

She gave him another I'm-on-to-you-mister look and he sighed in exasperation. "She's about eighty-seven and myopic and uses a vintage typewriter. The capitol *T* is always half a step up from the other letters. And she has a crooked *S*."

Narrowed green eyes glared up at him suspiciously. "Was that a subtle play on words?"

"No, I swear, but I'm glad you caught it anyway. It means you're not a totally hopeless case."

She ignored that and gazed around her. "You don't even have a typewriter."

"I'll buy one. Any kind you like."

The thought of being more productive was intriguing and challenging, but she knew she couldn't accept his offer. With a defeated stoop to her shoulders, she shook her head. "I can't, Cage."

"Why not?"

"Your parents need me too much."

"You hit the nail on the head. They need you too much. Do you think you're doing them any favors by waiting on them hand and foot? They're middle-aged, but if they don't have a purpose in their lives, they'll grow old very fast. They need to get their lives going again, but they won't ever do that if they become so reliant on you.

"I've never had a child, so I don't know what it's like to lose one. But I can imagine that the temptation would be to curl up and die yourself. If you keep catering to Mother and Dad, that's what they're likely to do."

He was right, of course. Every day the Hendrens seemed to shrivel up more. And as long as she was convenient for them to rely on, they would use her until all their lives had been wasted.

"How much would you pay me?"

His face broke into a strong, wide grin. "Mercenary little bitch, aren't you?"

"How much?" she demanded, not nearly as piqued by his vulgarity as she should have been.

"Let's see," he said, rubbing his jaw. "Two-fifty a week?"

She had no idea if that was fair or not, but she wanted to leap at it anyway. Still, she hedged, pretending to be considering it. "How many paid holidays do I get?"

"Take it or leave it, Miss Fletcher," he said sternly.

"I'll take it. Nine to five with an hour and a half off for lunch." That would give her time to go to the parsonage and take the meal with the Hendrens, though the thought of eating lunch out every day was much more exciting. "Two weeks paid vacation, plus all the holidays the postal service takes. And I'll work only until noon on Fridays.''

"You drive a hard bargain," Cage said, frowning. Actually he was thrilled. If he'd had to double the salary and meet any conditions, he would have done so to get her free of the parsonage and out from under his parents' control.

"I won't set foot in this place until it's been cleaned up. I mean *clean*.''

"Yes, ma'am." He clicked his heels together.

"And the calendar has to go."

He looked toward the closet door and his face drooped in comic disappointment. "Aw, shoot! I was really coming to like her." He shrugged. "Ah, well. Anything else?"

Jenny was thinking how absolutely adorable he was, but her mind snapped back to the problem at hand. "Yes. How am I going to tell your parents?"

"Don't give them a choice." He stuck out his hand. "Is that it? Do we have a deal?"

"Deal." She gave him her hand, but instead of shaking it, he drew it up and placed it on his chest.

"A handshake is no way to finalize a deal with a gorgeous woman.''

Before she could react, he bent his head down and slanted his mouth over hers. The hand now pressing hers to his chest went to her waist, where it settled lightly. His thumb gently stroked her lowest rib.

The kiss was long. His lips were open over hers, but he didn't use his tongue. He only kept her held in breathless suspension, teasing her with the possibility that at any moment he might send it delving into her mouth. But he didn't. And when he raised his head, he merely smiled.

Later, after he had deposited her back at the grocery store and she had finished her shopping, she wondered why she hadn't done something, anything, to stop the kiss. Why hadn't she slapped his face, or stamped her foot, or even laughed? Why, when he finally lifted his mouth off hers, had she just gazed up at him with limpid eyes and throbbing dewy lips, a pounding pulse, and melting thighs?

The only answer she could provide was that her limbs had felt leaden, deliciously so. And weak with pleasure. She couldn't have raised a finger to protect herself from Cage's kiss if she had wanted to. And she really hadn't wanted to.

The Hendrens didn't take the news of her job too well. Sarah dropped her fork on her dinner plate when Jenny made her announcement. "I start Monday."

"You're going to work—"

"For Cage?" Bob finished for his wife.

"Yes. If you have any projects for me to do before then, let me know."

She left the kitchen before their dumbfoundedness wore off. As Cage had advised her to do, she hadn't given them a choice in the matter.

One minute before nine o'clock the following Monday morning, Jenny entered the office. The door had been left unlocked. For a moment, she thought she had gone in the wrong door. The office hadn't only been cleaned, it had been transformed.

The gunmetal-gray walls were now painted a soothing cream. The hideous sofa had been replaced by two leather armchairs in a rich shade of chocolate brown. A walnut table was tucked between them.

The linoleum tile floor had been covered with parquet wood. An area rug of ethnic origin took up the center of the floor. Where the metal shelves had been, there was now a wall of wood shelves and cabinets. All the components had been tastefully arranged to maximize space so that everything was stacked neatly.

The surface of the desk now dominating the room was as glistening as an ice rink. Behind it was a leather chair of thronelike proportions. On the desk's shiny top was a bouquet of fresh flowers, still beaded with moisture from the florist's refrigerator.

"The flowers are for you."

Jenny spun around to see Cage standing just inside the closet. The door was open. "How did you do it?" she asked, aghast.

"With my checkbook," he said wryly. "That works better than magic wands these days. Do you like it?"

"Yes, but..." Jenny was suddenly contrite. "I shouldn't have criticized. You've gone to tremendous expense."

"Hey, don't go soft on me. You spurred me on to do something I should have done years ago. I've been entertaining clients at the drugstore's soda fountain because I was ashamed of this 'trash heap,' as someone we all know and love called it." He grinned when her cheeks flushed. "By the way, I have a selection of calendars for you to choose from."

He held up the first one and she gasped softly. "Buns of the Month," Cage said solemnly, trying hard not to smile. The muscular model, posed lying on his stomach, was wearing a jock strap, a football helmet, and a wicked grin. "This is Mr. October. Football season, you understand. Would you like to see the other months?" he asked guilelessly, thumbing through the calendar.

"That will be sufficient," Jenny said hoarsely. "What else do you have?"

Cage set that calendar aside and picked up another. "A Hunk a Day. No heads, just bodies." An oiled chest, bulging biceps, and a washboard stomach graced the picture he held up. Jenny made a squeamish face and shook her head. "Or," Cage said, spreading open the third choice, "Ansel Adams."

"Hang the Ansel Adams." Cage looked pleased and turned to do her bidding. "But leave the others in the closet," Jenny added mischievously. He gave her his most crestfallen expression, then they both burst out laughing.

"Cage, the office is beautiful, really. I love it."

"Good. I want you to be comfortable here."

"Thank you for the flowers," she said, moving behind the desk and tentatively sitting down in the leather chair.

"This is a special occasion."

Their eyes met and locked for a moment before he showed her where his business stationery was stored and how to operate the new typewriter. "You can start on these letters," he said, passing her a folder. "I've roughed them out in longhand, which I hope you can read. Gertie managed to."

"The friend with the crooked *S*?" Jenny asked innocently.

He yanked on a strand of her hair. "Right." He left shortly thereafter, saying he was going out to the Parsons ranch.

"How does it look?"

"The samples look great. If we don't strike oil, I'm an archangel." He put on his sunglasses and reached for the doorknob. "'Bye."

"'Bye."

He paused, staring at her for a long moment. "Goda'mighty, you look good sitting there."

Then he was gone.

He came back a few minutes before noon, carrying a large sack. "Lunchtime!" he yelled as he barged through the door.

Jenny waved her hand, motioning for him to be quiet. She was on the telephone, jotting down notes as the other party talked. "Yes, I have it and I'll give the information to Mr. Hendren when he comes in. Thank you." She hung up and proudly passed him the message.

He read it and thumped the paper. "Terrific. I've been waiting for permission to have a look-see at this property. You've brought me luck." He grinned and set the sack on the edge of the desk. "And I've brought you lunch."

"Can I expect this kind of treatment every day?" She stood up to peer into the sack.

"Absolutely not. But as I said earlier, today is a special occasion."

"I really should go home and check on Sarah and Bob."

"They'll be fine. Call them later if you must."

His lighthearted mood was infectious and she caught it as they unloaded the lunch he had carried out from the town's only delicatessen. "To top it all off..." He disappeared into the closet and came back carrying a bottle of champagne. "Ta-da!"

"Where'd you get that?"

"I've had it cooling in the refrigerator."

"There's a refrigerator in there?"

"A tiny one. Haven't you looked?"

"No. I've been busy." She pointed toward the stack of letters that were waiting for his signature.

"Then you deserve a glass of champagne," he said, working the cork free. The effervescent wine popped but didn't foam over. Cage poured her a paper cup full.

She took it, too overwhelmed not to. "I really shouldn't, Cage."

"How come?"

"You might find this hard to believe, but we don't usually serve champagne with lunch at the parsonage," she said sarcastically. "I'm not used to it."

"Good. Maybe you'll get drunk, strip off all your clothes, and dance naked on top of the desk."

He passed a speculative glance down her body that clearly intimated he wondered what such a sight would be like. Embarrassed, she watched him pour himself a cup of champagne. "Do you do this sort of thing often?"

"Drink champagne in the middle of the day? No."

"Then how do you know *you* won't get drunk, strip off all your clothes, and dance naked on top of the desk?"

He touched the rim of her cup with his. "Because, my Jenny," he whispered roughly, "if we were both naked on top of the desk, we wouldn't be dancing."

Her stomach did a backward somersault. She managed to tear her eyes away from the hypnotizing power of his and noticed that her hand was trembling.

"Take a sip," Cage urged in that same husky voice. Grateful for something to do, she did. The champagne was cold and biting on her tongue. "Like it?"

"Yes." She took another sip.

He moved his head closer until they were almost nose to nose. His eyes fairly smoldered. "How do you feel about..."

"About what?"

"Hot pastrami?"

Hot pastrami had never tasted so delicious. In fact, it was one of the most fabulous meals Jenny had ever eaten. As they ate he told her more about his business and was pleased with her intelligent and intuitive questions.

He couldn't coax her into drinking more than half the paper cup of champagne. When they were finished, he carefully picked up the empty cartons and put them back in the sack. "I wouldn't dare litter up your office," he said with a crooked smile.

For a long time after he left she couldn't stop thinking about both of them being naked. What had he meant when he'd said they wouldn't be dancing? But she knew what he'd meant.

And she couldn't stop thinking about that either.

The days fell into some sort of pattern, though life with Cage was always spontaneous and unplanned. It was like traveling down a mysterious jungle river. One never knew what unexpected surprise would be waiting around the next bend.

He left her small presents that shouldn't have been significant, but to someone who had never been courted, they were very much so.

A small cake with a single candle was waiting on her desk the morning of her first week's anniversary of employment. She found a red rose lying beside the coffeemaker another time. One morning when she opened the door she almost screamed. A giant teddy bear was grinning at her from her chair behind the desk.

She knew the town was buzzing with gossip about them. The tellers at the bank were shocked when she began to handle Cage's buisness banking. Now they were accustomed to seeing her come in on his behalf. But she could see them clustering together when she left.

The postmaster, who she had known for years, was still friendly, but now that she was handling Cage's mail instead of the church's, he looked at her in a way that made her skin crawl.

And Cage had begun attending church regularly, which really had the town gossips aflutter.

She loved the challenge of the new job and by the second week was handling every situation like a pro.

"Hendren Enterprises."

"Jenny, darlin', get your celebrating shoes on," Cage said, laughing.

Jenny could hear the racket in the background. "The well came in?" she squealed.

"The well came in!" he shouted. The roughnecks around him were already breaking out the coolers full of Coors. "Sweetheart, I'm going to buy you the biggest chicken fried steak lunch we can find. I'll be there in an hour."

"I have an errand to run. Why don't I just meet you somewhere?"

"All right. The Wagon Wheel at twelve-thirty?"

She agreed on the time and place.

But at twelve-thirty Jenny was wandering aimlessly down the main street of town, her brain registering nothing. Entranced, she stopped in the middle of the sidewalk and sightlessly gazed at the garish display of goods in the variety store's front window.

Cage drove by, spotted her, called out her name, and honked. She didn't turn around. She didn't even hear him.

He executed an illegal U-turn and whipped his pickup, which he had driven out to the drilling sight, into the only available parking space and hopped out onto the sidewalk. He jogged toward her. His boots and the hems of his jeans were caked with mud.

"Jenny," he said breathlessly, "you're going in the wrong direction. Didn't we say the Wagon Wheel?"

His broad smile collapsed when she turned and gazed up at him with vacuous eyes. Instantly alarmed, he caught her upper arm and shook her slightly. "Jenny, what's wrong?"

"Cage?" she whispered faintly. She blinked her eyes and looked around her as though only then realizing where she was. "Oh, Cage."

"God, don't scare me like that," he said, worry wrinkling his brow. "What's happened? What's the matter? Are you sick?"

She shook her head and lowered her eyes. "No. But I don't feel like going to lunch. I'm sorry. I'm very happy about the well, but I don't feel like—"

"Will you stop with all that apology crap. To hell with lunch. Tell me what's happened to you." She reeled against him as though she were going to faint. He caught her against his chest, cursing and feeling inept and stupid. "Come on, love. Let's go into the drugstore. I'll get you a Coke."

They walked half a block to the drugstore, where there was a soda fountain in back. At least Cage walked. Jenny stumbled along with his support. She virtually fell into the green vinyl booth as he called out, "Two Cokes, please, Hazel," to the waitress behind the counter.

Cage didn't take his eyes off Jenny, but she didn't look at him. She stared down at her hands where they were locked together on the Formica tabletop. Hazel set the icy fountain drinks on the table. "How're things, Cage?"

"Fine," he muttered absently.

Hazel shrugged and ambled back to the cash register. Folks were saying that Cage Hendren had undergone a change since his brother had gotten killed. They said he'd been hanging around the Fletcher girl like a fly around a jar of honey. Well, that just went to show that some gossip was true. Hazel could always count on Cage for a good half hour of bawdy joking. Today he was so taken with Jenny Fletcher, he was staring at her like she might go up in a puff of smoke if he took his eyes off her.

"Jenny, drink your Coke," Cage said, sliding it closer to her. "You're as pale as a ghost." Obediently she sipped through the straw. "Now tell me what's wrong."

Her head remained bowed for what seemed like hours to him. He was just about ready to lose control when she finally raised it.

Her eyes were glossy with tears. Two escaped simultaneously and rolled down her cheeks. "Cage," she whispered hoarsely, pausing to draw in a shuddering breath, "I'm pregnant."

Chapter 7

Cage felt like he had just been punched in the gut. His tawny eyes went blank. Except for swallowing hard, he remained perfectly still, his eyes trained on Jenny's face.

"Pregnant?"

She nodded. "I just came from the doctor's office. I'm going to have a baby."

He swiped his damp palms over his thighs. "You didn't know?"

"No."

"Aren't there signs?"

"I guess so."

"Hadn't you missed periods?"

Her cheeks were stained with hot color and she ducked her head. "Yes, but I thought that was because of Hal's death and all the turmoil afterward. I just never thought... Oh, I don't know," she said, wearily resting her forehead on the heel of her hand. "Cage, what am I going to do?"

Do? She would leave with him that very minute and get married, that's what. They were going to have a baby! Son-ofagun! A *baby!*

Joy pumped through Cage's body. He wanted to stand up and whoop, to rush out in the streets, stop traffic, and tell everybody that he was going to be a daddy.

But he saw Jenny's dejected posture, heard her quiet weeping, and knew that he couldn't let his true reaction show. She thought the baby was Hal's. Cage couldn't acknowledge that it was his because she would despise him, just when she was coming to trust him.

Was this to be his punishment for all the sins he had tallied up beside his name? He had always taken precautions to see that none of the wild oats he sewed produced an unwanted child. He had made certain every woman he slept with knew of those precautions so she couldn't frame him later for an accident that wasn't his.

But now, when he wanted to claim his paternity, he couldn't. He couldn't be granted the privilege of acknowledging the child he had created with the woman he loved, had always loved.

God played dirty pool.

Tell her, tell her now, a voice deep inside him whispered.

He wanted to. Lord, how he wanted to take her in his arms and reassure her that she had no reason to cry. He wanted to proclaim that he loved her and his child—yes, *his* child—and promise her that for as long as he lived he would take care of both of them. Selfishly that was what he wanted to do.

But he couldn't. Learning she was pregnant had been devastating enough for her. He couldn't bring her more misery by telling her that the father of the child wasn't who she thought he was.

For now, he had to be satisfied with being her friend.

"Crying won't help, Jenny." He passed her a handkerchief. She blotted her eyes and glanced around self-consciously. They had the small coffee shop to themselves. Hazel was engrossed in a movie star magazine.

"Everyone will think I'm trash. And Hal..." She bowed her head at the thought of what people would think of the young minister now.

"No one will think Jenny Fletcher is trash." Cage twirled the straw in his Coke, already feeling guilty for the way he was about to manipulate her. He cleared his throat. "I didn't know you and Hal had that kind of relationship."

"We didn't." She spoke so softly he had to lean across the table in order to hear her. "Not until the night before he left."

She raised her head to find him studying her intently. His unwavering attention made her even more uncomfortable about the subject they were discussing, and when she began speaking again, her voice faltered. "Remember you told me I should try to stop him from going? Well, I tried," she said with a shaky little laugh. "But it didn't work."

"What happened?" Cage was finding it hard to speak past the lump in his throat. But he wanted to know what she felt about that night. It wasn't fair to goad her into talking about it like this, but he had to know.

"He went upstairs with me. I..." She lowered her gaze and drew in a tremulous little breath. "I pleaded with him not to go. He wouldn't be swayed. Then I tried to lure him into bed. But he left me."

"Then I don't understand—"

"He came back awhile later and we...we made love."

Several moments ticked by while neither of them spoke, each lost in his own thoughts. Jenny was remembering that burst of joy she had felt when the door opened and she had seen Hal's silhouette against the narrow strip of light. Cage was recalling the same thing, only, from his perspective. Jenny sitting up in bed, her face awash with tears.

"That was the first time you ever..."

"The first and only. I never believed that a woman could become pregnant from one time." She plucked at the paper napkin growing soggy beneath her sweating glass. "I was wrong."

"Was it good for you, Jenny?" Her eyes flew up to meet his. "I mean, if you were a virgin," he improvised quickly, "didn't it hurt?"

"A little, at first." She smiled in a secretive, Mona Lisa way that made Cage's heart constrict. Then she looked him square in the eye. "It was wonderful, Cage. The best thing that's ever happened to me. I've never felt that kind of closeness to another human being. And no matter what happens, I'll never regret what I did that night."

Now it was his turn to drop his gaze. He felt dangerously close to tears. Emotion churned in his throat. His loins were thick with it. He wanted to hold her against him, to feel her body soft and warm against his. He longed to confess that he understood exactly how she felt because it had been the same for him.

"You must be about—"

"Almost four months," she supplied.

"And you haven't had any unpleasant symptoms?"

"Now that I know I'm pregnant, I recognize them. I wasn't looking for them before. I've been tired and listless. Right after we came back from Monterico I lost some weight, but I've gained it back. My breasts—" She stopped midsentence, glancing up at him modestly.

"Go on, Jenny," he coached softly. "Your breasts what?"

"They, uh, they've been tender and tingling sort of, you know?"

He grinned lopsidedly. "No. I don't know."

She laughed. "How could you know?" It felt good to laugh, but she covered her mouth. "I can't believe I'm laughing about something this serious."

"What else can you do? Besides, I think it's cause for celebration, not tears. It's not every day a man brings in an oil well and learns he's going to be a...an uncle."

She reached across the table for his hand and clasped it tightly. "Thank you for feeling that way, Cage. When I left the doctor's office, I was flabbergasted. I didn't know where to turn or where to go. I felt lost and alone."

"You don't have to feel that way, Jenny. You can always come to me. For anything."

"I appreciate your attitude about it."

If only she knew his real attitude about it. He was incredibly overjoyed and incredibly sad. He was having a child, but no one would know it was his. Not even its mother.

"What do you plan to do?"

"I don't know."

"Marry me, Jenny."

That stunned her speechless. She stared at him blankly while she tried to get her heart to calm down and stop hopping around in her chest like a wild bird in a cage. She knew he was motivated by pity, possibly family loyalty, but out of sheer desperation to grasp the security his offer promised, she was tempted to say yes. That was ridiculous, of course. "I can't."

"Why?"

"There are a thousand reasons against it."

"And one very good one for it."

"Cage, I can't let you do that. Ruin your life for the sake of me and my child? Never. No, thank you."

"Let me decide what would bring me ruination, please." He squeezed her hand. "Should we elope tonight or wait until tomorrow? I'll honeymoon anywhere you say. Except Monterico," he added with a grin.

Her eyes were soft and shiny with tears. "You really are wonderful, you know that?"

"That's what they tell me."

"But I can't marry you, Cage."

"Because of Hal?" His face lost all vestiges of humor.

"No. Not solely. It has to do with you and me. We would be getting married for all the wrong reasons. Jenny Fletcher and Cage Hendren. What a joke."

"Don't you like me anymore?" he asked, pouring all the charm at his command into his smile.

She smiled with him. "You know it's not that. I like you very much."

"You'd be amazed at how many married couples I know who can't stand each other. We'd have more going for us than most."

"But a wife and child hardly fit your life-style."

"I'll change my life-style."

"I won't let you make that kind of sacrifice."

He wanted to shake her and shout that he wouldn't be making any sacrifice. But now he had to give her room. She needed time to adjust to the idea of the baby before she could consider taking on a husband with a reputation for being a philanderer. This would only be a temporary postponement. Nothing in heaven or earth would keep him from marrying her, making her his forever, rearing his child in a home filled with love rather than censure.

"So if you're going to break my heart and turn me down, what are you going to do?"

"Can I still work for you?"

He frowned at her. "You have to ask?"

"Thank you, Cage," she murmured earnestly.

She let herself relax against the back of the booth and unconsciously smoothed her hands down her abdomen, which was still flat. *She's so damn tiny,* Cage thought. Was it possible that his child was growing inside her?

She had been so small. He almost groaned with the memory of his intrusion into that smooth sheath. He had loved her tightness then, but now it worried him. What if she had difficulty delivering the baby?

His eyes wandered up to her breasts. They weren't noticeably larger, but there was a ripe fullness to them. They were round and maternally plump and he wanted nothing more than to caress them softly and cover them with adoring kisses.

"Your parents will have to know."

Reluctantly Cage pulled his eyes away from her breasts and his mind from its fantasy. "Would you like me to tell them?"

"No. That responsibility falls to me. I only wish I knew how they are going to take it."

"How else can they take it? They will be delighted." It cost him tremendously to say it, but he added, "They'll have a living legacy of Hal."

She fiddled with the wet napkin. By now it was almost shredded. "Maybe. Somehow I don't think it will be that simple. They're very moral people, Cage. I don't have to tell you that. For them the boundaries of right and wrong are clearly defined. To their way of thinking, there are no gray areas of morality."

"But my father has preached Christian charity all his adult life. God's grace and loving forgiveness have been the topics of many sermons." He covered her hand with his. "They won't condemn you, Jenny. I'm certain of that."

She wished she could be as confident, but she smiled at him as though she were.

Before they left he made her drink a chocolate malt, saying that it was more important than ever that she gain weight and keep up her strength. They toasted the oil well and the baby with their glasses.

"I might have to share my teddy bear with the baby," she said as they walked outside, hands clasped and swinging between them.

"Put up a good fight," he said, smiling down at her. "For a long time, you'll be bigger than the baby." He walked her to her car and unlocked the door for her. "Go home and take a nap."

"But I've only put in half a day," she objected.

"And it's been a bitch. Rest this afternoon. I'll call and check on you tonight."

"Sometimes between now and then, I'll have to break the news to Sarah and Bob."

"They'll be as thrilled about the baby as I am."

That was impossible. No one was as thrilled about the baby as he was. God, he was bursting at the seams to declare how happy he was, how much he loved her, how much he loved the child they had made.

He was forced into silence, but he yielded to the temptation to hold Jenny. He drew her against him. She went into his arms willingly, and they held each other close in broad daylight, unaware of everything around them, prying eyes included.

His heart beat steady and strong beneath her ear. She drew warmth from his body. Cage had become important to her, almost unnervingly so. But she desperately needed a friend and he hadn't failed her. So she clung to him for strength and support. And while she was at it, she enjoyed the blended fragrances of sun and wind and spicy aftershave, scents that belonged so uniquely to Cage.

Cage cradled her against him, loving the feel of her lush breasts against his chest. He pressed his lips to the crown of her head for a prolonged kiss that really wasn't a kiss at all. It hurt like hell that he couldn't thank her for blessing him with a child. He couldn't lay his hands on her tummy and foolishly talk to the baby nestling inside. He couldn't fondle her breasts and tell her how he longed to see his baby suckling there. Worst of all, it hurt to have to let her go.

But eventually he did.

"Promise me you'll lie down as soon as you get home."

"I promise."

He tucked her into the front seat of her car and made her fasten the seat belt. "To protect you and baby from drivers like me," he said with a self-derisive smile.

"Thanks for everything, Cage."

He watched her drive away, wondering if she would thank him if she knew he was responsible for the predicament she now found herself in.

Cage arrived at the parsonage shortly after seven o'clock.

After sending Jenny home, he had spent the remainder of the afternoon at the drilling site. Busy as he was, she was never off his mind. He was worried about her, her mental state, her physical condition, her anxiety over telling his parents about the baby.

From the outside, the parsonage looked as it always did. Jenny's car was there, parked next to the one belonging to his parents. There were lights on in the kitchen and living room. Nonetheless, Cage had a gut instinct that something was wrong.

He knocked on the front door and then pushed it open. "Hello," he called out. He went in without invitation and found Bob and Sarah sitting together in the living room.

"Hello, Cage," his father said unenthusiastically. Sarah said nothing. She was twisting a handkerchief round and round her index finger.

"Where's Jenny?"

Bob was apparently finding it difficult to speak because he swallowed several times. When he did manage to make a sound, he spoke economically. "She left."

Anger and fear began to coil inside Cage. "Left? What do you mean she left? Her car's here."

Bob dragged his hand down his face, distorting his features. "She chose to leave without taking anything with her except her clothes."

Cage turned on his heel and bounded up the stairs two at a time, the way he had done in his youth. It had been an infringement of house rules, but he had ignored them then and he did now.

"Jenny?" She wasn't in her room. He lunged for the closet and yanked open the door. Except for a few garments, all the hangers were empty. In the drawers he frantically pulled from the bureaus, he found the same mute testament that she was gone.

"Dammit!" he roared like a thwarted lion and went charging down the stairs again. "What happened? What did you do? What did you say to her?" he demanded of his parents. "Did she tell you about the baby?"

"Yes," Bob said. "We were appalled."

"Appalled? *Appalled!* You found out Jenny is carrying your first grandchild and your only reaction is that you're appalled?!"

"She claims it's Hal's baby."

Had it been any man other than his father who maligned Jenny's integrity and virtue that way, Cage would have jerked him up by the shirt collar and beat him until he lived to regret ever having uttered so much as a breath of slander against her.

As it was, Cage only made a low growling sound in his throat and took a threatening step forward. That, in fact, it *wasn't* Hal's child didn't matter at the moment. Jenny thought it was. She had thought she was telling them the absolute truth.

"You doubt that?"

"Certainly we doubt it," Sarah said, speaking for the first time. "Hal wouldn't have done anything so...so...so sinful. Especially not on the night before he left for Central America as she claims."

"This may come as a surprise to you, Mother, but Hal was a man first and a missionary second."

"Is that supposed to mean—"

"It means that he had the same apparatus as every other man since Adam. The same drives. The same desires. It's only a wonder to me he waited so long to take Jenny to his bed." Hal never had taken Jenny to his bed, but Cage wasn't thinking very reasonbly at the moment.

"Cage, for heaven's sake, shut up," Bob hissed, rising to face his oldest son. "How dare you speak to your mother in such crude terms."

"All right," he said, slicing the air with his hands. "I don't give a damn what you think about me, but how could you have driven Jenny out at a time like this?"

"We didn't drive her out. She made the decision to leave."

"You must have said something to provoke her into taking such a drastic action. What was it?"

"She expected us to believe that Hal had...had done that," Bob said. "Mother and I conceded that he might have. As you pointed out, your brother was a man. But if he did, she must have tempted him to do it beyond his endurance to resist."

Frankly Cage didn't know how Hal had resisted her that night. He never could have. Not in a million years. Not if the jaws of Hell had opened up to welcome him as soon as it was over. "Whatever happened, it was done out of love." That much was the truth.

"I believe that. Even so," Bob said, stubbornly shaking his head, "Hal wouldn't have distracted himself from his mission unless he was sorely tempted. And possibly, just possibly, he was still distracted, or feeling guilty about the sin he had committed, or was otherwise in conflict with himself when he was in Monterico. Maybe that's why he was careless enough to get himself captured and killed."

"My God," Cage breathed, falling back against the wall as though he had just sustained a stunning blow. He stared at his parents, wondering how two such self-righteous, narrow-minded, judgmental people could have spawned him. "You told Jenny that? You blamed her for Hal's death?"

"She is to blame," Sarah said. "Hal's convictions were so steadfast, she must have seduced him. Can you imagine how betrayed we feel? We reared her as our own daughter. For her to turn on us like this...to have an illegitimate child...Oh, Lord, when I think of what this is going to do to Hal's memory. Everyone loved and admired him. This will destroy everything he stood for." Sarah clamped her lips into a thin white line and turned her head away.

Cage was torn by indecision. They were laying the blame for Hal's death on Jenny, thinking she had seduced him. Hal's death couldn't be blamed on anyone but Hal, because he hadn't been distracted or guilty over a night of passion with Jenny. Cage could absolve her now by telling them that she had been with him instead. But if they condemned Jenny for sleeping with Hal, they would stone her in the streets for sleeping with *him*.

Their attitude made him sick. He had reassured Jenny that they would be glad about the baby. Instead they had judged her and scorned her in a most unchristian way. He wanted to call them hypocrites to their faces, but he didn't have the time. And why waste the energy? As far as he was concerned, they were a lost cause. He had only one purpose in mind now. To find Jenny.

"Where did she go?"

"We don't know," Bob said in a tone that indicated he didn't care either. "She called a taxi."

"I pity the two of you," Cage said before storming out.

"How long ago?"

"Well, let's see." A gnarled finger traveled down the column of departure times, then traced a line across to the listing of cities. " 'Bout thirty minutes ago. It was due to pull out at six-fifty, and as well as I recollect, there weren't no delays."

"Does it make any stops?"

The clerk at the bus depot checked the schedule again with a meticulous precision that was driving Cage crazy. Didn't the man know anything without having to consult the damn schedule?

After talking with the owner of the town's only taxi service and learning that Jenny had been chauffeured from the parsonage to the bus depot, Cage had driven there at top speed. A rapid survey of the dingy passenger lounge assured him she wasn't there. Only one ticket had been sold to a young woman matching Jenny's description. A one-way ticket to Dallas.

"Nope. No stops. Not until Abilene, that is."

"Which highway do they take?"

The clerk told him and by the time he finished his painstaking directions, Cage was already running toward the door. The idling Corvette was shoved into gear, but Cage cursed when he checked the gas gauge. He couldn't go forty miles on what was in the tank. Turning into the next service station he came to he filled the tank with gasoline as fast as the pump would permit.

"You've only got a fifty-dollar bill?" the attendant whined. "Jeez, Cage, that's gonna take practically all the money out of my till."

"Sorry. That's all I have and I'm in a hurry." Damn, he needed a cigarette. Why had he promised Jenny he'd give them up?

"Heavy date?" The attendant winked lecherously. "Blonde or brunette tonight?"

"As I said, I'm in—"

"Yeah, a hurry, I know, I know," he said, winking again. "Is she the one running hot or are you? Well, let's see what we can do here." He peered down into the cash register's tray over the top of his eyeglasses. "There's a twenty. Nope, it's a ten. And here's a five."

Had the whole damn town been drugged with a mind-stealing chemical? Everyone had been reduced to an imbecile. "Tell you what, Andy, you keep my change and I'll pick it up later."

"Got the itch that bad, have ya?" he called to Cage's retreating back. "She must be somethin' special."

"She is," Cage said as he slid into the Corvette. Seconds later darkness swallowed his taillights.

Jenny had learned not to fight the swaying motion of the bus, but to let her body rock with it. It had become almost lulling. The sheer monotony of it was soothing, and it kept her mind off her future.

What future?

She had none.

The Hendrens had made their feelings plain. She was a Jezebel who had tempted their sainted son, who had tried to lure him away from his life's calling by getting herself pregnant by him.

Stinging tears filled her eyes, but she wouldn't submit to them. She closed her eyes and laid her head on the seat cushion behind her, wishing she could sleep. But that was impossible. Her mind was in turmoil and the passengers around her were becoming increasingly restless and vocal.

"Would you look at that."

"A maniac."

"Does our driver see him?"

"What does he think this is, the Indy Five Hundred?"

Curious as to what had captured their attention, Jenny peered through the window. She saw nothing but her own reflection in the glass and a stygian blackness beyond it. Then she saw the sports car skid alongside the bus, coming dangerously close to the oversized wheels.

"A madman for sure," Jenny heard someone mutter just as her eyes went wide and her mouth went slack with recognition.

"Oh, no," she breathed.

Suddenly the bus gave a lurch as the driver applied the brakes and steered it to the shoulder of the highway. "Ladies and gentlemen," he said into the microphone mounted near the steering wheel, "I'm sorry for this delay, but I'm making an unscheduled stop. This is obviously a drunk driver who's intent on running us off the road. I'll try to reason with him before he kills us all. Stay calm. We'll be on our way again shortly."

Several passengers leaned forward in their seats to see better. Jenny scrunched down in hers, her heart pounding. The driver pushed open the automatic door of the bus and made to leave his chair. Before he could, however, the "madman" bounded inside.

"Please, mister," the driver pleaded, obviously concerned for the safety of his passengers. He patted the air in front of him with raised hands. "We're just innocent folks and—"

"Relax. I'm not a robber. I'm not going to hurt anybody. I'm just going to relieve you of one of your passengers."

Cage's eyes were busily scanning the passengers. Jenny sat quiet and still in her seat. He began making his way down the aisle. "Sorry for this inconvenience," he said in friendly fashion to the passengers, who eyed him warily. "This will only take a minute, I promise." When he spotted his quarry, he stopped in the aisle and sighed with relief. "Get your things, Jenny. You're coming back with me."

"No, I'm not, Cage. I explained it all to you in a letter. I mailed it just before I left. You shouldn't have come after me."

"Well, I did, and I didn't make the trip for nothing. Now come on."

"No."

They had everyone's attention.

Aggravated with her the way a parent is with a lost child when he's found, he put his hands on his hips. "All right.

If you want to air the dirty laundry in front of all these nice people, it's fine with me, but you'd better think about it before we get down to the juicy details.''

Jenny's eyes skittered around the other passengers, who were looking at her with open curiosity. "What'd she do, mama?" a little girl piped up. "Was it bad?"

"What's it going to be, Jenny?"

"You don't have to go anywhere with him, miss," the driver said gallantly from behind Cage. It wasn't going to be said that he had let a wife-beater haul his hapless victim off *his* bus.

Jenny looked at Cage. His jaw was set. His eyes were glowing like yellow flame. He seemed as unmovable as the Rock of Gibraltar. He wouldn't relent, and she didn't want to be held responsible for a brawl aboard a Greyhound bus.

"Oh, all right. I'll go." She edged into the aisle after retrieving her small suitcase. "I have another bag in the luggage compartment," she told the driver softly, aware that every eye in the bus was focused on her.

The three of them stepped outside and the driver opened the luggage compartment beneath the bus. As he handed over her suitcase, he asked, "You're sure you want to go with him? He's not going to hurt you, is he?"

She smiled at him reassuringly. "No, no. It's nothing like that. He's not going to hurt me."

After shooting Cage a fulminating look and mumbling something about maniacal speedsters, he climbed back aboard his bus. A moment later it lumbered onto the highway, its passengers craning their necks in the windows to see the two people left behind.

Stiffly Jenny turned to face Cage. She dropped her suitcases with an emphatic plop. "Well, *that* was quite a stunt, Mr. Hendren. Just what did you expect to gain by it?"

"Just what I did. To get you off that bus and stop you from running away like a scared rabbit."

"Well, maybe that's what I am," she cried, giving vent to the tears that had been welling up since the scene in the parsonage.

"What did you have in mind, Jenny? Running to Dallas and having an abortion?"

Her hands knotted into fists. "That's a despicable thing to even suggest."

"What then? What was your intention? Were you going to have the baby and give it away?"

"No!"

"Hide it?" He stepped forward. How she answered the next question was of utmost importance to him. "Don't you want the baby, Jenny? Are you ashamed of it?"

"No, no," she groaned, covering her stomach with both hands. "Of course I want it. I love it already."

Cage's shoulders slumped with relief, but his voice still had an angry edge to it. "Then why were you running scared?"

"I didn't know what else to to. Your parents made it obvious they didn't want me around any longer."

"So?"

"*So?*" She jerked her arm in the direction the bus had just taken. "Not everyone is brave enough or *crazy* enough to come chasing after a Greyhound bus. Or drive ninety miles an hour down the highway on a motorcycle. I can't be like you, Cage. You don't give a damn what people think about you. You please yourself." She splayed her hands wide over her chest. "I'm not like that. I do care what people think. And I am scared."

"Of what?" he asked, thrusting his chin out belligerently. "Of a town full of petty minds? How can they hurt you? What's the worst they can do to you? Gossip about you? Scorn you? So what? You're better off without the people who would do that.

"Are you afraid of besmirching Hal's name? I hate it that some righteous hypocrites will think badly of him. But Hal is dead. He'll never know. And the work he instigated will continue. You've seen to that yourself by setting up that fund-raising network. For godsake, Jenny, don't be so hard on yourself. You are your own worst enemy."

"What are you suggesting I do? Go back and work in your office?"

"Yes."

"Flaunt my condition?"

"Be proud of it."

"Have my baby knowing he'll be labeled with a dirty name all his life?"

Cage pointed a steely finger toward her middle. "Anyone who labels that kid anything but wonderful is risking his life."

She could almost laugh at his ferocity. "But you won't always be around to protect him. It won't be easy for this child in a small town where everyone knows his origin."

"It won't be easy for him to grow up in a big city where his mother doesn't know anyone either. Who would you call on for help, Jenny? At least any hostile faces you encounter in La Bota will be familiar ones."

She hated to admit how the thought of moving to another city without much money, without a job or a place to live, without friends or relatives, had terrified her.

"Isn't it time you showed some backbone, Jenny?"

Her head snapped up. "What do you mean by that?" she asked tightly.

"You've been letting other people make your decisions for you since you were fourteen."

"We had this same argument a few months ago. I tried to direct my own destiny. Look what a mess I made of it."

He looked offended. "I thought you said the lovemaking was beautiful. You're going to have a baby as a result of it. Do you really consider that a mess?"

She hung her head and pressed her hands to her stomach. "No. It's wonderful. I'm awed by the thought of the child. Awed and humbled by the miracle of it."

"Then hold that thought. Come back to La Bota with me. Have that beautiful baby and thumb your nose at everybody who doesn't like it."

"Even your parents?"

"Their reaction tonight was a knee-jerk reflex. When they think about it, they'll come around."

Meditatively she stared at nothing. "I suppose you're right. I can't *find* a future for me and the baby. I have to make one. Right?"

He grinned and gave her the thumbs-up sign. "I couldn't have put it better myself."

"Oh, Cage," she sighed, her arms dangling uselessly at her sides. She was suddenly sapped of energy. "Thank you once again."

He moved toward her, his boots crunching on the gravel. Cupping her face between his hands, he whisked his thumbs over her cheekbones. "You could make this a lot easier on yourself if you'd just marry me. The baby would have a daddy and everything would be neat and nice and legal."

"I can't, Cage."

"Sure?"

"Sure."

"That's not the last time I'll ask."

His breath was hot and sweet on her lips before they actually made contact with his. He eased her face upward to his descending mouth and kissed her with gentle possessiveness.

As before, his lips were open and moist. But unlike the other time, his tongue touched hers. Just the tip. Just enough to make her breath catch in her throat and her heart beat erratically. Just enough to make her breasts flare in instantaneous response.

He slid the end of his tongue back and forth over hers in a lazy movement. Then he withdrew and left her wanting. When he stepped away from her and took her arm to guide her to the car, she felt chilled with the absence of his body heat.

He stored her suitcases behind the seats of the Corvette as best he could. "The first thing on the agenda is finding you a place to live," he remarked when they were under way.

Somehow her hand had come to rest on his thigh. "Have any ideas?" she asked vaguely.

"You could move in with me."

Their eyes locked across the console. His were inquiring and mischievous; hers were chastising. "Next suggestion."

He chuckled good-naturedly. "I think I can fix something up with Roxy."

Chapter 8

"Roxy *Clemmons*?" Jenny asked, snatching her hand away from his thigh.

"Yeah. Do you know her?"

Only by reputation, Jenny thought snidely. Only by reputation as one of Cage's regulars. "I've heard of her." She turned her head away to gaze out the car window. Despair and disappointment tasted acrid in her mouth.

He had kissed her with such sweet intimacy. His embrace had been warming and security-lending. She was coming to like it when he touched her, liking it even more when he kissed her. But he wasn't doing to her what he hadn't done to hundreds of others. His kisses might set off fireworks in her head, but that kind of passion wasn't a new experience for him. His kissing technique could have been perfected only by hours of practice.

Was she destined to become one of Cage Hendren's "women"? Did he plan on lumping her into that sorority, actually ensconcing her under a roof where she would always be convenient to visit?

"You don't sound very enthusiastic about the idea," he commented.

"I don't have much choice, do I?"

"I offered you an alternative. You rejected it."

She sat in stony silence. She was angry and couldn't quite pinpoint why. Why should she be feeling mad and insulted? She certainly had nothing in common with that Clemmons woman. There was one major distinction between them.

Jenny Fletcher wasn't one of Cage's women...yet.

Had she been subconsciously harboring the thought that they would become lovers? Why? Because he had kissed her a few times? Because of the night in Monterico? Or because she had always felt an inexorable gravitation toward him? It had frightened her and she had resisted it. Until recently.

Well, if he thought she was going to join the ranks of his other women, he had another think coming. Roxy Clemmons and so many other women were strung like beads on a thread of sexual encounters that wound through several counties. Maybe because of her fall from grace with Hal, Cage now considered her fair game. He couldn't be more mistaken.

They didn't speak for the reminder of the trip back. The streets of town were deserted by the time they reached La Bota. Cage pulled his car into the parking lot of an apartment complex and cut the engine. "What's this?" Jenny asked.

"Your new address, I hope. Come on." He led her up to the apartment with a discreet sign reading Manager stuck in the front yard.

He rang the bell. Through the walls, they could hear Johnny Carson amusing his audience. When the door opened, Jenny came face to face with Roxy Clemmons. The woman looked at her with polite curiosity, then spotted

Cage in the shadows. "Hiya, Cage." The smile she flashed him caused Jenny to whither inside. "What's going on?"

"May we come in?"

"Sure." Without reservation Roxy stood aside and held the door open for them. After she closed it, she went to the television set and turned the sound all the way down.

"I'm sorry to bother you so late, Roxy," Cage began.

"Hell, you know you're welcome anytime."

Jenny's heart twisted and her gaze dropped to the floor.

"Roxy, this is Jenny Fletcher."

"Yeah, I know. Hi, Jenny. It's nice to meet you."

Her open friendliness surprised Jenny and she raised her head. "Nice to meet you too, Ms. Clemmons."

Roxy laughed. "Call me Roxy. Y'all want something to drink? I've got a cold beer, Cage."

"Sounds good."

"Jenny?"

"Uh, nothing, thank you."

"A Coke?"

She didn't want to appear impolite, so she answered with a weak smile. "Yes, all right, a Coke."

"Sit down and make yourselves at home."

Roxy turned toward the swinging barroom doors, which led to the kitchen. Her hips showed full and shapely in a pair of tight jeans. Voluptuous breasts swung free beneath her sweatshirt. She was barefoot. Her coppery hair was tousled, but attractively so. She looked either like she had just gotten out of bed or was on her way. She was the kind of woman a man could curl up and relax with, custom made to be a mistress. Friendly, hospitable, warm, and willing. The thought brought a scalding rush of nausea to Jenny's throat.

Cage had settled down on the sofa and was leafing through an issue of *Cosmopolitan* that Roxy had left there. "Sit down, Jenny," he said, noting that she was standing awkwardly in the middle of the room.

Uneasily, as though she might dirty her skirt if she wasn't careful, she lowered herself onto a straight chair. Cage looked amused. That irritated her.

Roxy came back with their drinks, and after Cage had taken a long swallow from the can of beer, he said, "Do you have any vacancies? We need an apartment."

Roxy cast a dumbfounded glance at Jenny, then her eyes swung back to Cage. "Gee, that's great, congratulations. But what's wrong with your house?"

He laughed. "Nothing that I know of. I think you misunderstood. Jenny will be living in the apartment alone."

Jenny could have killed Cage for making it sound like they would be living together. Her cheeks were flaming scarlet. Now that he had clarified the situation, she watched Roxy for signs of relief. Surely Roxy would be glad that he wasn't going to move in another mistress right under her nose. But all Jenny saw on Roxy's face was chagrin at her mistake.

"Oh!" She looked at Jenny and smiled. "You're in luck. I have a one-bedroom apartment vacant."

Jenny opened her mouth to speak, but Cage cut in before her. "How large is the bedroom? Jenny's going to have a baby. Is there enough room for a crib?"

Roxy's reaction to that piece of news was shock. Her mouth hung slack for several moments as she stared at Cage. When she turned back to Jenny, her eyes moved unerringly down to Jenny's still-trim middle.

"You don't have any restrictions on tenants with babies, do you?" Cage asked.

"No. Hell, no." Visibly Roxy collected herself and put things in their proper perspective. She bent down to slip her bare feet into a pair of sandals. "Let's go see the apartment and you can decide if it's what you're looking for."

"It's in a good location," she said over her shoulder a few minutes later as they followed her down the sidewalk between the buildings. She had gotten the key to the vacant apartment from the spare bedroom in her unit, which served as an office. "Private and quiet, but not so isolated that you'll be afraid to live here alone, Jenny." She prattled on about the complex's amenities, pointing out the laundry facilities and the pool area.

Jenny wasn't listening. She was casting murderous glances at Cage for blurting out her condition to this...this *woman*. By morning everybody in town would know she was pregnant.

"Here we are." Roxy unlocked the apartment and led them inside. She switched on the light. "Whew! It's a little close. I haven't opened it since the cleaning crews and painters were here."

The apartment did smell of disinfectant and new paint, but Jenny didn't mind that. It was spotlessly clean as a result.

"This is the living room, of course. You have a kitchen in here." Roxy led Jenny through a louvered half door like the one in her own apartment. The built-ins were all clean and shiny. Jenny opened the refrigerator. It was clean, too.

They finished touring the apartment, which didn't take long. There was only a bathroom and bedroom beyond the living room. "How much is the rent?" Jenny asked.

"Four hundred a month plus utilities."

"Four hundred?" Jenny squeaked. "I'm afraid—"

"Unfurnished?" Cage asked, butting in.

"Oh, Jeez," Roxy said, swatting her forehead. "I misquoted. Unfurnished one bedrooms are two-fifty."

"That's more like it," Cage said.

Jenny calculated her income and expenditures. She might be able to afford it if she were frugal. Besides, this was one of the nicer apartment complexes in town, and her choices were limited. She was lucky there was an apartment available. Trying to forget that she would be living doors away from one of Cage's lovers, she said, "Do I need to sign a lease?"

"You'll take it, then?" Roxy asked.

"Yes, I suppose so," Jenny answered, wondering why the other woman was so obviously pleased.

"Fantastic. I'm glad you'll be a neighbor. Come on, let's go back to the office."

Within fifteen minutes Jenny had a copy of the contract and a set of keys in her hand. "You can move in tomorrow. In the morning I'll go over and air it out a bit."

"Thank you." She and Roxy shook hands. Cage escorted Jenny to the car, saw that she was settled in the front seat, and then returned to Roxy, who was still standing in her opened front door.

"Thanks for playing along about the rent."

"You threw me a curve ball, but I picked up on it," Roxy said, smiling up at him. "Are you gonna fill me in on the details of this 'arrangement,' or am I gonna have to use my vivid imagination?"

"Nosy?"

"Damn right."

He laughed. "We'll talk later. Thanks for everything."

"Don't mention it. What are friends for?"

He kissed her quickly on the lips and patted her fanny before he sauntered down the steps and joined Jenny in the car. She was sitting as rigid as a statue staring straight ahead, spears of jealousy knifing into her chest.

She hadn't overheard the conversation at the door, but she had seen the way they smiled at each other and how Cage had bent down to kiss Roxy. The easy familiarity with which they touched each other wrenched at Jenny's composure. Despite her avowals that she didn't care, her heart was slowly tearing in two.

"First thing in the morning we'll hit the furniture stores," Cage was saying.

"You've done enough. I can't ask you—"

"You didn't ask, all right?" he said testily. "I volunteered. Make a list tonight of everything you'll need."

"I won't be able to afford much. Just the essentials. By the way, where are we going now?" Until that moment she hadn't remembered that for tonight she was still homeless. Where would she spend the night?

"I didn't think you wanted to go back to the parsonage."

"No."

"You could come home with me."

"You don't have the room."

"In that big house?"

"There's only one bed."

"So? We've shared a bed before." The reminder was quietly and huskily spoken. She didn't comment on it. After several seconds he sighed and said, "I'm checking you into a motel."

It was no sooner said than he pulled his car under the porte cochere of a chain motel. "Wait here."

Jenny watched him enter the well-lighted lobby. Through the plate-glass front she saw the night clerk swing his legs down from his desk and set his spy thriller novel aside. That he recognized Cage was obvious by the wide grin and hearty handshake he gave him.

He didn't even require Cage to sign the register, but immediately reached for a room key and slid it across the counter. Leaning forward in a conspiratorial, lets-have-a-man-to-man-chat posture, he said something that caused Cage to wave his hand in negligent dismissal.

The clerk squinted through the window toward the car. Jenny saw his surprised expression when he recognized her. Grinning up at Cage, he made another comment that drew Cage's brows into a deep scowl. It was still there when he returned to the car after bidding the clerk a brusque good night.

"What did he say?"

"Nothing," Cage ground through his teeth.

"He said something. I saw him."

Cage didn't respond, but drove straight to the room without even having to check the numbers on the doors. He brought the car to a jarring halt and angrily cut the engine.

"You've been here before," Jenny said intuitively.

"Jenny—"

"Haven't you?"

"—drop it."

"Haven't you?"

"Maybe."

"Often?"

"Yes!"

"With women?"

"Yes!"

Her chest was in danger of caving in around her heart. She could barely speak, it hurt so much to draw sufficient air. "You've brought women here to affairs and that's what the clerk thinks I'm doing with you. What did he say about me?"

"It doesn't matter what he—"

"It matters to me," she shouted. "Tell me."

"No."

He got out of the car and jerked her bags from behind the seat. Without waiting to see if she followed him, he strode toward the door of the motel room and unlocked it. He flung the luggage on the rack in the closet and flipped on the lamp.

"What did he say?" Jenny demanded from the doorway.

Cage spun around and saw her resolved expression. She looked tired and distraught, angry and vulnerable. Her hair was disheveled and her cheeks were pale. Her eyes were ringed with violet shadows of fatigue. Her mouth was trembling slightly. She looked like a lost child and an unvanquished soldier.

He had never wanted her more. But he couldn't have her and that only fueled his anger. She was his, dammit, but he couldn't claim her. He needed her just as much as she needed him, but circumstance was keeping them apart. He was paying dearly for that one night of heaven. Desire to possess her again was making his life hell on earth.

Wanting to hurt her as much as he was hurting, he lashed out. "All right, Miss Fletcher. You want to know what he said? He said that I was keeping it in the family this time."

She clamped her top teeth over her bottom lip to keep from screaming in outrage. Indignation boiled up inside her, seeking an outlet. Cage was the only one to vent it against.

"Do you see what you've done?" she cried. "You announced to Roxy Clemmons, whom everybody knows is one of your sluts, that I'm pregnant. Now you've brought me to a motel where you regularly bring other women. It'll be all over town tomorrow that I was here with you. Well, I don't want to be dragged from lair to lair like a prize. I don't want anybody to mistake me for one of your lovers, Cage."

"Why? Because I'm so rotten? You don't want to be associated with the 'bad boy,' that wild preacher's kid that no one can control, the one who's always in trouble, always in a scrape, always involved with the wrong woman?"

He had advanced toward her with a predatory gait. She tried to back away from him, but was trapped by the dresser. "I didn't mean it that way."

"The hell you didn't," he snarled. "Well, you've got every right to be cautious where I'm concerned. I am bad. I must be. Damn bad." One hand shot out and cupped the back of her head. The strong fingers knotted in her hair and pulled her head back. "Because I have brought a lot of women to this room, but I never wanted one as much as I want you."

He encircled her wrist with his other hand and dragged her hand down. *"No!"* she cried when she realized his intent. She pulled on her hand, but he wouldn't release it. He shoved it past his waist and forced it flat against his body, pressing, making sure she felt the steely evidence of his arousal behind the fly of his jeans.

"That's how much I want you. I've wanted you for a long time and I'm tired of hiding the fact. Now, does that make you scared? Sick? Disgusted? Does it make you want to cringe? To scream? Or skulk back to the safety of the parsonage?" He ground himself into her palm. "Well, that's just tough, Jenny, because this is the way it is."

He kissed her with barely controlled savagery. Unleashing all his emotions, he twisted his mouth against hers, tilting his head first to one side then to the other. His tongue plunged deep, withdrew, sank again more slowly and thoroughly into her mouth, evocative of coupling.

Then just as furiously as he had possessed her, he released her. He stormed out of the door and pulled it closed behind him with a resounding slam.

Jenny staggered to the bed and collapsed. She tried to deny that she was disappointed he hadn't finished what he had started. But she was. Her body was weak and fluttery with longing. Garnering what little strength was left her, she stumbled into the bathroom and peeled off her clothes. She avoided the mirror, not wanting to see the flags of color in her cheeks or the rosy readiness of her breasts.

The shower was hot and punishing, just the ticket for the self-flagellation she deserved. The jetting spray stung her skin like driving needles. It was still tingling when she took a nightgown from her suitcase and pulled it on. She climbed into bed and squeezed her eyes shut, hoping that would close off her mind as well.

But the kiss was too recent to be banished from her memory. She could still taste him on her lips, still feel the rigid proof of his sex against her hand, still recall the cadence of his kiss as his tongue thrust against hers.

When the telephone rang near her ear, she jumped as though lightning had struck her. "Hello."

"I'm sorry."

Neither of them said anything for ponderous moments. Jenny's breasts trembled with emotion beneath her batiste nightie. She cradled the receiver between her cheek and shoulder as though inclining her head toward Cage. "It's all right."

"I lost my temper."

"I provoked you."

"We've been through an ordeal today."

"We were both touchy."

"Did I hurt you?"

"No, of course you didn't hurt me."

"I was rough." His voice dropped significantly. "And crude."

She looked down at her hand as though to see an imprint there. She swallowed. "I survived."

"Jenny?"

"What?"

A long pause. "I'm not sorry I kissed you. I'm only sorry for the *way* I kissed you." He let that sink in, then added, "And if you were ever in any doubt about how I feel about you, it's no secret now."

Touched by the gentle, but imperative, tone of his voice, her throat ached with the need to cry. "I'm not ready to think about that, Cage. So much has happened."

"I know, I know. Get a good night's sleep. Sleep late. The office will be closed tomorrow. I'll pick you up, feed you breakfast, and then take you shopping. Be ready at ten sharp."

"Okay."

"G'night, Jenny."

"G'night, Cage."

"Good morning, Jenny."

"Hm?"

"I said good morning."

Jenny yawned broadly into the pillow, stretched her pointed toes as far as she could reach beneath the covers, and pried her eyes open. Then she popped erect. Cage was sitting on the edge of her bed, smiling down at her. "Welcome back to the land of the living."

"What time is it?"

"Ten after ten. I arrived at ten o'clock on the dot, knocked, and got no answer. I went to the lobby to pick up an extra key and let myself in."

"I'm sorry," she said, raking the hair out of her eyes. She blushed becomingly under his ardent perusal of her sleepy disarray and inched the sheet up higher over her breasts. "I was exhausted."

"Hungry?"

"Starving."

"I'll go order breakfast in the coffee shop while you get dressed." He dropped an airy kiss on the tip of her nose before pulling himself off the bed.

"I'll be right there," she called to him as he closed the door behind him.

She looked fresh and rested when she joined him twenty minutes later in the coffee shop. She had dressed in a simple skirt and blouse, but had accessorized them with a paisley shawl tied at her waist under one arm. Her shoes had low heels and narrow ankle straps that captured Cage's attention as she crossed the casual dining room toward him.

He knew she had taken one of her first pay checks and used it to refurbish her wardrobe. She was dressing with more flair than she had when she was engaged to Hal.

"Am I late?"

"Your food just got here. I like your shoes, by the way."

"They're new," she said absently, eyeing the platters of food at her plate setting. "All of this is for me?"

"Yep."

"You don't expect me to eat it all, do you?"

"I expect you to make a big dent in it. Get busy. I'm outlining our attack."

"Aren't you eating?" she asked, spreading the napkin in her lap.

"I went ahead." His head was bent over a note pad where he was jotting down an extensive list of households items she would need.

Jenny was taken by the endearing picture he made. There were a thousand shades of blond and brown and ash in his hair, but it all added up to dusty blond color that looked rugged and perpetually wind-tossed.

His cheeks and chin had been closely shaved and the brisk scent of his cologne overwhelmed even the aroma of fresh coffee as the waitress filled Jenny's cup. His tawny brow was furrowed with concentration.

He was dressed in jeans and a sport shirt, but there was a raw silk jacket draped over the back of his chair. It was an odd wardrobe combination, and one only a man who flagrantly broke all the rules could get by with.

He was gorgeous in a sexy, dangerous way. Jenny knew just how dangerous his appeal could be. It drew a woman out of her shell until she didn't recognize herself anymore. Jenny had to consciously settle her stomach down before she could take a bite of food.

By the time she had eaten enough breakfast to suit him, he had their itinerary mapped out. "Remember my budget," she said when he enumerated the stores they would shop in.

"Maybe your boss will give you a raise."

She stoped on her way to his car and turned to face him. Her chin was stubbornly set. "Get this straight, Cage. I won't accept your charity."

"Will you marry me?"

"No."

"Then shut up and get in." He held the door of the Corvette open for her and she knew further argument was futile. She'd just have to put her foot down when it came to what she could buy and what she couldn't.

He had expensive taste and everything he liked was exactly what she would have selected had money been no object. "I can't afford this sofa. The other one costs half as much."

"It's ugly as sin."

"It's functional."

"It's hard and...boxy. This one has cushions a foot thick and is so comfy."

"That's what makes it expensive. Comfy and cushions aren't that important."

His grin was Satan-inspired and his voice was slurred with innuendo. "That all depends on what you're going to do on the sofa."

The sales clerk standing near enough to overhear snickered, but drew a serious face when Jenny turned around and glared at him. "I'll take the other one," she said with prim hauteur.

They had the same argument over the bed, chairs, a dinette, linens, dishes, pots and pans, even a can opener. In every case he urged her to pay a premium price for top quality merchandise. She was adamantly stingy.

"Tired?"

She was resting her head on the back of the car seat. "Yes," she sighed. "I'll probably never move from this apartment. I couldn't go through this again."

He laughed. "I've arranged for everything we bought to be delivered this afternoon. By nightfall that apartment will be like home sweet home."

"How'd you manage to get everything delivered today?"

"Bribes, threats, blackmail, any way I could."

He was smiling mischievously, but she believed him.

"That looks like my car!" She sat up straight when he stopped in front of her apartment.

"It is your car," Cage said nonchalantly as he assisted her out of the Corvette.

"How did it get here?"

"I had it towed." He opened the door of her compact and leaned down to fish the keys from beneath the floor mat where he had instructed the tow truck driver to leave them. He tossed them to her. "Frankly I think it's a pile of no-class junk, but I know you're attached to it."

She looked distressed. "Cage, I didn't want to take anything from your parents."

Placing his hands on his hips, he said, "For godsake, Jenny, they gave you this car as a present years ago. Why do they need three cars—theirs, Hal's, and yours—in their driveway when Mother rarely even drives?"

She marched toward the car and moved him aside so she could get in. "I'm taking it back."

He bent down and stuck his head in the open window after she had shut the door. "Then I'll be your only means of transportation," he reminded her in a singsong voice.

In weary surrender, she laid her head on the steering wheel. "That's blackmail."

"That's right."

Laughing in spite of herself, she let him lead her into the apartment. Roxy had made good on her promise. The windows had been opened and the fresh air had rid the rooms of their stuffiness.

Within a half hour her purchases began to arrive. "Oh, you've made a mistake!" Jenny exclaimed as she opened the door for the first delivery.

"No mistake, miss. Excuse me." The man transferred his fat cigar from one side of his mouth to the other and casually brushed past her as he carried in a chair. "Bring the sofa on in," he yelled back to his helpers, who were climbing down from the truck.

"But wait, that's the wrong one."

"It's the one written on the ticket." He sat the chair down and handed her the green invoice.

Her eyes quickly scanned the invoice, then went back over it more carefully. "Oh, no! Cage, there's been some terrible—"

She broke off when she saw his smile. His backside was trying out the cushiony couch he had chosen, his arms stretched out along its back. He was smiling like a gratified Santa Claus on Christmas morning.

"What have you done?" she grated.

"Sabotage is the word that comes to mind."

That was exactly the word that applied. As piece after piece of merchandise was delivered, she realized that he had gone behind her and ordered the things she had wanted but couldn't afford. "How am I supposed to pay for all this?" she cried.

"Credit. Whatever you paid today went as a down payment. I arranged monthly terms for you that you can afford. A single woman should establish credit. So what's the problem?"

"I can't let you do this, Cage. You're railroading me into making decisions that go against my better judgment. But it's going to stop right now. I won't stay in this apartment if it means keeping all this furniture."

"All right." Those two words of concession should have been accompanied by a sigh and a dejected slump of his broad shoulders. Instead he was grinning broadly. He went to the front door and whistled piercingly. "Hey, fellows, load it all back up and take it out to my place. She's decided to marry me instead of living here alone."

"Oh, Lord," Jenny groaned and covered her face with her hands. "Uncle, uncle!"

Laughing, Cage closed the door and moved toward her.

"Haven't you got anything better to do than baby-sit me?"

"Nothing I can think of."

"Since Hal went away, you've been wonderful. Why are you doing all this for me, Cage?"

The golden eyes wandered over her face. With one index finger, he brushed a strand of her hair off her forehead. "Because I like the color of your hair. Especially when the afternoon sunlight shines on it the way it is now."

He moved closer. Her head tilted back naturally so she could gaze up into his chiseled face. "And I like your eyes," he said softly.

He reached beneath her arm and untied the ends of her shawl. He drew it off slowly, as though he were peeling away a much more personal article of clothing, and dropped it negligently onto the floor.

"I love the way you laugh. And the way the sound of it makes me feel on the inside."

He settled his hands on either side of her waist and lightly seesawed them up and down. "I like the way your body is made."

He lowered his head and nuzzled her ear. "And the shape of your mouth."

A heartbeat later his lips drifted over hers. He pecked her mouth softly, repeatedly, until her lips parted, all but begging to be possessed.

He heeded her silent yearning and melded their mouths together. His tongue slid deep into her mouth and prowled at will. The violence of last night's kiss was gone, but this tender one was just as potent and awakened her body as earth-shatteringly as it had been stirred the night before. Driven by a craving to get closer, she took unconscious steps toward him. When her body was plastered against his from chest to knees, she was almost surprised to find it so.

"God, Jenny," he whispered. His breath was hot and fragrant against her flushing cheeks. His lips were dewy as he caught her earlobe between his teeth and arousingly worried it with small nibbles.

She felt herself slipping into silky surrender again, losing control, turning her common sense and her senses over to a reckless master.

"Cage, we shouldn't do—"

"Shh, shh."

Her memory quickened. She should remember something. She knew it.

But before she could grasp the elusive memory, his mouth was making love to hers again and all thought scattered.

He lifted her arms and folded them around his shoulders. Then his hands slid from her elbows down the undersides of her arms to the shallows of her armpits. He paused an instant before continuing downward to the outer curves of her breasts. He massaged them with the heels of his hands. Jenny sighed into his mouth.

"Feel good?"

She murmured an affirmation. The kiss deepened.

She angled her head so that one of her cheeks was lying on his chest. He bent his head down low over hers, seeking, always seeking, for her taste with his agile tongue. His arms went around her and drew her closer still. One of his hands slipped below her waist to her derriere. He pressed her against him, positioning her so she would feel the full urgency of his desire.

She moaned and rubbed her middle against his. The heart of her femininity felt feverish and swollen, but it was a delicious malady she suffered from. She throbbed, achingly but wonderfully.

"Jenny, I want you."

He moved his hand between their bodies, covered her breast, kneaded it lovingly. The pad of his middle finger found the sensivitve crest and coaxed it into hard arousal.

"Ah, that's sweet." He complimented her as though she had done something miraculous. "So sweet. I want to see it, taste it, taste you."

He ducked his head and kissed her breast through her blouse. His tongue moistly nudged the tight peak. "I want to make love to you." He moved his mouth to her throat, where his lips could touch her warm skin. His voice was hoarse. "Do you understand? I want to be inside you. Deep, deep." His lips claimed hers again, wildly, more demanding.

"Hey, you two, open up." There was banging on the door. "I've brought the party."

Cage lifted his mouth from Jenny's and uttered a vicious obscenity. Then he drew in a shaky breath. He looked back down at Jenny and smiled crookedly. "We can't deliberately hurt her feelings."

Jenny worked herself free of his arms.

He went to the door and welcomed Roxy inside.

Chapter 9

Roxy bounced in, carrying a jug of wine in one hand and a grocery sack in the other. "Hey, what's all this?" Cage asked, relieving her of the sack. He peeped inside. "Chips, dips, popcorn, and cheese."

"Just as I said, a *party*," Roxy chirped happily. "Hi, Jenny. Is the apartment all right?"

"It's fine, thank you."

"Gee, it looks terrific." Roxy whistled as she surveyed the new furniture. Cage had had the delivery men arrange it as they carried it in, after having consulted with Jenny on where everything was to go. The pieces fit well within the dimensions of the room.

"Got glasses?" Roxy asked. "Come on, let's toast your new place." Without invitation she made her way into the kitchen, with Cage right behind her. Jenny had no choice but to follow, though it was crowded in the small kitchen with all three of them.

Cage ripped open a package of corn chips and popped the lid off a plastic container of prepared dip. He gouged into it with his chip and offered it to Roxy. She took a bite of it, laughing because she was trying to pull the cork out of the wine bottle at the same time. What Roxy didn't eat of the chip and dip, Cage put into his own mouth. Then he licked his fingers.

Jenny remained in the background, feeling out of her element in the midst of their hilarity. She wasn't in a party mood.

"I don't provide this service to all my tenants, you understand," Roxy told Jenny as she washed the price tags off the glasses they had bought that afternoon. Apparently Roxy had no qualms about making herself right at home in a stranger's kitchen. "But since you're a friend of Cage's and he's a friend of mine... Ugh!" She grunted when he reached around her from behind and hugged her hard, his hands locked beneath her lush breasts.

"You betcha. Friends to the bitter end."

"Get away from me, you fool, and slice the cheese."

Jenny felt like a fifth wheel. She didn't belong with them. She didn't know how to participate in their kind of teasing banter. Roxy seemed to know exactly what to say to make Cage burst into laughter. His hands were unintimidated about touching her frequently.

Why their shared familiarity should bother her so much Jenny didn't know. How had she expected them to behave around each other? After all, they were lovers. She knew that. But *knowing* it and actually *witnessing* it were two different things. It hurt her to the core that Cage had been kissing her with such tender fervor only seconds before Roxy made her untimely appearance.

Could he turn his passions off and on at will? Had he already forgotten that he had been kissing her, telling her how much he wanted her? Could he transfer his affection from one woman to another so quickly? Apparently he could. The evidence of his chameleon desires was right in front of her.

When the wine was poured, they toasted her new home. Jenny took one sip of the inexpensive vintage. She set her glass down, and, with an "Excuse me" that she wasn't even sure they heard over their laughter, went into the bathroom and closed the door. She barely made it in time to be sick in the commode.

"Jenny?" Cage tapped on the bathroom door a few moments later. His voice was laced with concern. "Is something wrong?"

"I'll be right out," she called through the door. She washed her face, rinsed out her mouth, and combed her fingers through her hair.

"Are you mad at us?" Cage asked the moment she opened the door. "I know how you feel about drinking. This is your place. We didn't mean to offend you."

It was then that she knew she loved him.

Probably she always had. But it wasn't until that moment, that instant, when he was gazing down at her with such contrition, that she realized she did.

She had been deluding herself for all these years, telling herself that if she stayed away from him, her attraction to him would wane. But all this time it had been secretly nestling inside her like an oyster in its shell, gathering grains of knowledge about Cage, a glance, a touch, a sound, until her love for him was like a rare and precious pearl imbedded in her soul.

She wanted to walk into his arms, to be held close, to cling to his strength. But she wouldn't. Couldn't. It was unheard of. Jenny Fletcher and Cage Hendren? Impossible. She was pregnant with another man's child, his brother's child. Even if that weren't so, they were totally unsuited to each other. Had any two people ever been more different? Their being together in any kind of romantic relationship was a hopeless prospect.

Oh, but she loved him!

"No, it isn't that, Cage," she said, giving him a weak smile. "I don't feel too well."

He tensed. "The baby? Is it bad? Cramps? Blood? What? Should I call the doctor?"

"No, no." She put a restraining hand on his arm but immediately withdrew it. "I'm just tired. I was on my feet all day and I think it's catching up with me."

"I should be shot at sunrise," he said. "I should have tucked you into bed the minute we got home."

"I didn't have a bed then."

He scowled at her attempt at humor. "Well, as soon as it was delivered I should have tucked you in." He took her hand and led her into the living room. "Say good night, Roxy. We're leaving the lady so she can get some rest."

Roxy sprang off the new sofa and looked at Jenny closely. "You're pale as a ghost, honey," she said, laying the back of her hand on Jenny's pallid cheek. "Is there anything I can do?"

Yes, leave, Jenny wanted to shout. *And keep your hands off Cage.* Her primary illness was jealousy. She acknowledged it, but she couldn't ward it off. She just wanted Cage's mistress out of her house. "No. I'll be fine after I get to bed," she said tactfully.

Over her protests, Roxy and Cage made up her new bed, spreading the crisp sheets over it. "Tomorrow you might want to wash these and soften them up a bit," Roxy suggested. "If you need any help carrying them into the laundry room, call me."

"Thank you," she said, knowing good and well she'd never be asking Roxy Clemmons for any favors.

When the bed was made to their satisfaction, they gathered up the party snacks and wine. At the front door Cage took both Jenny's hands in his. "Lock up after us."

"I will."

"If you need me, in the middle of the night, anytime, for anything, go to Roxy's and call me."

"Don't worry about me."

"I'll worry about you if I damn well feel like it," he said crossly. "You'll have a phone installed tomorrow."

"But I didn't order—"

He placed his index finger against her lips. "I did, when you went to the ladies' room after lunch. Now, good night and get some sleep." He kissed her mouth softly. His tongue whisked across her lower lip so lightly and fleetingly, she wasn't sure she hadn't imagined it. As he stepped into the night he took Roxy's arm. "Come on, Roxy sweet, I'll walk you home."

Jenny closed the door after them. Cage was going home with Roxy. They would no doubt pick up the party where they'd left off. Images of them together, their mouths sealed, their bodies entwined, flickered through her mind. Miserable, she lay in her new bed for a long time, unable to fall asleep. She was tormented by the thought of Cage with Roxy. Cage with anybody.

It was very late when she heard the Corvette start up where it was still parked outside her door and drive away.

The next day was Saturday, so there was no rush about getting up and going to work. Jenny stripped the sheets off the bed, having already decided before Roxy mentioned it that they would be more comfortable to sleep on after they'd been washed.

Still wearing her robe, she brewed herself a pot of coffee in her new coffeemaker, which had been only one of a hundred items she and Cage had purchased in the housewares department the day before.

She was lifting the first cup to her lips when someone knocked on the door. Peering out the window first to see who it was, she sagged against the wall dispiritedly. She wasn't up to facing Roxy so soon after last night.

"Hi," Roxy said gaily when Jenny opened the door no more than a discouraging crack. "I didn't wake you up, did I?"

"No."

"Good. Cage would have killed me. Listen, I just made this yummy pastry. It's too much for me to eat alone, and if I don't share it, that's exactly what I'll do." She slapped her generous hip. "Then I'll live to regret it."

It would have been ungracious not to invite her in, so Jenny stepped aside, manufactured a smile of sorts, and said, "Come on in. I just made coffee."

"Great." Roxy set her foil-wrapped package on the new butcher block table and eased herself into one of the bentwood chairs. "You have terrific taste," she commented, glancing around the apartment. "I really like your stuff."

"Thank you, but Cage helped me pick it out."

"He's got terrific taste, too." She winked, but Jenny wasn't sure what the wink was supposed to mean. She concentrated on pouring Roxy a cup of coffee. "Cream and sugar?"

"Black with Sweet 'n Low...the chubby one says as she slices the gooey dessert," Roxy said, mocking herself as she peeled back the foil. "Got a knife and two plates?"

When the pastry had been sliced and Jenny's portion passed to her, she said politely, "This looks good."

"Doesn't it? I got the recipe out of a magazine." Roxy dug into hers. Jenny was more reserved but found the pastry to be delicious. "Did you need me to help you with anything today, like carrying those linens to the laundry room?" Roxy asked her between bites.

"No, thank you."

"Sure? I'm free."

"I can manage."

"Want another slice?" Roxy said, holding the knife poised over the dessert.

"No, thank you. I appreciate your bringing it, though."

Roxy dropped the knife and placed her forearms on the table. She stared at Jenny with disconcertingly candid brown eyes. "You don't like me, do you?"

Jenny was taken aback. All her life she had avoided confrontations and she couldn't believe she was being forced into this one. She opened her mouth to deny the allegation as diplomatically as she could, but Roxy forestalled her.

"Don't bother denying it. I know you don't and I know why. Because I've slept with Cage."

The color that surged to Jenny's cheeks and the way her eyes fell away from Roxy's were as good as an admission of guilt. Roxy leaned back in her chair. "Well, save your hostility and cut the cool politeness. The truth of it is, I've never been to bed with Cage. Surprised?" she asked when she read the incredulous expression on Jenny's face.

"Most folks would be." Roxy laughed. "Well, it wasn't for lack of wanting to, or even for lack of opportunity," she said ruefully. "Cage is a very sexy guy. A woman would have to be dead not to wonder what it's like to ride that stallion."

Jenny swallowed hard.

"Did Cage tell you how we met?" Jenny shook her head. "Wanna know?" She took Jenny's silence for consent.

"It was at a dance after a rodeo. My husband...did you know I'd been married?" Again Jenny shook her head speechlessly. "Well, I was. That night my husband was in a bad mood because he couldn't stay on some damn Brahman bull and lost the prize money to another guy. Anyhow, he took it out on me as he always did. Nearly beat me to death."

"He *hit* you?"

Roxy chuckled at Jenny's innocence. "Yeah, lots of times. Only, that night he was really drunk and got a little carried away. Cage heard me screaming out in the parking lot where Todd—that's his name—had dragged me. Cage beat the hell out of Todd and told him if he ever did that to me again he could expect another going over."

She dipped her finger into the slice of dessert left on her plate and licked the cream cheese off. "This had gone on for years. Todd would get mad, get drunk, get jealous, and beat up on me. But I loved the guy, you know? Besides, I had no one else. Nowhere to go. No money to get there if there was."

"Your parents?"

"My mama died when I was ten. Daddy was a roughneck. He dragged me from one oil field to another. When I got married at sixteen, he felt like he'd done his last fatherly duty and hightailed it to Alaska. Haven't heard from the lousy bastard since. So I was stuck with Todd.

"One night he got so mad, I thought he was going to kill me. He had threatened to before, but this time I think he meant it. Cage had given me his telephone number. I called and he came to get me. He took me to the hospital and paid the bill for having me fixed up. I stayed at his house for over a month after that. That's when folks started saying we were shacking up." She laughed harshly. "I wouldn't have been much fun in the sack. I was busted up real good.

"Todd was furious. He accused us of carrying on behind his back for months, which wasn't true. He drove to Mexico and got a divorce. That was fine with me. Only, then I *really* had nothing, and I knew I couldn't go on living at Cage's place.

"Cage talked some of his buddies into going partners with him and buying this apartment complex. He installed me as the manager. I get the apartment, plus a salary."

Jenny was transfixed by the tale. She read the newspapers, she watched television. She knew this sort of melodrama went on. She had just never known anyone who had actually experienced that kind of life.

Roxy met her stare levelly. "Cage is the best friend I've ever had. He was the first person in my whole life to care anything about me. I owe him everything, even my life."

She leaned forward across the table. "If he'd asked me to pay him back in bed, I would have. And probably would have loved every minute of it." She lowered her voice for emphasis. "But he never did, Jenny. I think he knew all along what I came to realize. If we'd become lovers, it would have messed up the friendship. And we both valued that more than getting laid." Her hand reached out to cover Jenny's. "You don't have to be jealous of me."

After long moments of looking at each other, Jenny lowered her gaze. "You misunderstand. Cage and I don't have...we aren't...it's not..."

"Maybe not yet," Roxy said intuitively.

Jenny would have had little doubt as to the future of her relationship with Cage if she could have seen him the night before in Roxy's apartment. It was downright comical. Roxy had seen men in every human condition, but she'd never seen one so lovesick.

Cage had sat on her floor, his back propped against her couch, staring into space, wearing the silliest expression on his face. He had talked about Jenny until Roxy had physically hauled him up and ordered him to go home, telling him that she was sleepy and if she heard Jenny's name one more time, she was going to throw up.

As much to divert the conversation away from her and Cage as to apologize, Jenny said, "I've been so rude to you."

"Naw," Roxy said, dismissing Jenny's apology with a wave. "Forget it. I'm used to being snubbed as a fallen woman."

"I like you," Jenny said bluntly, realizing that it was true. One knew exactly where one stood with Roxy. There was no pretense. She didn't put on airs and wouldn't let anyone else get by with it, either.

"Good," Roxy replied as if they had reached an agreement after days of debate. "Now eat the rest of this fattening temptation before I do. Your cute little butt can stand it, but my big fat one sure as hell can't."

Laughing, Jenny sliced herself another piece. "I promised Cage I'd eat to gain weight."

"He's worried about the baby."

"He is?" She tried to appear nonchalant but failed.

Roxy grinned. "He thinks you're too dainty to carry it. I assured him you would come through the pregnancy with flying colors."

"I'm not concerned about me. I worry about people punishing the child for something I've done."

"Forget 'people.' "

"That's what Cage says."

"And he's right. Are you glad about the baby?"

"Yes. Very," Jenny confirmed, her eyes shining.

"With his mama and his uncle Cage loving him, the kid'll have no problems," Roxy assured her.

"You never had children?"

Roxy's smile faded. "No. I always wanted kids, but Todd, he, uh...hurt me one time, you know? Ruined all the plumbing and it had to come out."

"Oh, Lord, I'm so sorry!" Jenny exclaimed in a soft voice.

Roxy shrugged. "Hell, I'm getting too old to have a kid anyway and Gary says it doesn't matter to him."

"Gary?"

"He's the guy I'm seeing," Roxy said, her ebullience restored. "Cage introduced us. He works for the phone company. In fact, he should be here soon to install your phone."

From Roxy's description Jenny was expecting Gary to be a cross between a *Playgirl* centerfold and Prince Valiant. He was neither. He had big ears, a long nose, and a toothy grin, but his face beamed wholesomeness and a self-effacing good humor.

It was obvious to Jenny within moments of his arrival that he and Roxy were madly in love.

"I wanted to come to the party last night and welcome you to the neighborhood," Gary said, pumping Jenny's hand, "but I got called out on an emergency. Where do you want your phones?"

"Phones? Plural?"

"Three."

"Three?"

"That's what Cage ordered. I suggest the bedroom, living room, and kitchen."

"But—"

"You might just as well go along with it, Jenny, if that's what Cage ordered," Roxy said.

"Oh, all right."

While Gary went about his business Roxy helped Jenny organize her kitchen. Later they laundered all the new bed linens and towels before folding and storing them. They talked nonstop. By noon Jenny felt she had known the other woman all her life. Despite their separate backgrounds, they liked each other immensely.

"Anybody hungry?" Cage stuck his head through the front door, which Gary had left open on one of his trips to his truck.

Jenny was so relieved to learn that Cage and Roxy hadn't been lovers, she turned toward the door at the sound of his voice and flashed him a dazzling smile. She rushed forward, stopping just short of flinging herself in his arms.

"Well, don't stop there," he said softly.

She closed the remaining distance between them and hugged him, even going so far as to boldly slide her hands beneath his denim vest. "Hi," she whispered shyly when she backed away.

"Hi." He made three syllables out of one. His eyes were busily scanning her face. "Tell me what I did to deserve that welcome and I'll do it some more."

"I'm mad at you."

"Stay mad. I like it. Hug me again."

"Once is enough."

"But my hands are full and I can't hug back, so you've got to hug me twice."

It was pure madness, but in her state of mind it made perfect sense. She reached around him again and linked her hands behind his back, tilting her head back to look up at him. "Now, what are you mad about?" he asked.

"What am I going to do with three telephones?"

"Save yourself a lot of steps." He kissed her quickly. "But you were glad to see me. I could tell. Why?"

"You brought lunch," she quipped, nodding toward the sacks he held in his hands.

"You like cheeseburgers?"

"With onions?"

"Yes," he answered warily.

"Love 'em."

The four of them had a riotously gay lunch together. "I think you guys planned this," Roxy said suspiciously, biting into a fat golden french fry.

"I didn't plan this," Cage swore, crossing his heart. "Did you plan this, Gary?"

"I didn't plan this," he said, licking salt off his fingers. "Pass me one of those little catsup doodads, please."

"Roxy and I might have made other plans for lunch," Jenny said loftily.

Cage grinned at her, pleased that she could easily join in the joking now. "We *assumed* you didn't."

"Assumed, huh? Don't start taking us for granted," Roxy warned. "Right, Jenny?"

"Right."

She would have taken a bite of her cheeseburger then, but Cage leaned down and kissed her solidly on the mouth.

She never remembered being happier or feeling freer. Despite her pregnancy, Jenny felt like she had shed a hundred pounds. She had left the parsonage behind like an old skin. Her whole being breathed new life.

But she didn't shirk her responsibilities at the church. She attended regularly and Cage went with her. They sat near the back and rarely saw Bob except in the pulpit. If he knew they were there, he gave no sign. They didn't see Sarah where she sat in her usual place in the second row.

She and Cage could feel the furtive glances cast in their direction and hear the whispered conversations they left in their wake, but they spoke politely to everyone. With Cage by her side, it was easy for Jenny to hold her head high and walk proudly.

She became more involved with work in the office. She had graduated from answering the telephone and writing correspondence to handling filing and research that Cage had never intended her to do.

"You're going to wear yourself out," he said one day when he stopped by to leave some mail and found her still there.

"What time is it?"

"Long after five o'clock."

"This is so interesting. I lost track of time."

"Don't expect me to pay you overtime."

"I owe you the time. I went to the doctor today on my lunch hour."

"Your lunch hour *and a half.*"

"Whatever. Anyway, they were running behind and that put me late getting back, so stop bugging me."

"You're getting pretty feisty, Miss Fletcher. If you don't watch your step, I'm going to give up the idea of marrying you and start looking for a nice docile girl who will treat me with the respect I deserve."

She folded the chart. "If you were treated with the respect you deserve, you'd get a thrashing."

"Hm, that sounds…interesting." He came up behind her where she was now standing at the file cabinet, encircled her waist with his arms, and nuzzled her neck.

"Don't tell me you're into S and M."

"S and M?" He laughed, lifting his lips from her neck but keeping her imprisoned between him and the file cabinet. "What do you know about S and M?"

"Lots. Roxy has a book that gives step-by-step instructions."

"Roxy's corrupting you. I should have known better than to entrust you to her. Don't look at any more of her books."

"You don't have to worry that I'd get involved in anything involving whips and chains. It all looks painful. Besides," she teased, "I don't think those skimpy black leather outfits would look very good on my new figure."

"I think your new figure would look delicious in anything. It's lovely."

He lowered his hands to her abdomen and massaged soothingly, before moving them down to stroke the tops of her thighs through her skirt. Jenny whimpered and struggled to turn around. He allowed her to, but facing him didn't give her any freedom. If anything, it made her situation more precarious. "I've got to go, Cage."

"Later." He moved her hair aside with his nose and dedicated himself to pleasuring her ear.

"It's getting late," she gasped when she felt the wet stroke of his tongue. "I should be getting home."

"Later."

The word was spoken against her open lips and when he closed his mouth over hers, all her resistance melted. He braced his hands on the file cabinet and leaned into her, pressing his body against hers. He eased away, then leaned forward again, as though doing push-ups against the cabinet. Every time his body brushed against hers, the contact set off electric charges in her.

Moving his hands to her neck, he closed his fingers around it loosely, deepening the kiss as he did so.

"Hm, Cage, no," she protested feebly when she managed to work her mouth free. It was a bone-melting, mind-stealing kiss and she could feel herself succumbing to it.

"Why not?"

"Because it's unhealthy."

He moved against her suggestively. "I beg to differ."

The proof of his healthy condition probed the soft delta between her thighs. "We shouldn't…" He moved again and she groaned in spite of her best intentions to remain immune. "We shouldn't do this in here, in your place of business."

"How about my house?"

"No."

"Your apartment?"

"No."

"Then where?"

"Nowhere. We shouldn't be doing this anywhere."

Recently, every time he kissed her, she was reminded of the night with Hal. Cage's kisses evoked memories that were startlingly vivid. The brothers kissed with similar intensity, their caresses were equally stimulating. But somehow, by responding to Cage's kisses, she felt she was betraying Hal. Had she trembled in his arms the way she did every time Cage touched her?

"Jenny, please."

"No."

"I ache. I haven't been with a woman since—" He stuttered to a halt just before saying, "Since making love to you." He changed it to "For a long time."

"Whose fault is that?"

"Yours. I don't want anybody but you."

"Go to one of your old haunts. I'm sure you'll find an obliging lady." She would die if he did. Each day she figuratively held her breath, wondering when Cage would tire of spending so much time with her and resort to his carousing. She felt compelled to press her luck. "Or check out the grocery store."

"Invite me over tonight."

"No."

"You've been living in your apartment three weeks and I've been invited inside exactly twice."

"And that was two times too many. You stay too long and don't behave while you're there." Lord, she wished he'd stop kissing her neck that way. It felt so good. "People are seeing us together around town and they're starting to talk."

"What else have they got to talk about? It isn't football season."

"Don't you see? When word gets out that I'm pregnant, everybody will jump to the conclusion that—" She didn't finish.

His head came up and his eyes drilled into hers. "What conclusion will they jump to?"

"That the baby is yours," she answered, staring at the collar button on his shirt, unable to meet his eyes.

"And would that be so terrible?" His voice was as gravelly and emotion-packed as hers.

"I don't want you to be blamed for something you didn't do."

"I wouldn't consider it being *blamed*. I wouldn't mind in the least taking the *credit* for fathering your baby."

"But that wouldn't be right, Cage."

"I've been blamed for things I didn't do before. People make up their own minds. If they get the facts jumbled, there's little you can do to change public opinions."

"I don't believe that."

"Didn't you think that Roxy was my lover?"

"No!"

"You can't lie worth a damn, Jenny," he taunted. "You even called her one of my sluts. You thought we were having an affair. That's why you pouted all the way home that night after I took you off the bus."

"If I was pouting, it was because I'm not used to being chased down by a maniac who has the unmitigated gall to stop a Greyhound bus and haul somebody off it."

Her flare of temper delighted him. "God, you're cute." He kissed the end of her nose. "But you're not going to get off the hook by changing the subject. You thought Roxy and I had a thing going, didn't you?"

"Well, can you blame me?" she said defensively. "You can't keep your hands off her."

He squeezed her ribcage where his hands were currently resting. "I can't keep my hands off you either, so we know that's not conclusive evidence that two people are sleeping together."

She felt flustered from the inside out. "Which only brings me back to my original point. You shouldn't touch me all the time." Her voice lacked conviction even to her own ears.

"You don't like it when I touch you?"

Who wouldn't like it? Who wouldn't like the way his thumbs lightly grazed the undersides of her breasts while his strong fingers aligned themselves to her ribs? "I sure like touching you," he whispered as his hands slid around her back and drew her close for another kiss that she was powerless to resist.

"Ask me to supper, Jenny. What's the harm in having dinner at your house?"

"Because when Cage Hendren has dinner at a woman's house, it automatically implies more than eating a meal."

Their mouths continued to come together and drift apart in soft, damp caresses. "Gossip."

"Based on truth."

"Okay, I confess. I want to spend an evening alone with you. Get in a little necking and heavy breathing. What's wrong with that?"

"Everything."

"All right," he sighed. "I asked you nice, but you want to play rough. I'm not letting you leave this office until you invite me to your apartment for dinner. Now, I can stand here till doomsday kissing you, only, I'm getting very aroused."

He wedged his legs between hers and fit their hips snugly together. "Soon, kissing's not going to be enough. I'll be driven to undo those buttons on your blouse. I've counted. There are exactly four. That should take three seconds, three and a half at the most. Then I'll know if your brassiere is lilac or blue. I know it's sheer, but I can't quite tell the color. And then—"

She pushed him away. His grin was undiluted deviltry, but he spoke like a good little boy who had just gotten all *A*'s. "I'm free Friday night."

"Don't play so hard to get, Cage," she said sarcastically.

"Jenny, where you're concerned I'm as easy as Ruda Beth Graham was in the tenth grade."

"Oh, you're horrible!" She shoved him aside and picked up her purse. "You're blackmailing me again, but come at seven o'clock."

"Six."

She shot him a disparaging look and reached for the doorknob. "Jenny?" She turned back. "What color *is* that brassiere?"

"That's for me to know," she said saucily as she swung out the door.

"And for me to find out," Cage said with a sly grin.

Chapter 10

Jenny flattened her hand over her stomach in the hope of subduing the butterflies inside. She wet her lips. She touched her hair. She drew a deep breath and opened her front door.

Cage was standing on her threshold. He was wearing a pair of tailored brown slacks, a light cream-colored shirt, and a camel sport jacket. The ensemble couldn't have been better coordinated with his own sandy coloring.

His hair was clean and shiny, but, as usual, any styling had been left to chance. As tousled as it was, he could have just gotten out of bed. Indeed, that was what his expression insinuated. His eyes looked like smoky Mexican topaz as they toured Jenny. One corner of his sensuous mouth was hiked into a sly smile.

"Hi," she said timidly.

"Are you dessert?" he drawled. "If so, I'm opting to skip dinner."

The butterflies soared and sailed despite her previous efforts to calm them.

The sensations pulsing through her were ridiculous. She had spent the morning with Cage in his office, catching up on the week's correspondence. They had worked companionably, in carefree camaraderie.

Where had this tension between them come from? What had caused this tingling awareness? The air crackled with suppressed sexuality, and she knew Cage felt it as keenly as she did.

As long as they were working, they were able to control these undercurrents. But the moment they let down that professional barrier, the latent desire between them began to churn and bubble like the waters in a hot tub.

Jenny had left the office at noon, as she did every Friday. But this afternoon she hadn't rested. She had thrown herself wholeheartedly into preparations for the evening. She wanted the meal, the apartment, herself to be perfect.

With each passing hour her expectancy had mounted until now, when she stood face to face with him, she felt like fainting.

"Are those for me?" He was holding a large bouquet of pink roses and baby's breath. The long stems were wrapped in green tissue and they filled the air with nature's sweetest perfume.

"Do you have a twin?"

"No."

"Then I guess they're for you." He passed them to her and she moved aside so he could step into the room. He halted before he had taken two steps. "What the—"

He gazed around him in awe. The room had undergone a transformation since he'd last seen it. Jenny had spent her lunch hours and afternoons browsing through thrift shops and garage sales looking for "goodies."

With Roxy's help she had made the apartment into a home, and she was proud of the results. She was twenty-six years old, yet this was the first time in her life that she'd had the priviledge of choosing her own decor in her own home.

Unlike her room in the parsonage, there wasn't a ruffle to be found. Her taste was simple and elegant, but warm.

"Do you like it?" she asked anxiously, wringing her hands.

"Like it? I may move in tonight."

She laughed, knowing he wasn't suggesting anything illicit, only complimenting her on a job well done.

"I paid a decorator an astronomical fee to do my house. I should have let you do it. I didn't know you had a hidden talent for this kind of thing." Cage scoured her speculatively with narrowed eyes. "What else do you have a hidden talent for?"

She felt a swell of emotion and rushed to lighten the mood. "You should have seen Roxy bargaining over the plants. We found them at a garage sale. The man was asking fifty dollars for all of them. Roxy got him down to ten, then called Gary to come over in his pickup and load them up before the man changed his mind. I rode in the back of the truck so none of them would get crushed."

"I would protect my *benjaminia* with my life. I couldn't stand for it to get crushed."

His face was too angelic for her not to be suspicious. There was a play on words in there somewhere, but she had better sense than to ask him to expound.

She cleared her throat. "I bought the bentwood rocker there, too, for five dollars. All it needed was a coat of paint."

"I like what you did to that wall."

"The fabric was a remnant I found at K mart. Roxy helped me tack it to the wall so I would get the pattern straight." She had used what was left over to make small throw pillows for the sofa.

The colors she had selected to accent her new furniture were restful, yet oddly stimulating—mulberry, navy, slate, and beige. "The candles smell good," Cage said, nodding toward the attractive arrangement on the end table.

"I found the brass candlesticks in an antique store, one of those dim, ratty places out on the Pecos highway. I had to move aside cobwebs to get to them. It took two cans of Brasso and three nights of elbow grease to polish them up."

"Everything looks great."

"Thank you," she replied demurely.

"Especially you." He suddenly bent his head to kiss her. She expected a soft, faternal, hello-type kiss. Instead, his lips were commanding and his tongue bold. After several moments, she pulled away breathlessly.

"I'd better get these flowers in water before they wilt."

Or before I do, she thought as she hurried into the kitchen to look for something to serve as a vase worthy of the roses. She didn't have anything, and they ended up in an orange juice carafe. She had already arranged a bunch of heather to serve as an abstract centerpiece for the dining table, so she carried the roses into the living room and, with an apologetic smile for their humble container, placed them on the coffee table.

"Is that a new outfit?"

"Yes," she answered nervously. "Roxy picked it out and made me buy it."

"I'm glad she did."

The long skirt and oversized blouse were raw silk in its natural color, and unlike anything that Jenny had worn before. A wide braided belt was knotted around her waist. She had on the flat, ankle-strap shoes Cage had admired before. Her hair had been swept up, but with a calculated messiness so that soft wisps escaped to lie on her neck and cheeks.

"It's sort of a Gypsy look," she said, self-conscious under his assessing eyes. "I only let Roxy talk me into it because the blouse has a long tail and will be full enough to wear when I start showing."

"Turn around." She made a slow three-hundred-and-sixty degree pivot until she faced him again. "I love it," he said with a slow smile. "But are you sure you're in there? All that cloth is camouflaging."

"I'm in here, all right," she said, patting her tummy. "I've gained two pounds."

"Good for you! Does the doctor say everything is okay?" His brow wrinkled with concern. "You're half way through your pregnancy, but you barely show."

"Barely show? You should see me without my clothes on."

"I'd like that."

His expression was altogether too sexy. "What I mean is," Jenny said quickly, "I'm showing a little in my tummy. The doctor said the baby is growing nicely. He's just the right size for almost five months."

"He?"

"The doctor thinks it's a boy because of the heartbeat. Typically, boys have a slower heartbeat than girls."

"Then I'm atypical," Cage whispered. "My heart's racing."

"Why?" His amber eyes seemed to pull at her like a magnet. She inclined toward him slightly.

"I'm still thinking about seeing you without your clothes on."

The impulse to gravitate toward him was almost irresistible, but she drew on enough self-discipline not to. Pulling herself both mentally and physically away from him, she turned toward the louvered half doors that led into the kitchen. "I need to check on dinner."

"What are we having? It smells scrumptious."

He reached the swinging doors in time to see her bending down to check the simmering contents in the oven. The view was captivating and stirred up another of Cage's appetites, one more ravenous than that in his stomach.

"Stuffed pork chops, asparagus with hollandaise... Do you like asparagus?" He nodded and she looked relieved.

"Potatoes with parsley and butter, hot rolls, and Milky Way ice cream."

"You're kidding! Milky Way ice cream?"

"No, I'm not kidding, and I *paid* for the Milky Way bars."

He ignored the jibe and pushed through the swinging doors. As soon as she had slid a cookie sheet of rolls into the oven, he clasped her arms and turned her to face him. "Trying to impress me?"

"Why do you ask that?"

"You went to a lot of trouble for me." He captured a free strand of her hair and wound it around his index finger. "Why, Jenny?"

"I like to cook." She watched, mesmerized, as he lifted the strand of her hair to his lips and kissed it, at the same time drawing her face dangerously close to his. "And...and...uh, your parents didn't like to experiment. I like to try out new recipes, but they always wanted to eat the same—"

His mouth stopped the flow of nervous chatter with a kiss. "Do I get to choose dessert?" he asked in a soft murmur when he lifted his lips from hers.

"No."

"I choose you," he said, heedless of her denial. "You're the sweetest thing I've ever tasted."

He moved forward until he had backed her against the countertop. It caught her in the small of her back. Cage molded his body to hers in a complementing fit that left little doubt as to who was female and who was male. Seconds later she was shamelessly responding to the subtle nudges against her middle, and her hands were crawling up his back. The fiery embrace lasted until the smell of warm yeast rolls permeated the small kitchen.

"Cage," Jenny gasped, drawing enough breath to dispel the ringing in her ears, "the rolls are burning."

"Who gives a damn?" he growled against her throat.

"I do." She pushed him away. "I worked hard on them."

He sighed and stepped back so she could retrieve the rolls from the oven. "Do you mind if I take off my jacket?"

"Are you too warm?"

For answer one of his sand-colored eyebrows arched upward. "Hot, Jenny darling, hot."

He joined her at the table a few moments later in his shirtsleeves. "This looks delicious," he said, seating her before he sat down. She served him and waited anxiously for his verdict after the first bite. "Better than my mother used to make," he said.

Pleased, she smiled and began eating. "Have you seen them, Cage?"

"Who? Oh, Mother and Dad? No. At least not to speak to. Have you?"

"No. I feel guilty about driving this wedge between them and you."

He laughed mirthlessly. "Jenny, that wedge has been there since I was old enough to toddle."

"But my moving out and the baby have made things worse. I hate that. I was hoping you'd be drawn closer together. They need you now."

His eyes wandered around the apartment. "You know, I think they'd be jealous if they could see what you've done here."

"Jealous?"

"Yes. I think they wanted you to need them as much as they needed you. And you didn't. You don't. They were afraid to let out your leash on the chance you'd discover that. So they kept you bound to them by obligation."

"That's unfair, Cage. They're not manipulative."

"Don't get me wrong," he said, covering her hand briefly. "I didn't mean to suggest that they did all this consciously. They'd be horrified to think themselves capable of such selfishness.

"But think about it, Jenny. I wasn't what they wanted their son to be, so they gave up on me completely and poured all their hopes and energies into Hal. Luckily he was a perfect candidate for what they had in mind and they groomed him meticulously. Then you came along. You were a sweet, obedient little girl who would make them a charming daughter-in-law."

"I'm sure they don't feel that way now."

"I'm sure they don't either, but it's healthier for everyone this way. You're a free agent. That doesn't mean you love them less." He shook his head in puzzlement. "That's what they never could understand. I loved them. I wanted them to love me. If they had shown me any affection, I wouldn't have been so unmanageable. It wouldn't have been necessary." His eyes came back to hers. "You've rebelled in your own way. Maybe this time they'll see the light."

"I hope so. I hate to think of them alone in that big house after having suffered Hal's death. I guess sooner or later, with or without our support, they'll adjust to the loss."

"And what about you, Jenny? Have you adjusted to it?"

Finished eating, she laid her knife and fork diagonally on her plate. "I miss him. Hal and I were very close. We used to talk for hours." A vein was ticking in Cage's temple, but she didn't notice as she went on musingly. "He was such a sweet person. I don't think he would have intentionally hurt anybody."

"Do you still love him?"

She was on the verge of saying, "I'm not sure I ever did," but she caught herself in time. For years she had thought she was in love with Hal. Had she only been trying to convince herself that it was so?

She had had a deep and abiding affection for him, but his kisses had never made her dizzy as Cage's did. Her heart hadn't begun to flutter each time Hal walked into a room. No, she had never felt this yearning, aching need for Hal the way she did for Cage. It was a persistent longing, as constant as her heartbeat.

Out of respect for Hal, she couldn't discuss her feelings for him with Cage. She evaded giving him a definitive answer. "I'll always love Hal in a special way."

Cage was unaccustomed to being put off. He never skirted an issue and wasn't going to tolerate it from Jenny. "If he were still alive, would you want to marry him?"

Her eyes flickered toward his, then away. "There would be the baby to—"

"If the baby weren't a consideration?"

She hesitated, because she had to come to terms with that hour spent in bed with Hal. Had it only been one of those magical comets of emotion that rocket through one's life before burning out? Had it been a fluke? Had each of them been so emotionally high strung that particular night that it had been easy to lose their heads?

She was beginning to believe that such was the case. As splendid as it had been for her, she now knew that her passion wasn't necessarily limited to one person. She had been just as aroused by Cage's kisses as she had been by Hal's that night.

Knowing that he was waiting for her answer, she softly replied, "No, I don't think so. After living on my own, I realize that Hal and I weren't intended to be man and wife. Friends. Good friends. Perhaps brother and sister. But I don't think I would have been the kind of wife Hal needed for the life he chose."

Cage kept his features under control so that his relief and elation wouldn't show. "Let me help you with the dishes," he said, standing.

"You haven't had your dessert yet."

"I'm letting the anticipation build."

His inflection hinted at an underlying meaning, but again Jenny thought it best not to pursue it. His eyes held a golden glint that was only partially due to candlelight.

They conversed easily while they cleared up the kitchen. The second oil well had come in on the Parsons property and a third was already being drilled. Cage had his eyes on another tract of land he was sure topped a basin of oil.

Jenny loved the excitement that he emanated when he talked about wildcatting. He was successful, but money wasn't his incentive. The challenge, the gamble, and the flirtation with disaster were what motivated him. Most would call him reckless, but she knew better. He drove fast, but he knew what he was doing behind the wheel of a car. He used the same dashing skill in his business dealings.

He dished up the ice cream, unabashedly licking the dipper as he did so, while Jenny arranged the coffee things on a tray. Together they moved into the living room. "Don't drip any of that on my new sofa," Jenny scolded as Cage raised a spoonful of the ice cream to his mouth.

"Sinful, positively sinful." He let the ice cream melt in his mouth.

"Then it's true what they say?"

"What's that?"

"That the way to a man's heart is through his stomach."

He was holding the spoon upside down in his mouth. His tongue cleaned out its shallow bowl, then he pulled it through his lips slowly as he gazed at Jenny. "That's one way to get there, I guess, but I can think of another route that's much more fun to take. Want me to give you the guided tour?"

"Cream or sugar?" she asked in a thin, high voice.

He chuckled at her shaking hand as she poured his coffee. "Jenny, you've been pouring coffee for me for years. You know I drink it black."

"I forgot."

"Like hell. You're just all atremble over what I said."

"It was outrageous and uncouth." She still couldn't look him straight in the eye. Her cheeks were burning.

"You're a paradox," he observed, learning back against the cushions to drink his coffee. He had finished his ice cream and had set the empty bowl on the tray.

"A paradox?"

"Yes. You're carrying a child, yet any time the subject of sex is even hinted at, you come all undone."

Her sweet tooth suddenly went sour and she set aside her bowl of ice cream after having taken only a few bites. "You think I'm a prude, a holdover from another era, a Victorian dinosaur trying to survive in the age of sexual enlightenment?"

"Don't put words in my mouth. I didn't mean to imply any such thing. Your innocence is endearing."

"I'm hardly innocent," she mumbled, her chin tucked against her chest. She closed her eyes, recalling the sound of her own breathing at the point of climax. The moans of fulfillment echoed in her head even now when she remembered how her body had exploded into full bloom like an exotic neon flower. She could feel again her back bowing, her hips lifting, her limbs quaking, all greedily experiencing the pleasure.

"You said you were a virgin the night—"

"I was."

"Never before?"

"No."

"Close?"

"No."

Cage placed his coffee cup on the tray. He moved closer to her, resting his bent elbow on the back of the sofa. He lightly stroked her cheek with his knuckles. "You must have been deeply moved that night to give away what you had cherished for so long."

"I've never felt like that in my life."

Cage's heart leaped in his chest. What he was about to do was unforgivable, but that had never deterred him. "Tell me how you felt."

Deep in thought, Jenny unconsciously lifted her hand to his chest. Her fingers strummed the placket of his shirt. "It was like I had stepped out of myself and was watching what was happening to someone else. I shed all my inhibitions. I cast aside the restrictions I normally impose on myself. I existed only for those moments. I became purely carnal, and yet my spirit had never felt more elevated or expanded." She raised her eyes to his like a confused little girl. "Do you understand what I mean?"

"Yes. Perfectly," he answered honestly.

"Nothing that we did seemed sordid or wrong. It was all beautiful. I wanted to love and to be loved. It wasn't enough to verbalize our love; I wanted it demonstrated."

"And Hal was willing?"

"Not at first."

His hand cradled one side of her face. "But you talked him into it."

"That's a nice way of saying I seduced him."

"All right, you seduced him. What happened then?"

She smiled and ducked her head shyly. "Then he was more than willing. He'd never been that way with me before."

"What way?" If Jenny had been looking at Cage's face, she would have read the hungry expression there.

She closed her eyes briefly, as though to get a hold of herself and carefully choose her words. Cage studied the path her tongue took as it wet her lower lip before she continued. "Lusty, a trifle wild, sensual." She laughed lightly. "I don't know how to describe him."

"Rough? Too rough?"

"No, I didn't mean to imply that."

"Tender?"

"Yes. Through it all, he was extremely gentle, but... passionate."

"Were you afraid when he slipped your nightgown off?" Her eyes swung up to his inquiringly and Cage cursed himself for a careless damn fool. "You *were* wearing a night-gown, weren't you?"

For the last few minutes his soft, sand-raspy voice had been inducing a trance, and like someone who is hypnotized, she had responded to it. But his last question snapped her out of her stupor. "I shouldn't be talking to you about this, Cage."

"Why not?"

"It's embarrassing," she cried softly. "Besides, it's not fair to Hal. Why do you want to know about that night?"

"Because I'm curious."

"That's sick!"

"Not sick, Jenny, normal." He leaned over her, forcing her against the corner cushions of the sofa. He braced one hand on the back cushion, the other on the armrest, and trapped her in the triangle his arms formed. "I want to know what you think about making love."

"Why?" she asked on a near sob.

He lowered his head until his words fell as soft, emphatic puffs of air against her lips. "Because I want to make love to you. You've resisted me at every turn. I want to know what made you step out of yourself that night. What made you live only for the moment? What did your lover do that made you shed those inhibitions and lift the restrictions you normally impose on yourself? What made you purely carnal? In short, Jenny, what turned you on?"

In spite of herself, she was aroused by his demanding tone and the hard strength of his body as it stretched across hers. Her chest was rising and falling with accelereated breathing. Her eyes were incapable of leaving the magnetic field of his.

"Was it the setting that broke through your reserve?" he asked. "Did he set such a romantic scene you couldn't restrain yourself?"

She shook her head and heard herself answer. "It happened in my room."

"God knows that wasn't sexy."

"It was dark."

Cage reached above and behind her, almost covering her, and switched off the lamp on the end table. She hadn't noticed until now that he had turned off the lights in the kitchen and dining alcove as they left them. They were plunged into darkness, save for the incandescent glow of the candles. They cast long, wavering shadows on the walls and highlighted the rugged planes of his face. "Like that?"

"No. Totally dark. I couldn't see anything."

"Nothing?" His strong fingers delved in her hair and held her head steady, forcing her eyes to do battle with his.

"No."

"You couldn't see your lover's face?"

"No."

"Didn't you want to?"

"Yes, yes, yes," she moaned and tried to turn her head away. He wouldn't let her.

"Then this is better. Look at your lover's face this time, Jenny. For godsake look at all of me."

His mouth came down hard on hers and she was ready for it. Her lips responded to the possessive fury of his and parted to receive the thrilling thrust of his tongue. Her arms slid under his and around his back. She kneaded the rippling muscles beneath his shirt.

"What did he say to you, Jenny?" He breathed kisses across her cheeks and mouth. "Did he tell you all the things you wanted and needed to hear?"

While his lips toyed with hers, her mind went on a probing search into her memory. "He said..." She drew a blank. "He didn't say anything."

"Nothing?"

"No. I think he sighed my name...once."

"He didn't tell you how beautiful and desirable you are?"

"I'm not."

"You are, my love, you are. So beautiful." His breath was warm and moist as he whispered directly into her ear. "You can feel how hard I am, Jenny. How can you think you're not desirable? I desire you. I want you more than I've ever wanted any woman."

"Cage," she whimpered when he finally released her mouth from an inflaming kiss. He licked her lips gently, flicking at the corners teasingly.

His hand slid to her waist and untied her belt. He touched her throat and caressed her chest with his callused fingertips. "Did he tell you that your skin is as soft as silk?"

His head dipped lower to nuzzle her neck with his nose and mouth. "And that you smell heavenly?" He planted a hot kiss in the hollow of her throat, applying his tongue.

She was unmindful of the buttons on her blouse being undone until she felt him moving it aside. His harsh whisper could have been a curse but might have been a prayer. He groaned. He touched her lovingly. Jenny closed her eyes and reveled in the sensations his stroking fingers and soothing palms elicited.

"He should have told you that your breasts are beautiful." He kissed her through her brassiere. "That your nipples are delicate and sweet and perfect. He should have said all that. Because it's true." Deftly he unhooked the fastener and peeled away the veil-sheer cups. "Ah, Jenny, let me love you."

And, holding her cupped in his hands, he did.

Jenny hadn't known kisses could be so adoring and yet so hedonistic, that lips could suckle so ardently without causing pain, or that a tongue could be so nimble but still unhurried.

His caresses went on and on until she was swirling in an effervescent ocean of feeling. Geysers of sensation sprung up along her nerve endings. She knew it was wrong to relive her night of loving Hal with his brother.

But she had stepped through the boundaries of common sense long ago and there was no retreating now. She had fallen victim to Cage's legendary charm. Jenny Fletcher would now be listed on the roster of his lovers, but somehow she couldn't help but believe that tonight was different for Cage, too.

"Did you like the feel of his body against yours, Jenny?"

"Yes."

"The touch of his skin?"

"He didn't undress," she confessed breathlessly as his mouth continued to play upon her breasts.

"And you?"

"Yes, I was..."

"Naked?"

"Yes."

"And how did you feel about that?"

She thought back to that moment when her nightgown had been stripped from her body and she had lain naked and vulnerable beneath her lover. "I felt no shame. I only wanted..."

"What?"

"Never mind."

"What?" he pressed.

"To feel him against me."

He levered himself up and penetrated her eyes with his. "Unbutton my shirt."

She hesitated only a moment before she lowered her eyes from his and looked at the first fastened button on his shirt. She watched her fingers move toward it mindlessly, as though obeying an unspoken command. The button slipped through its hole. All the others followed.

She sighed a soft yearning sound deep in her throat when his chest was revealed. The sun-kissed brown hair spread over the sculpted muscles like a wide golden fan. His nipples were dark in the dim light.

Tears gathered in Jenny's eyes. His masculine perfection made her want to weep. He was beautiful. She caught the fabric of his shirt in her hands and peeled it back over his shoulders and down his arms as far as it would go. Her hands smoothed over him. His skin was tan and sleek, spattered with coppery freckles on the tops of his shoulders. Her fingertips traced the faint blue lines of veins in the bluging biceps.

Gradually he lowered himself over her until they were chest to breast, hair-roughened skin to smooth, masculine muscle to feminine softness.

"Jenny, Jenny, Jenny."

Their mouths meshed as surely as their bodies did. He settled against her carefully, rolling slightly to his side, so she wouldn't absorb all of his weight. He felt the pounding of her heart against his. The tips of her breasts felt achingly sweet against his furred skin.

He loved her. God he loved her. And he couldn't believe that she was finally going to be his.

"Aren't you glad we got the soft couch?"

"Hm. Is this what you had in mind when you persuaded me to buy it?"

"This and more."

They kissed. Eternally. Erotically.

"Jenny, let's go to bed."

"Cage—"

"I won't hurt you. I swear it."

"It's not that."

"Then what?"

"Oh, please don't touch me there," she gasped.

"Isn't it good?"

"Oh, Lord. Too good. Cage, please—"

"Like that? There?"

"Yes."

Their mouths dissolved together.

"Touch me," he pleaded.

"Where?"

"Anywhere."

She laid her hand on his breast. His nipple shrank to a tiny tight pebble against her fingertips.

"Oh, God, I'm dying. Come to bed with me, Jenny."

"I can't."

"Don't you want me?"

She answered with an arching thrust against his hardness. He took it to mean yes. Easing up, he offered her his hand. She placed hers in his palm and rose off the couch willingly. They headed toward the bedroom.

The front door vibrated with a resounding knock, which was followed by a blistering curse from Cage.

"What the *hell*!"

Jenny dove for the sofa, yanked up her blouse, shoved her arms in the sleeves, and fumbled with the buttons. She stuffed her discarded brassiere beneath the nearest cushion.

Apparently Cage wasn't worried about his give-away dishevelment. He stormed to the front door with his shirttails flapping and hauled it open with a vicious jerk.

Roxy and Gary were standing on the threshold.

"Is the building on fire?" Cage snarled.

"No."

"Then good night."

He tried to slam the door in their faces, but Roxy caught it just in time. "It is, however, a matter of life and death. If Gary and I don't get married tonight, I'm going to kill myself."

Chapter 11

"Married!" Jenny exclaimed, stepping around Cage. Astonishment had overriden modesty. She had forgotten her mussed condition until Roxy's eyes lit up with amusement.

"Did we interrupt something important?" Roxy asked, batting her eyelashes with comic innocence. Cage's scowl deepened.

"Sorry about that, pal," Gary mumbled apologetically.

"Then make this quick and leave."

"Cage, didn't you hear what Roxy said? They're getting married."

"That's right." Roxy looped her arm through Gary's and squeezed it against her voluptuous breast. "That is if you'll go with us to El Paso and drive Gary's car back."

"You're serious, aren't you?" Cage asked, his eyes going back and forth between the two of them. He was just now recovering from his frustration. "You're really getting married?"

"Yes!" Roxy said, beaming.

"Well, hey, that's great!" Cage pumped Gary's hand, then gave Roxy a bear hug.

"Congratulations, Gary," Jenny said. Getting into the spirit of the occasion, she gave him a big hug, which made the tops of his large ears turn beet red. She clasped Roxy to her. "I'm so happy for you."

"Me, too, kid, me, too. He's the best thing that's ever happened to me. I don't deserve him."

"Yes, you do." Jenny smiled at her and they hugged again.

"Now, what's this about driving to El Paso?" Cage asked when the two women fell apart, dabbing at their moist eyes.

"We've got reservations on a noon flight from there to Acapulco tomorrow. Gary's so conventional," Roxy teased, "he thinks we should get married before the honeymoon.

"So we're driving to El Paso tonight to a justice of the peace. We want you to go along so you can bring Gary's car back, *if* you don't mind picking us up in a week and bringing us home. Besides, it'll be more fun having you there with us when we tie the knot."

Gary stood by, wearing a silly grin and nodding his head in agreement to Roxy's explanation.

Cage flashed his notorious grin. "I'm game. Jenny?"

It was after ten o'clock. She couldn't imagine striking out on such a trip in the middle of the night. Between here and El Paso there was nothing but sand, tumbleweeds, and jackrabbits.

But the idea of such an impetuous trip was exciting and unlike anything she'd ever done before. She had come to like Roxy and Gary tremendously and wanted to be a witness to their marriage.

"It sounds great to me!"

Everyone went into a flurry of motion and decision-making that finally culminated at Roxy's front door twenty minutes later.

"I think we got everything," Roxy cried, waving a bottle of champagne high over her head. She locked her door behind her after having made sure the apartment was secure for a week. Her and Gary's luggage had been stored in the trunk of the car. "The assistant manager, Mrs. Burton, is going to keep an eye on things while I'm gone, Cage," she explained as she climbed in the front seat beside Gary.

"No problem. Jenny and I will be around, so don't worry. You just concentrate on having a fantastic honeymoon."

"I intend to," Roxy said, snuggling next to Gary. She touched him in a place intimate enough to make him jump. The car lurched when he momentarily lost control.

"This is no good," Cage said. "Gary can't drive and neck with Roxy at the same time. Let's stop at my house and get my Lincoln. Then you two can have the backseat all the way to El Paso."

"I like that idea even better!" Roxy agreed enthusiastically. "Honey, is that all right with you?" Gary bobbed his head.

"Besides," Jenny added dryly, "if Cage is driving, we'll get there in half the time."

"You know, woman, if you don't stop smarting off like that, I'm gonna have to take drastic measures to shut you up." Cage drew her into an unyielding embrace and sealed her mouth in a hot kiss that didn't end until they pulled up to his garage.

"Time!" Roxy called out like a referee in a wrestling match.

Cage cursed softly as Jenny disentangled her limbs from his. "I had to come up for air anyway, Cage," Jenny whispered as she self-consciously straightened her clothes and smoothed down her hair.

Everybody thought that comment was hysterically funny and they were laughing as they transferred the luggage from Gary's car to Cage's. The Lincoln was as vintage as the Corvette, and had been restored to the same mint condition. It seemed half a block long and was as silver and shiny as the Lone Ranger's bullets.

"Make yourselves at home." Cage grinned over his shoulder at the passengers in the backseat.

"We intend to," Roxy answered. She fell back into the corner, dragging an unsuspecting, but certainly willing, Gary with her.

Cage laughed as he steered the car onto the highway. "That's the last we'll hear from them until we get to El Paso." Just then a contented groan rose from the shadows of the backseat. "Well, maybe not," he corrected himself, chuckling.

The Lincoln straddled the center stripe of the two-lane highway as it ate up the miles. Cage had it cranked up to ninety or better, but Jenny felt safe. They could see the headlights of other vehicles for miles before they met them. There was nothing on the landscape to block them from sight.

"Comfy?" Cage asked her after several moments of silence. He had tuned to a soft FM station on the radio. The stereo mood music was interrupted infrequently by a modulated, disembodied voice that kept the listeners apprised of the time and weather conditions.

"Hm, yes," Jenny sighed.

"Sleepy?"

"Not particularly."

"You're awfully quiet."

"Just thinking."

"You know, even though this car is monstrous by modern standards, we're not required to use the entire front seat."

"What does that mean?"

"To put it in the vernacular, haul your buns over here."

She smiled and slid over to sit hip to hip beside him. "That's better." He draped his right arm over her shoulders and immediately covered her breast with his hand.

"Cage!" She flung his hand off.

"I developed and perfected that move in junior high school. Don't tell me that after all these years it doesn't work."

"It doesn't work with me," she retorted primly.

"It never did work with the nice girls," he grumbled. "But you can't blame a guy for trying." He crooked his elbow and drew his hand back so that his fingers were free to strum her neck. "What were you thinking about?"

Quite naturally she let her head fall fack onto his shoulder. Her hand landed on his thigh and she left it there. "That this is really fun. I've never done anything this wild and reckless before."

"This is wild and reckless? We're merely driving down the highway. Of course, there's a little harmless petting going on between two people who are obviously in love with each other and are soon to be married."

"I haven't said I'll marry you."

His pause was brief but significant. "I was referring to Roxy and Gary."

Mortification swept through Jenny like a tidal wave. She yanked her hand off his thigh and tried to put space between them. Cage would have none of it. He held her against him, though she strained away.

"Come back here," he whispered fiercely. "And you can stop that wiggling because I'm not going to let you go." When her struggles subsided, he said, "I'm thrilled that you thought I was talking about us. You took it to mean that we are two people obviously in love with each other. *Are* we two people in love, Jenny?"

"I don't know," she mumbled, her head bowed.

"I can only speak for myself, of course." His eyes left the highway. "I love you, Jenny."

She raised her head and became captivated by the eloquent expression in his eyes. They stared at each other for long moments as the car roared down the highway. Finally he returned his attention to the road.

"I know what you're thinking. You're thinking that I've said those words to dozens of women. Well, I have. I've said whatever was necessary at the time to get them into bed with me. I've made love because I was drunk, or horny, or angry, or blue, or happy. For just about every reason you can think of.

"And sometimes I did it even when I didn't want to, but because I felt sorry for the woman and knew she needed a man. I've been with beautiful women and some not so beautiful. I haven't been discreet or discriminating.

"But I swear to you, Jenny," he said earnestly, turning his head toward her again, "that I've never been in love. Until now. You're the only woman I've ever loved. It started a long time ago. Years ago.

"But I didn't see any sense in pursuing it. Everyone would have thought I was wrong for you. You would have run in terror if I'd approached you seriously. Mother and Dad would have had conniption fits. And besides all that, there was Hal, and I didn't want to hurt him."

Tears were rolling down the cheek she pressed against his shoulder. "Why are you telling me this now?"

"Don't you think it's time you knew?" His arm hugged her possessively and he pressed a kiss to her temple. "Do you love me, Jenny?"

"Yes, I think so. I mean, I do, I know I do. It's just that I'm confused."

"Confused?"

"My life was so well planned and organized, so carefully controlled, until a few months ago. Since the night Hal left for Central America nothing has been as it was before. That night changed me. I'm different. I can't explain it."

Cage squeezed his eyes shut for a moment. He wanted to tell her then. He wanted to say, "You're changed because we made love and it was beautiful and our bodies told us something we had secretly known but had ignored for years—you were involved with the wrong brother.''

But he couldn't tell her that. Not now. Not ever. It was a secret he would live with for the rest of his life, even if it meant that he couldn't acknowledge his own child. Jenny had been hurt enough. He wouldn't hurt her any more.

''I'm like an animal raised in captivity who has just been thrown into the wild. I'm feeling my way into the mainstream of life. Taking things a day at a time. It has to be a gradual process.''

She raised her head and spoke to his profile. ''Don't ask me for a commitment, Cage. Everything is so complex. I barely had time to straighten out my feelings for Hal before I realized how I really felt about you.'' Again her hand was on his thigh. Her fingers curled into the hard flesh. ''I only know that if you were to suddenly leave my life, I couldn't bear it.''

He covered her hand with his. ''You know what would have happened if Roxy and Gary hadn't interrupted us, don't you?''

''We would have made love.''

''We would still be making love.''

''And it would be wrong.''

''How can you say that when we've just admitted we love each other?''

''There's someone else involved.''

''Hal?''

''Hal's child,'' she answered softly.

Cage was quiet for a long time before he said thickly, ''The child is yours, too, Jenny, a living part of you. I love you. I love the child. It's as simple as that.''

''Hardly simple.'' She returned her head to his shoulder and after several moments she confessed, ''I wanted to make love with you tonight. But even that confuses me.''

''Why?''

"I can't honestly say. Is it *you* I want, or just another night of loving like the one I spent with Hal? That sounds shabby and sordid, I know, but somehow when it comes to lovemaking, I can't separate the two of you in my mind."

Cage's heart soared. "It will be incredible with us. I promise. It'll be exactly what you want it to be. But once I have you, I won't ever let you go." He had had to give her up for Hal's sake. He wasn't willing to give her up again. "Be sure you're ready to make a commitment before you make love with me."

She smiled up at him, a shy, sexy smile that made his heart accelerate. But instead of pressing down harder on the gas pedal, he applied brakes and slowed the car to a halt on the shoulder of the highway.

"What are we stopping for?" Gary asked groggily from the backseat.

"I'm hungry," Cage said.

"Who can think of food at a time like this?" Roxy complained.

"I wasn't thinking of food." Cage pulled Jenny into his arms and lowered his mouth to hers.

It was awhile before the Lincoln was once again under way.

"I thought it was extremely romantic," Jenny said with a huge yawn she unsuccessfully tried to cover with her hand.

"I thought we looked like the seediest bunch since the Barrow gang," Cage said. "If I'd been that justice of the peace, I'd have barred my door."

They had routed the public official out of bed, and he had grudgingly consented to perform the wedding ceremony. The bride and groom had then been driven to a hotel where they would spend a few hours before leaving for the airport. After drinking several cups of coffee in a twenty-four-hour diner and refueling the Lincoln, Cage had turned it toward home.

"We could get a room and sleep a few hours," he had suggested to Jenny.

"No. I feel so gritty. I think I'd rather just go the distance, then crash."

Cage looked at her now and laughed. At some point during the night she had surrendered the losing battle of keeping her hair up and had removed all the pins. The caramel-colored strands hung around her shoulders in tumbled disarray. Her new skirt and blouse were hopelessly wrinkled. She looked like the starlet of a sexy French movie during the morning-after scene.

"That funny looking, am I?"

"That adorable. Stretch out and go to sleep," he said, patting his thigh to indicate she should lay her head on it.

"I'm afraid you'll fall asleep if I'm not keeping you company."

"No, I won't. The coffee will keep me awake. Besides, I'm used to doing wild and reckless things like this." She made a face at him and he laughed. "Come on," he urged.

"Are you sure?"

"Positive."

She lay down on her side, stretching out as much as possible, and settled her head on his thigh. Closing her eyes, she breathed deeply. "That feels good."

Keeping a careful eye on the road, he pulled her blouse from underneath her belt and reached beneath it to massage her back. She sighed. "You're going to spoil me."

"That would be my pleasure." Her skin was as smooth as satin. And warm. His hand stroked up and down her spine, gently kneading away the tiredness and tension. Eventually he caressed his way around her ribs to her front. Beneath her raised arm he found the soft fullness of her breast.

"Cage..."

"It's all right," he said soothingly.

It felt so right, Jenny silently fell into agreement and relaxed again.

"Where's your bra?"

"I had to hide it under the cushion of the sofa when you answered the door." He chuckled and she smiled against the fabric of his pants leg. "I didn't have a chance to retrieve it before we left."

"I'm glad," he whispered meaningfully, and the ministrations of his hand echoed his words.

"So am I."

He continued to caress her. His intention wasn't to arouse but to soothe. His heart swelled with love to know she had come so far in trusting him, enough to permit this kind of familiarity. In a few short minutes he knew from her even breathing that she was asleep.

Temptation got the best of him and he let his fingers sweep across her nipple. His touch was airy light, but it was enough to bring an instantaneous response, even in sleep. She stirred, shifting her weight and rubbing her head against his lap, until she once again settled and became still.

Cage ground his teeth in an agony of pleasure. "Jenny," he whispered for his ears alone, "there's one thing you don't have to worry about. As long as your head is lying in my lap, I won't be accidentally falling asleep."

The car sped through the gray predawn.

"Where are we?" Jenny sat up and blinked her eyes against the sunlight. She rolled her head around her shoulders once and stretched her neck.

"Home. Well, almost. I thought you might be hungry. I'm starving."

Through the bug-splattered windshield she saw that they were at the same motel on the outskirts of La Bota where Cage had brought her before. He was parked in front of the coffee shop.

"I can't go in there looking like this!" she cried.

"Nonsense. You look terrific."

He swung out of the car door and, after stopping to arch his back and stretch, came around to Jenny's side. She was making futile efforts to smooth the wrinkles out of her clothes and straighten her hair.

"I look terrible," she said as he helped her out, a hand under her elbow. She swayed against him and clutched at his arm. "Oh, my foot's gone to sleep. You may have to hold me up."

"I won't mind," he growled in her ear. "You might as well know that I took liberties while you were asleep."

"That sounds like something you'd do." She tried to look angry, but the sparkle in her eyes gave her away.

"Hey, what's this?" Something had caught his eye in the morning sunlight. He reached behind her seat and came up with the unopened bottle of champagne. "Well, what do you know? We forgot to make a toast with the champagne."

Jenny made a *tsking* sound and grabbed the bottle. "We'll save it for after breakfast."

"Uh-oh. I've created a monster. You're going to be an expensive woman to keep. I should have started you out on beer."

Slaphappy and tired, they staggered up the steps toward the door of the coffee shop. Cage reached for the door just as another couple pushed through it on their way out.

Bob and Sarah Hendren.

It had been a tradition of theirs to go out to breakfast alone every Saturday morning. Since their boys had been old enough to fend for themselves, the Hendrens had indulged in that two hours of solitude every weekend. The demands of Bob's work allowed them little time to themselves, so they treated each Saturday as an occasion and spent all week deciding on where they would go next, always choosing a different restaurant.

The couple stood rooted to the spot as they took in the condition of Jenny's clothes and Cage's day-old beard.

Jenny's attempt to brush her hair back only called attention to the tangles in it. Her lips were naturally rouged from the frequent and passionate kisses the night before. Her mascara had been smeared during her nap. Had the older couple looked closely, they would have seen a smudge of it on Cage's trouser leg.

But their attention was focused mainly on Jenny, who had undergone such a metamorphosis since they had last seen her and who was now unconsciously hugging a bottle of champagne to her breasts.

"Mother, Dad, hi." Cage was the first to break the tense silence. He would have removed his arm from around Jenny's waist to relieve the awkwardness of the moment, but he was afraid she couldn't stand up under her own power. She had slumped against him heavily.

"Good morning," Bob said with a discernible lack of civility.

Sarah said nothing, but continued to stare at Jenny. They hadn't come face to face since that awful scene in the parsonage when she had accused Jenny of seducing Hal. Her hard expression revealed that she thought she had been right in her accusation.

"Sarah, Bob," Jenny said pleadingly, "this isn't what it looks like. We...Cage and I drove...drove..."

Cage picked up for her when she faltered. "We drove two friends to El Paso last night so they could get married. We made a turn-around trip and just got back." He was trying to emphasize that they hadn't spent the night away together, though he thought now it would have been better if they had. At least Bob and Sarah wouldn't have known about it, and this scene, which he instinctively felt was about to get nasty, would have been avoided.

Jenny laughed nervously, fearfully, as though someone had just arrested her for a hideous crime and she couldn't determine if it was a joke or not. "The champagne was for the wedding. We forgot all about it. See? It isn't even opened. Just now we were acting silly and—"

"You don't have to explain anything to them," Cage lashed out irritably.

He wasn't angry with her. He knew she was embarrassed and he would have given anything to have spared her that. But he was furious with his parents for being so judgmental and automatically jumping to the wrong conclusion. He couldn't blame them for thinking the worse about him, but couldn't they have given Jenny the benefit of the doubt?

"You were like a daughter to me," Sarah said in a trembling voice. Tears were collecting in her eyes. She blinked them back while she pursed her lips tighter.

"I still am," Jenny moaned with soft earnestness. "I want to be. I love you both and I've missed you."

"Missed us?" Sarah's harsh tone dismissed that notion. "We've heard about your new apartment. You didn't bother to let us know your address, much less take the time to come see us."

"Because I didn't think you wanted to see *me*."

"You forgot us as quickly as you forgot Hal," Sarah accused her.

"I'll never forget Hal. How could I? I loved him. And I'm carrying his child."

That gently spoken reminder lifted the floodgate of Sarah's tears and she sobbed against Bob's arm.

"She's been upset," he said quietly. "She misses you terribly, Jenny. I know we didn't take the news of the baby too well, but we've had time to reevaluate. We want to be a part of his life. Even this morning we talked about calling you and making amends. It's our Christian duty to keep the family intact. I can't be the kind of example I should be with this thing between us."

The minister glanced at Cage, at the incriminating champagne, at the disreputable picture the two of them made. "But now, seeing you like this, I just don't know." He shook his head sadly and turned away, holding Sarah protectively under his arm as she cried.

"Oh, please," Jenny said, taking a step forward and extending her arms as though reaching out to touch them.

"Jenny, no," Cage said softly and drew her back. "Give it time. They have to work it out in their own minds."

He escorted her back to the car without argument. She surely wasn't up to being seen in public now. Indeed, as soon as she was in the car, she began to cry.

It seemed to Jenny that for each giant step forward, she took two backward. She had humbled herself and begged Hal to make love to her, but he had left anyway.

While he was away she had come to realize she didn't love him as a wife should love her husband. He had died, leaving her with the guilt, as though she had deserted him and not the other way around.

Piecing her life back together, she had embarked upon a new job, only to discover she was pregnant. Now she was a pariah to the beloved people she had considered her family since adolescence.

She didn't want to return to the life she had lived before Hal left. It had been stifling and she couldn't bear that kind of slow suffocation again. After having tasted independence, she wanted to feast on it. She had achieved a level of freedom, but at what price? The liberation of Jenny Fletcher had been expensive. It had cost her the love and respect of those she held most dear.

Her tears were bitter as they rolled down her face into her mouth. Knowing that fatigue and pregnancy were partly responsible for this weeping binge, she let herself indulge in it. The outpouring of emotion was cleansing and she let it happen, paying no attention to where Cage was driving until the motor of the Lincoln was turned off.

She raised her head from her hands and wiped her eyes. "This is your house," she remarked unnecessarily.

"Right."

He got out and came around to assist her. "What are we doing here?"

"I'm going to see to it that you eat a good breakfast. And," he stressed when she opened her mouth to protest, "there will be no argument about it."

She was too weary to argue anyway, so she said nothing. He unlocked the front door and she trudged upstairs behind him into the master suite. "The bathroom's yours for ten minutes." He rummaged in a drawer and came up with a Texas Tech T-shirt. The red double *T* against the black cotton was faded from many washings. "Take a hot shower and put this on when you get out. If you're not downstairs in ten minutes, I'm coming to get you." He kissed her swiftly and she was left alone.

The water was scalding, the soap fragrant and sudsy, the shampoo luxurious, the towels plush. When she pulled the T-shirt over her head, she felt one hundred percent better and ravenously hungry.

Hesitantly she stood on the threshold of the kitchen, feeling vulnerable and exposed. Her hair was wet and all she had on under the T-shirt was a pair of panties. The hem of the shirt reached mid-thigh, but she still felt awkward and self-conscious.

Cage seemed not to notice either the brevity of her costume or her bashfulness. The moment he saw her he said, "Well, don't just stand there. Two hands are better than one."

"What can I do?"

"Butter the toast."

She did and within minutes they were sitting down to a steaming platter of bacon and eggs. Hunger made manners dispensable and she dug right in. After several hefty mouthfuls, she caught Cage's amused eyes on her. Chagrined, she blotted her mouth with a napkin and took a demure sip of cold orange juice. "You're a good cook."

"Don't let me slow you down." By the time she had cleared the plate of food, she was so exhausted she could barely lift the cup of herbal tea Cage had steeped for her.

"Come on before you drop," he said, pushing back his chair.

"Where am I going?"

"To bed." He swept her into his arms.

"Your bed?"

"Yes."

"I should dress and go home. Put me down, Cage."

"Not until we get to the bed."

She should stop him before he took another step up the stairs, but she couldn't collect the energy. The long nap in the car hadn't been sufficient. She couldn't remember ever feeling so wrung out. Her head fell against his chest and her eyes slid closed. He was so strong. Capable. Trustworthy. And she loved him.

The sleeve of his shirt felt rough against the backs of her bare thighs. She was reminded of that night in bed with Hal and the way his clothes had felt against her skin, how sensuous it had been.

Cage set her down beside the bed but kept an arm around her as he flung back the suede spread. Then he gently lowered her to the fresh-smelling sheets. "Sleep tight," he whispered as he pulled the top sheet over her. He brushed a strand of damp hair away from her cheek.

"What are you going to do?"

"Wash the dishes."

"That's not fair. You drove all night. You cooked the food." Her mind had a difficult time organizing the words in the right order. Her lips had an even harder time forming them.

"You can make it up to me another time. Now you and baby get some rest." He kissed her lips softly, but she didn't feel it. She was already asleep.

Chapter 12

It took her a moment to orient herself when she woke up. She lay without moving, taking in her surroundings with sleepy eyes until she recognized Cage's bedroom.

Memory came back intact then. She remembered the sequence of events that had led to her sleeping in his bed. So much had happened since she had opened her front door to him last night and seen him standing there holding the roses.

It was almost night again. The sky seen through the shutters was violet, deepening into purple. A milky moon seemed within touching distance of the window. And one brilliant star, like a beauty mark juxtaposed to a smile, was positioned just below and to one side of the moon.

She yawned and stretched and rolled to her back. She sat up and shook her tousled hair. The T-shirt was twisted around her waist. Her legs, bare and silky, since she had availed herself of Cage's razor when she showered, slid smoothly against the covers she kicked off as she raised her knees and bowed her back to stretch forward.

She gasped softly.

Cage was lying beside her, perfectly still, an arm's length away. Not a single muscle moved as he lay on his back, his arms raised, his hands folded beneath his head, watching her. It seemed inappropriate to say anything, so Jenny returned his silent stare and said hello only with her eyes.

He had taken a shower while she was asleep. He smelled of the same soap she had used. His jaw had been shaved clean of whiskers, and she wondered with a half smile if she had dulled his razor.

His hair was arranged as haphazardly as usual. The disorder of those dusty blond strands was rakish, cavalier, and so typically Cage, she longed to run her fingers through them. But touching him seemed inappropriate, too.

For the moment the most provocative caress was eye contact. So Jenny did nothing at all but look at him with the same intensity with which he was looking at her. Longing vibrated between them like humming harp strings. Their senses were perfectly attuned to each other, but for the time being they tacitly agreed to indulge only their sense of sight.

His eyes hadn't wavered, but she knew he was looking at all of her at once—her hair, her face, her mouth, her breasts. How could he miss seeing her breasts? Jenny could feel them trembling with emotion, their crests thrusting against the soft cloth of the T-shirt as though vying for his attention.

Nor could he miss the vee where the wedge of her panties showed above her bare thighs. Surely that spot hadn't escaped those smoky topaz eyes. Under their ardent stare, the erogenous parts of her body warmed considerably and began to throb with a pleasant ache. Still, Jenny couldn't tear her eyes away from him.

She noticed that the undersides of his arms weren't as darkly tanned as the rest of him. She wanted to sink her teeth into the hard muscles of his biceps, but she knew Cage would be shocked if she did. Women were supposed to be passive, weren't they? Besides, such conduct was beyond her experience.

The tufts of hair in his armpits looked soft and downy. Would they tickle? No doubt. Did she dare find out? Her eyes fell away shyly for a moment before she raised them again.

Ever since that night in Monterico she had been dazzled by his naked torso. Leisurely now, she studied it thoroughly and took in every detail, the curved muscles of his chest, the dusting of hair, the way the broad expanse tapered into a trim ribcage. His stomach was hard and flat. His navel dimpled the center of a narrow abdomen.

He was lying with his legs crossed at the ankles. His feet were bare. He was wearing a pair of jeans.

And they were unbuttoned.

They were the regulation jeans of roughnecks and cowboys, with the old-fashioned button fly. The seams were faded white and the denim was frayed in spots. They gloved his long thighs and cupped his sex. A ribbon of hair arrowed down into the shadowed opening.

Jenny realized she had been holding her breath for a long time. She closed her eyes and exhaled on a slow sigh. It was easy to figure out what had happened. As soon as Cage had finished showering, he had given way to sleepiness and fallen onto the bed without bothering to button his jeans. After all, he had driven all night.

He was *covered*, it was just...

Her heart hammering, Jenny opened her eyes again. Almost against her will they trained on Cage's lap. With each breath his stomach rose and fell, setting his muscles into play in a hypnotizing and erotic ballet.

Jenny was entranced. She felt compelled. Why resist?

She touched him.

Her fingertips found that sleek center stripe of hair that bisected his torso. They rode it down to his navel. Her index finger shyly tested the depth of that beguiling indentation and twirled in the hair encircling it.

He was so warm and alive. Energy emanated from him and sent electric currents chasing up her fingertips. He was raw masculinity. She felt weak and defenseless against his power.

Inexorably drawn, her hand moved down. The hair she encountered just inside the opening of his jeans was darker and denser and springy.

She hesitated and turned her head. When she looked into his face, she cried out softly.

Tears were glistening in his eyes. He hadn't moved, hadn't altered his position in the slightest, hadn't said a word, but his eyes were filled with emotion. That touched Jenny in a way that transcended the physical.

Love had never been demonstrated for him. He had never been fondled or smothered with affection. Loving touches had been absent from his young life. He had been deprived of unselfish giving.

Jenny didn't hesitate. Indeed, she didn't even think about it. Her mind had nothing to deliberate.

Her hand disappeared inside his jeans.

A heartfelt groan erupted from Cage's chest. Lowering his hands, he clutched at the sheet beneath him. He bared his teeth in a grimace of ecstasy and ground the back of his head into the pillow. The tears were squeezed from the corners of his eyes when he clamped them shut against the passion that flooded through him like a rushing river.

He hooked his thumbs in the waistband of his jeans and pushed them down over his hips, then bicycled his legs until he could kick them away.

Jenny, her eyes glazed with wonder, looked down at her hand. He more than filled it. He was full, thick, hard, and hot. She admired him with uneducated yet eager eyes.

Acting purely on instinct, she turned and lay down close to him, resting her cheek on his thigh. Her hair spilled over him like a silky mantle. He sifted through it with unthinking fingers guided only by touch.

She ached with love for him and wanted him to know how marvelous she thought he was, body and soul. She lifted her head from his thigh, bent down, and kissed him.

What happened then was beyond her imagination or comprehension. With a soft moan Cage turned his head and began nuzzling her. Her panties were somehow discarded, though she could never recall quite how that came about.

She felt his hands on her thighs, stroking and caressing and parting. He touched her in the most supremely intimate way.

Then his mouth was there, warm and wet and gentle.

He made love to her and she caressed him with her lips and tongue. The world became a bowl of cream and she was submerged in it. The atmosphere was rich and delicious and velvety. In this realm there existed no jagged edges of feeling, no difficult emotions, no harsh realities. Everything was smooth and complete and understood. There was an absence of ugliness and ambiguity. All was beauty and light.

When he turned and braced himself above her, he whispered, "Open your eyes, Jenny. See the one who loves you."

Her eyes drifted open. They were hazy with passion, but Cage knew she saw and recognized him. With one swift thrust he sheathed himself in her satiny warmth. When he was secured deep inside, he smiled down into her radiant face.

He watched the patterns of expression dance across her features in response to his rhythmic stroking. He saw the wonder dawn in her slumberous eyes when he changed tempos and brought her to ever-higher levels of arousal.

He watched the light burn inside her soul when she experienced her fulfillment...and he saw her shine with love when he experienced his.

"You're precious to me and I love you, Jenny. I always have." His lips were close to her ear. The dusty blond strands of his hair mingled with the richer brown tones of hers on the pillow. His cheek felt as fevered as hers when he pressed them together. "I love you."

He raised his head and gazed down into her eyes, which were glimmering like emeralds. "I love you, too, Cage." She reached up to touch his cheek, his eyebrows, his lips, as though to convince herself that he was truly there and that it hadn't all been a dream.

"Remember what I promised you?"

"Yes. You kept your promise. It was beautiful, just as you said it would be."

"*You're* beautiful." He moved.

"No, stay inside me."

"I intend to," he whispered against her lips. "But I haven't even kissed you yet." He remedied that with a thorough kiss that kept his tongue nestled inside her mouth for breathless moments.

Working the T-shirt up, he pulled it over her head and tossed it aside. He lowered his gaze to her breasts and caressed one softly.

"I meant what I said, Jenny. I've loved you for a long time, but I couldn't do anything about it. You belonged to Hal. I accepted that without argument just as everyone did, including you."

"I sensed there was something between us. I didn't know what it was."

"Lust."

She smiled and combed her fingers through his hair. "Whatever it was, I was afraid of it."

"I thought you were afraid of me."

"No. Only of the way you made me feel."

"Is that why you avoided me?"

"Was I that conspicuous?"

"Hm." He was intrigued with her breasts, their shape, their dusky crests. He examined them lovingly. "I'd come around and you'd duck for cover."

"You were dangerous to be around. I would go to any lengths not to be left alone in the same room with you. You seemed to consume all the oxygen. I couldn't breathe." She groaned softly as he dipped his head and bathed the tip of her breast with his tongue. "You still take my breath away."

"I can't keep what you do to me a secret." He stirred inside her. He was hard again.

She palmed the firm muscles of his buttocks and drew him deeper inside. He fondled her breast, finessed the nipple until it was firm and flushed, then lowered his mouth to it.

Jenny watched him caress her, watched the flexing of his cheeks as he gratified his need for her. She wished she could fill the void inside him, erase from his past all the times he had needed loving and went lacking.

"Cage, use me. Use me."

"No, Jenny," he rasped, his tongue flicking. "I've used other women. This is different."

She wanted to concentrate on ways to please and satisfy him, but she became too caught up in the pleasure he was giving her. His arousal had heightened until he filled her again. The walls of her body closed around his hardness like a miserly fist. She thrilled to each powerful thrust and arched up to meet them.

Then another sensation spiraled through her middle. At first the rippling movements were so faint she thought she had imagined them. But then the flutterings became stronger and she realized what had caused them.

When she did, she panicked. Her body went rigid beneath Cage's and instead of striving to know more of him, she shrank away. "No, no, stop." She clasped his head and lifted it from her breasts. She squirmed free of him and pressed her thighs together tightly. "Stop, stop."

"Jenny?" His breathing was harsh and loud. It took several seconds for him to bring his eyes back into focus and set the world on its rightful axis. "What's wrong, Jenny? Did I hurt you?"

His heart contracted with fear when she turned her back on him, raised her knees to her chest and formed a ball with her slight body. "Oh, my God, something's wrong. What's wrong? Tell me."

Cage had never felt so afraid and useless in his life. Seconds ago he and Jenny had been making love. Her body had been responsive and eager. Now she was weeping and acting as though agonizing pains were ripping through her.

He laid a hand on her shoulder. She flinched at his touch. "What is it? Should I call a doctor?" His only answer was a racking sob. "For godsake, Jenny, at least tell me if you're in pain."

"No, no," she moaned. "Nothing like that."

"Then what?" He crammed his fingers through his hair, impatiently pushing it off his forehead. "What happened? Why did you stop me? Was I hurting you?"

"I felt the baby move."

The words were mumbled into the pillow in a papery voice. At first Cage couldn't decipher them, but when he broke apart the unintelligible syllables and pieced them back together, he went weak with relief. "That's the first time?"

She nodded her head. "The doctor said I should start feeling him soon. This is the first time."

Behind her, Cage smiled. His child had spoken to him. But Jenny was obviously concerned about it. He touched her shoulder again and this time didn't remove his hand even when she stiffened with aversion. In fact, he lay down beside her and tried to take her in his arms.

"It's all right, Jenny. It won't hurt the baby if we're careful."

She sat up abruptly and glared at him. "You don't get it, do you?"

Cage stared at her incredulously as she lunged off the bed, pulled on the blanket until it came free of the other rumpled covers, and wrapped it around herself. She stalked to the window and braced her shoulder against the frame with her back to the room.

He was hurt and angry and it showed as he got off the bed as well, yanked up his jeans, and shoved his legs into them, hiking them up over his hips with a definitely angry tug.

"I guess I don't get it, Jenny. Why don't you tell me?"

She hadn't heard his footfalls on the thick, lush carpet, and it alarmed her when she turned around to find him standing so close. His eyebrows were lowered into a glower. The jeans had been left unbuttoned again and his hair was mussed from her fingers plowing through it.

He was the personification of male sexuality and was so appealing, she had to struggle to resist him.

"You might not have any morals against that alley cat type of behavior, but I do."

"You thought what we were doing was alley cat behavior?" he demanded, his voice quaking with rage.

"I didn't until I felt my baby move."

"I think it's beautiful. I wish you had shared it with me."

"It's another man's baby, Cage! Do you realize what kind of woman that makes me?"

Her anger was spent and in its place were shame and misery. She hung her head as the tears began to fall. Cage watched her shoulders begin to shake with weeping. Her small, frail hands gripped the blanket around her as Eve must have clung to that first fig leaf to hide her shame.

"What kind of woman does that make you?"

She shook her head, at first unable to voice her thoughts aloud. She sniffed back tears. "What we did together...the way I acted when we were...making love..."

"Go on," he prodded when she hesitated.

"I don't know myself anymore. I love you, but I carry your brother's baby."

"Hal is dead. We're alive."

"I've denied it, even to myself, but your parents were partially correct when they said I tried to lure Hal away from his misson."

"What do you mean?" Cage's brow knit in concern.

"That night when he came to my bedroom to tuck me in, he had no intention of making love to me. I kissed him and begged him to stay with me, to give up the trip and marry me."

"You've told me this before. You said he left, then came back."

"That's right."

"So you can't condemn yourself for seducing him. Hal made up his own mind without any coercion from you."

She rested her head against the window jamb and stared sightlessly through the shutters. "But don't you see? He might have only come back to check on me, to kiss me good night one more time. I was desperate and he must have sensed that."

Cage's insides were knotted. How much longer could he perpetrate this lie? Why wouldn't it die a natural death and leave him the hell alone? Why must it come back to haunt him every time he glimpsed happiness with Jenny? Like a malicious gatekeeper, that one sin was keeping him from knowing heaven.

"It was still Hal's decision," he said firmly.

"But if that night had never happened, he might still be alive. I didn't have sense enough to worry about pregnancy, but maybe Hal did. Maybe that was what he was thinking about when he became careless enough to get arrested.

"I had no more conscience than to seduce him away from a God-called mission when all the time I really loved you, a love I was too weak and frightened to admit to. Now I'm sleeping with you while carrying Hal's child. The baby will never know his father because of me."

Cage stood silently for a moment before going to the foot of the bed and sitting down on its edge. He spread his knees wide, propped his elbows on them, and rested his forehead against his raised fists as he stared down at the carpet between his feet.

"You have no reason to feel guilty, Jenny."

"Don't try to make me feel better. I disgust myself."

"Listen to me, hear me out," Cage said sharply, raising his head. "You're *not* guilty of any of that, not of seducing Hal into your bed, not of distracting him from his mission, certainly not of his death. Nor are you guilty of making love to me while carrying Hal's child."

She turned to look at him with perplexity. The moon shone only on one side of her face, keeping the other in shadow. That was just as well, Cage thought. He feared what he might see in her expression when he told her.

He drew in a heavy breath and spoke quietly, though there was no hesitation in his confession. "Hal didn't father your baby, Jenny. I did. I came to your bedroom that night, not Hal. It was me you made love with."

Her eyes remained still and wide as she stared at him from across the room. Slowly she slid down the wall and sank to the floor. The blanket mushroomed out around her. All that was visible was her face, pale with disbelief, and her hands, the knuckles of which had gone white.

"That's impossible," she said on a filament of breath.

"It's the truth."

She shook her head furiously. "Hal came into my room. I saw him."

"You saw me. The room was dark. I was standing against the light when I opened the door. I couldn't have been anything but a silhouette."

"It was Hal!"

"I was walking past your door and heard you crying. I intended to go get Hal. But he was downstairs, engrossed in conversation with Mother and Dad. So I went in to check on you instead.''

"No," she said soundlessly, still shaking her head.

"Before I could say anything, you sat up and addressed me as Hal."

"I don't believe you."

"Then how do I know how it happened? You reached for me. There were tears on your face. I could see them reflected in the light before I closed the door. I'll admit I should have identified myself the moment you called me Hal, but I didn't. I didn't want to then and I'm damn glad now that I didn't."

"I don't want to hear." She covered her ears with her hands.

Unpertrubed, he went on. "I knew you were suffering, Jenny. You were hurt and needed comforting. Frankly, I didn't think Hal would give you what you needed."

"But you would," she hissed accusingly.

"I *did*." He came off the bed and walked toward her. "You asked me to hold you, Jenny."

"I asked Hal!"

"But Hal wasn't there, was he?" Cage shouted, his own ire rising. "He was downstairs talking about visions and callings and causes, when he should have been ministering to his own fiancée."

"I made love with Hal!" she cried in one last frantic attempt to deny what he was telling her.

"You were upset. You had been crying. Hal and I were close enough in build for you to mistake me for him. We were dressed alike in jeans and shirts. I didn't say anything so you couldn't distinguish my voice."

"But I would know the difference."

"Who could you compare me to? You'd had no other lover."

She tried to forget how anxiously she had enticed that "lover" to hold her and kiss her, just as she tried to forget the sleeping pills she had taken that night. Hadn't she been sedated, her mind foggy? Hadn't she thought afterward that it almost could have been her imagination? Hadn't it all seemed dreamlike?

"You weren't looking for me," Cage said. "You were looking for Hal. It simply never occurred to you that it could be anyone else."

"Which is as good as admitting what a deceitful creep you are."

His eyes narrowed perceptibly. "You didn't seem to think I was a creep that night. You didn't seem to mind me at all."

"Stop it. Don't—"

"You lapped me up like a bear does honey."

"Shut up."

"Admit it, Jenny, you'd never been kissed like that before. Hal never kissed you like that, did he?"

"I—"

"Admit it!"

"I'll do no such thing!"

"Well, you can deny it to yourself all you want, but you know I'm right. I touched you and we both went off like rockets."

Jenny squeezed her eyes shut. "I didn't know it was you."

"It wouldn't have mattered."

Her eyes popped open. "That's a lie!"

"No, it's not, and what's more, you know it's not."

She mashed her fingers against her lips. "How could you be so low? How could you deceive me like that? How could you..." She choked on the rest of it.

Cage dropped to his knees in front of her. His anger had diminished and his voice trembled with earnestness. "Because I loved you."

She stared back at him wordlessly.

"Because I needed to be enveloped in you as much as you needed a man's love. I had wanted you for years, Jenny. Lust, yes, but more, much more than that. That night, you were there, in bed, naked and warm and sweet and aroused. At first I thought I'd only hold you, kiss you a few times before I identified myself. But once I'd held you, tasted you, felt your tongue against mine, touched your breasts" —he shrugged helplessly— "there was just no stopping the avalanche.

"I was surprised that you were a virgin. But even discovering that wasn't enough to stop me. Everything I am went into loving you that night. All I thought about was relieving your pain with my loving. It was the first time in my life I felt like I was doing something good. It was clean and right, Jenny. You've told me that yourself."

"I thought I was talking about Hal."

"But you weren't. *I* was your lover. Think back on that night and compare it to tonight. You know I'm not lying."

He stood up again and began pacing the stretch of carpet between bed and window. "Once I had made love to you, I couldn't give you up. I wanted to win you over slowly. I planned on courting you so that by the time Hal got home you'd be willing to break your engagement with him as painlessly as possible and come to me."

He stopped his pacing and smiled down at her. "The day you told me you were pregnant, I could barely keep still. I wanted to jump up, take you in my arms, and waltz you around that drugstore. Tonight when you told me the baby had moved, I felt the same way."

With the reminder of what had transpired only minutes ago, Jenny glanced toward the bed. It was terrible. Horrible. But she believed him. It all made sense. Why she hadn't seen it before she didn't know. It was obvious now. So damnably obvious. But as he had said, she hadn't been looking for it.

Or had she? Had she known? In the secretmost part of herself, *had she known?* No. God, please, no!

"Why didn't you tell me, Cage? I made love to one man thinking it was another! Why didn't you tell me?"

"At first because I thought you still loved Hal. It would have destroyed you to think you'd been unfaithful to him."

"I was."

"You weren't, dammit. If anyone was, I was!"

Her breasts heaved with emotion as she struggled to her feet. "Months have gone by. Why haven't you told me?"

"I didn't want to hurt you."

"You don't think I'm hurting now?"

"You shouldn't be. You're free of it. It was my sin, Jenny, not yours. You were innocent and I was trying to spare you."

"Why?"

"Because you have a masochistic penchant for taking the responsibility for other people's failures. You hold yourself accountable for everyone's shortcomings. My parents, Hal, me."

He sighed deeply. "But that's not the only reason." He bored into her eyes with his. "I wanted to do the right thing. I felt as if I owed it to Hal not to tell you. While I was out raising hell, drinking and womanizing, he had devoted his life to doing good. I took something that rightfully belonged to him...although I could argue that, because I had loved you for so long."

He stepped closer to her. "I wanted you to be a part of my life, but I knew the price I would have to pay for you would be high. Hellions like me don't get rewarded without paying a premium."

"What are you talking about, Cage? It seems to me that until tonight you've gotten off scot-free. What kind of dues have you paid?"

"One of them was having you cry out my brother's name the moment you climaxed for the first time." She ducked her head. "Another was having you think all this time that it was Hal who had first introduced you to ecstasy. Another was the night in Monterico when I could hold you while you slept, but still couldn't express my love. The highest price was having you think that my child, *my* child, had been fathered by anyone other than me."

She almost forgave him then. She almost succumbed to the tremor in his voice and the fierce possession in his eyes. She almost walked into his arms and claimed his love.

But she couldn't. What he had done had been dreadful, and a sin of that magnitude couldn't be lightly dismissed. "So why tell me now?"

"Because you're blaming yourself for Hal's death. I can't have that, Jenny. He left on his mission with a pure body and a pure conscience. His death had nothing to do with you. There was no way you could have prevented it. I won't let you go through the rest of your life blaming yourself for it and thinking that you're even remotely responsible for making your child an orphan."

He reached for her hand. It lay cold and lifeless in his. "I love you, Jenny."

She snatched her hand away. "Love isn't built on deception and lies, Cage. You've been lying to me for months. What do you want me to do?"

"Love me back."

"You made a fool of me!"

"I made a woman of you!" He spun away from her, making an effort to control his temper. "If you'd stop sifting everything through your filter of propriety and conscience and guilt, you'd see things clearly. That night was the best thing that had ever happened to either of us. It freed us both."

"Free?" she cried. "Free? I'll have to bear the burden of that night the rest of my life."

"Are you referring to my baby as a burden?"

"No, not the baby," she ground out. "The guilt. Of making love to one brother while being engaged to another."

"Oh…" He blistered the walls with his expletive. "Are we back to that again?"

"Yes. And I'm weary of it. Take me home."

"Not a chance. Not until we've thrashed this thing out."

"Take me home," she said adamantly. "If you don't, I'll steal the keys to one of your automobiles and drive myself."

"You're staying here or I'll—"

"Don't threaten me. I'm not afraid of you anymore. Your threats are empty anyway. What could you possibly do to me that would be worse than what you've already done?"

His jaw bunched with fury. She watched his eyes fill with hot rage, then just as quickly harden coldly. Abruptly he turned away from her. Going to the closet, he ripped a shirt from a hanger and picked up a pair of boots. "Get dressed," he said tersely through barely moving lips. "I'll come back for you in five minutes."

When he did, she was ready. She preceded him downstairs and through the front door. It was dark as they crossed the yard to the garage. He opened the door of the Lincoln and she got inside.

They were silent during the entire trip into town. His hands gripped the steering wheel as though he'd like to tear it from its mounting. He drove fast. When he braked outside her apartment, she rocked forward with the impact. Leaning across her, he opened the door and shoved it open. She stepped out.

"Jenny?" He was leaning across the seat. "I've done some terrible things. Mostly out of pure meanness. But this is one time I tried to do the right thing. I wanted to do right by my folks, you, and my baby." He laughed mirthlessly. "Even when I try to do what's right, it gets shot to hell. Maybe it's true what people have always said about Cage Hendren. He's just no damn good." He reached for the door and slammed it closed.

Then with a grinding of gears and a shower of gravel, the car shot forward and out of the parking lot.

Jenny let herself into the apartment. She felt drained, listless. Had it only been last night that she and Cage had shared the candlelight dinner? Yes, there were their ice-cream bowls and coffee cups still on the coffee table, forgotten there when they had left to drive Roxy and Gary to El Paso. It could have happened in another lifetime.

She left the lamps unlit as she went through the apartment toward her bedroom. It seemed dark, cold, empty, unlike the bedroom at Cage's house.

No, she wouldn't think of that.

But she did and there was no stopping the memories that rushed to her mind. Every touch, every kiss, every word.

She remembered the bleak expression in his eyes just before he had left. *Had* he been trying to do the right thing by holding his silence?

He certainly hadn't acted smug the morning Hal left. She remembered the attention he had paid her. He had been tense and watchful, but not cocky or obnoxious as he could have been. If it had only been a cruel trick he'd played, he certainly hadn't gloated over it afterward.

Did he love her? He had been willing to forfeit claiming his child. Wasn't such a sacrifice the ultimate testimony of love?

And if he loved her, what was she really upset about?

Cage had been her only lover. Didn't that give her a warm, glowing feeling inside? The enchantment of that night had been hers and Cage's. She should have known! She had never felt that way in her life before or since...until last night.

When he was inside her, hadn't his body felt familiar, like an extension of hers? Both times, hadn't she felt complete? Hadn't the addition of his body to hers brought together all the pieces of the complex puzzle that was Jenny Fletcher and made it whole?

Was she accusing Cage of deceit only to alleviate her own conscience? Because for years she had been deceitful to Hal, to the Hendrens, to the town. She had gone along with their marriage plans, knowing full well that the love she bore Hal wasn't the kind to base a marriage on.

There had been no sympathetic cord struck between them as there was with her and Cage. Hal hadn't satisfied the restless hunger of her spirit. With him she would have gone on suppressing that spirit and living under constant restraints. Cage dared her to be herself.

Couldn't she forgive Cage for keeping his secret all these months? She had been prepared to keep hers for the remainder of her life. If Cage hadn't made love to her that night, if Hal hadn't died, she would have married her fiancé. And no matter how unhappy it had made her, she would have stuck it out. Before her relationship with Cage, she wouldn't have had the courage to seek her own happiness, but would have continued letting others do it for her.

Cage had taught her to make her own future. Wasn't that alone reason enough to love him?

Tomorrow she would think about it some more. Maybe she would call Cage, apologize for her intolerance tonight, and together they would sort it all out.

Wearily she stripped off her clothes, pulled on a nightgown, and slipped into bed. But she couldn't sleep. She had slept most of the day, and the world seemed to be against her getting the peaceful rest she needed. Sirens screamed through the streets of town, and just when she had rubbed Cage from her mind enough to fall asleep, her telephone jangled loudly.

Chapter 13

Thinking it might be Cage, she weighed the wisdom of answering. Was she ready to talk to him yet? The phone was on its sixth ring before she gave in and reached for the receiver.

"Hello?"

"Miss Fletcher?"

It wasn't Cage and she felt a momentary pang of disappointment. "Yes."

"Is this the Jenny Fletcher who used to live with Reverend Hendren?"

"Yes. Who is this, please?"

"Deputy Sheriff Rawlins," the caller identified himself. "You wouldn't happen to know where we can locate the Hendrens, would you?"

"Have you checked the church and the parsonage?"

"Sure have."

"Then I'm sorry, I don't know where they are. Can I help you?"

"We really need to find them," the deputy said, convoying urgency. "Their son's been in an accident."

Jenny went cold. Nausea churned in her stomach. Yellow sunbursts exploded against a field of black when she closed her eyes. By an act of will she fought off fainting. "Their son?" she asked in a high, reedy voice.

"Yeah, Cage."

"But he was just...I just saw him."

"It happened a few minutes ago."

"Is he...was it...fatal?"

"I don't know yet, Miss Fletcher. The ambulance is rushing him to the hospital now. It's bad, all right. A train hit his car." Jenny stifled her outcry with a bloodless hand. A train! "That's why we need to find his next of kin."

Lord, what an awful official expression. "Next of kin," the phrase reserved in police jargon for those who have to be notified when someone they love dies in an accident away from home.

"Miss Fletcher?"

Several moments of silence had ticked by while Jenny tried to absorb the tragic enormity of this telephone call. "I don't know where Bob and Sarah are. But I'll be at the hospital in a few minutes. Good-bye. I have to hurry."

She hung up the phone before giving the deputy a chance to say anything more. Her knees buckled beneath her when she lunged off the bed. She stumbled to the closet, where she pulled out the first garment her hands fell on.

She had to get to Cage. Now. Hurry. She had to tell him she loved him before—

No, no. He wouldn't die. She wouldn't even think of his dying.

Oh, God, Cage, why did you do it?

Ever since the deputy had told her about the accident, Jenny had questioned whether it was an accident or not. What was the last thing Cage had said to her? "I'm just no damn good." Had her rejection of his love been the last rejection he could stand? Was this "accident" an attempt to win approval by ridding the world of Cage Hendren?

"No!"

She didn't realize she had screamed the word aloud until it echoed off the silent walls of her apartment. She ran through the darkened rooms on her way to the front door. Tears were streaming down her face and her fingers shook so badly, she could barely insert the key in the ignition of the car.

She saw the scene of the accident from several blocks away. A wrecker had pulled Cage's car off the tracks, but police still had the area cordoned off with flares to discourage curious onlookers.

The silver Lincoln looked like a piece of aluminum foil a petulant giant had balled up in his fist and thrown away. Jenny's chest compressed painfully. Nothing could have come out of that mangled mess of metal alive. Her arms were too weak to steer the car, but she forced herself to keep going. She had to reach the hospital in time.

When she arrived, she parked and dashed toward the emergency room doors. *Don't die, don't die, don't die,* her heart chanted with each footfall. This kind of emotional upheaval and physical exertion weren't good for the baby, but Cage was first in her thoughts now.

"Cage Hendren?" she gasped breathlessly, slapping her hands on top of the nurses' station desk.

The on-duty nurse looked up. "He's already gone up for surgery."

"Surgery?"

"Yes. Dr. Mabry."

If they were operating on him, he was still alive. *Thank you, God, thank you.* Jenny gulped for breath. "What floor?"

"Three."

"Thank you." She ran for the elevator.

"Miss?" Jenny turned around. "He might be in there for a long time."

The nurse was diplomatically cautioning her not to hold out much hope. "I'll wait, no matter how long it takes."

On the third floor the woman at the nurses' station confirmed that Cage was in surgery. "Are you a relative?" the R.N. inquired politely.

"I...I grew up with him. His parents adopted me when I was orphaned."

"I see. We haven't been able to contact his parents, but we're still trying."

"I'm sure they're just out for the evening and will return soon." Jenny couldn't believe she was capable of making casual conversation. She felt like screaming the walls down. She wanted to fall to the floor and keen while she tore at her hair.

"There's a policeman waiting at the house to bring them here."

Jenny bit her lower lip. "They'll be frightened. They lost their youngest son only a few months ago."

The nurse made a clucking sound of regret. "Why don't you sit down over there to wait," she said, indicating a waiting room. "I'm sure we'll hear something about Mr. Hendren's condition soon."

Like an automaton, Jenny moved to the waiting room and sat down on the sofa. She should go to the parsonage herself, be there to break the news of Cage's accident when the Hendrens came home. But she couldn't leave him. She couldn't! She had to stay right here telegraphing her love and encouragement through the walls into the operating room where he precariously clung to life.

His life was precious to her. Didn't he know that? How could he have—

Oh, God, she had let him leave her thinking the worst of himself. Just as his parents had rejected him on the night of Hal's funeral, she had cruelly shut him out tonight after he had opened his heart to her. The Hendrens might be too ignorant of Cage's psyche to realize what they had done to him all his life, but *she knew better.*

How many times had he doubted the value of his life? Wasn't he flirting with death every time he challenged authority, or got behind the wheel of a car and defied the speed limit? Hadn't he pulled his outrageous pranks only to win the attention always denied him?

Oh, Cage, forgive me. I love you. I love you. You're the most important person in the world to me.

"Miss Fletcher?"

She jumped at the sound of her name. Her eyes had been closed in anguish as she prayed, bargaining with God to spare Cage's life. She had expected to see a doctor bending over her in commiseration. Instead the man who had addressed her was wearing a police uniform.

"Yes?"

"I thought it was you," he said. "I'm Deputy Rawlins. I spoke to you on the phone."

She rubbed the tears out of her eyes. "Of course. I remember."

"And this here's Mr. Hanks. It was his family Cage saved."

For the first time Jenny noticed the man standing slightly behind the deputy. He stepped forward, his overalls and brogans a jarring contrast to the modern sterility of the hospital corridor. His eyes were red with tears and his balding head was humbly bowed.

"Saved?" Jenny mouthed. Very little sound came out. "I don't understand."

"His wife and kids were in the car that was stalled on the tracks. Cage came up behind them and pushed them off. He barely got them out of the way in time. 'Course, the engineer had seen what was happening and had slowed the train down as much as he could, but there wasn't time to stop it." He cleared his throat uncomfortably. "It's a good thing he hit on the passenger side and damn lucky for Cage he wasn't in his Vet. That would have been squashed like a bug."

Cage hadn't tried to take his own life! He had roared away from her angry and hurt, but it had never been his intention to kill himself. What a fool she had been to even suspect that.

A fresh batch of tears streamed down Jenny's face. He had been trying to save other lives. If he died, it would be as a hero and not as a suicide. She looked up at Mr. Hanks. "Is your family all right?"

He nodded. "They're still shaken up, but thanks to Mr. Hendren, they're alive. I'd like to tell him myself how grateful I am. I pray to God he pulls out of this."

"I pray so, too."

"You know," Hanks said, lowering his head and shaking it sadly, "I've always thought bad things about Cage Hendren, because of the stories goin' around. His drinking and women and all. I've seen him ripping around town in his fancy cars, driving like a bat out of Hades. I thought he was a damn fool to risk his life like that." He sighed. "Reckon I've been taught the hard way not to condemn a man I don't know. He didn't have to run up on that track and knock my wife's car out of the path of that freight train. But he did." His eyes began to fill again. Embarrassed, he covered them with his hand.

"Why don't you get on home, Mr. Hanks," Deputy Rawlins said kindly, laying a hand on the man's shoulder.

"Thank you, Mr. Hanks," Jenny said.

"For what? If it hadn't been for my sorry ol' car—"

"Thank you anyway," she said softly. Hanks gave her a solemn, encouraging nod before Rawlins led him to the elevator.

The nurses's prediction that they would soon hear something about Cage's condition proved to be false. Jenny sat alone in the waiting room. No one came out of the operating room to report on Cage.

She had been there for almost two hours when the elevator doors opened and Bob and Sarah rushed out. Their eyes were frantic, their faces wild with worry and ravaged with renewed grief.

Jenny watched them stop at the nurses' station and identify themselves. They got the same polite, tepid reassurance from the nurse that she had. Leaning into each other for support, they turned toward the alcove. When they saw Jenny, their footsteps faltered.

At first Jenny's eyes indicted them. *You didn't love him, but now you come to weep over his deathbed,* her expression said.

But she couldn't incriminate them without incriminating herself, too. If she hadn't been so frightened of what it would mean to her placid life, she would have faced up to her love for Cage years ago.

And today, *today*, when he had needed to know that he was forgiven and that she loved him, she had rejected his apology. The irony of it was, he had been apologizing for making love to her, for giving her the most splendid night of her life. And she had refused to accept it! How could she blame the Hendrens for their shortsightedness when hers had been so much more hurtful?

She stood and extended her arms toward Sarah. With a glad cry the older woman staggered forward. Jenny hugged her hard. "Shh, Sarah, he'll be all right. I know it."

Hiccupping on every other word, Sarah explained where they'd been. "We drove out of town to visit a sick friend. When we got back, the sheriff's car was parked outside our house. We knew something terrible had happened." Together they sat down on the sofa. "First Hal, now Cage, I can't bear it."

"Would it matter to you so much if Cage died?"

Jenny couldn't believe she had so boldly asked them the question uppermost in her mind. They looked back at her through stricken eyes. Knowing she should go easily on them in the face of tragedy, she nonetheless could find no mercy in her heart. If cruelty would wake them up to the shabby way they had treated their son, then cruel she would be. She was fighting this battle for Cage.

"I don't think Cage believes that you would care."

"But he's our son. We love him," Sarah cried.

"Have you ever told him you love him? Have you ever told him how much you value him?" Bob lowered his eyes guiltily. Sarah swallowed hard. "Never mind answering. As long as I lived with you, you never did."

"We...we had a difficult time with Cage," Bob said.

"Because he didn't fit into the mold you thought he should. He never felt accepted. You didn't appreciate his individuality. He knew he could never measure up to your expectations, so he gave up trying. He acts hard and cold and cynical, but that's a defense mechanism. He wants desperately to be loved. He wants you, his parents, to love him."

"I tried to love him," Sarah said. "He never stood still long enough. He didn't cuddle like Hal did. He wasn't well behaved like Hal. It was difficult to love Cage. His rambunctiousness, that wild streak, frightened me."

"I know what you mean," Jenny said, smiling privately and patting Sarah's hand in understanding. "I learned to see through that into the man. I love him deeply."

Bob was the first to speak. "Do you, Jenny?"

"Yes. Very much."

"How can you, so soon after Hal's death?"

"I loved Hal. But he was more like a brother to me. I only realized when Cage and I began spending time together that I had loved him for a long time. I, like you, was afraid of him."

Bob said, "It may take us some time to get used to the idea of you and Cage together."

"It's taken me some time."

"We know we haven't been fair to you," Sarah said. "We wanted to keep you with us to fill the vacancy in our lives that Hal's death made."

"I have my own life."

"We realize that now. The only way we can keep you is to let you go."

"I won't be going far," she assured them with a smile. "I love you both. It broke my heart for there to be this rift between us."

"The baby was a shock to us, Jenny." Bob's eyes flickered down to her stomach. "Surely you can understand that. But, well, it's Hal's child, too. We'll accept it and love it for that reason."

Jenny opened her mouth to speak, but another voice interrupted. "Reverend Hendren?" They turned and recognized Dr. Mabry in his operating room greens. They were sweat stained. He looked haggard. Jenny clutched her middle, as though to protect her child from hearing bad news about his father.

"He's alive," the doctor said, relieving them of their primary fear. "Barely. He's still in critical condition. He was in shock when they brought him in. His insides were a mess. He was bleeding internally. We had to give him several pints of blood. It was a real patch-up job, but I think we got everything sewed back together. His right tibia has a clean break and there's a hairline fracture in his right femur. Bruises and lacerations all over him. They're the least of his problems."

"Will he live, Dr. Mabry?" Sarah asked the question as if her own life hinged on the answer.

"He has a good chance because he's as strong as a bull and tough as a boot. He came through the crash and the surgery. If he can survive those two traumas, I'm laying good money on his making it. Now, if you'll excuse me, I'd better get back."

"Can we see him?" Jenny asked, catching the doctor's sleeve.

The doctor pondered the question, but the anxiety on their faces convinced him. "As soon as he's moved to an ICU, one of you can go in for three minutes. I'll be in touch." He turned and headed back down the hall at a brisk pace.

"I have to see him," Sarah said. "I need to tell him how much we do care about him."

"Of course, darling," Bob agreed. "You go."

"No," Jenny said firmly. "I'm going in to see him. You had all his life to tell him you love him, but you didn't. I hope you have the rest of your lives to make that up to him. But I'm going to see him tonight. He needs me. Oh, and about the baby..." She felt the last string of oppression being clipped from her heart. "Hal didn't father him. Cage did. I'm carrying Cage's child."

Their mouths fell open in mute surprise, but Jenny was beyond caring whether they approved or not. This time she wouldn't let convention or the habits of a lifetime intimidate her.

"I hope you'll love us all—Cage, me, and the baby." Jenny laid a hand on each of their shoulders and spoke from her heart. "We love you and would like to be a family." She drew a ragged breath and let her hands fall to her sides. The tears she felt flooding her eyes were sniffed away quickly, lest Cage's parents mistake their source as weakness rather than relief. "But if you can't accept us for what we are, if you can't accept the love we have for each other, then that's all right, too. It will be your loss."

Courage and hope bubbled up inside her, and she took heart, smiling through her tears. "I love Cage and he loves me, and I refuse to feel guilty about that. We're going to marry and raise our child, and he'll know every day of his life that he's loved for what he is, not for what we want or expect him to be.''

And half an hour later when the doctor returned to lead one of them down the hall to Cage's ICU, it was Jenny who left the waiting room and went with him.

Epilogue

"What is going on in here?"

"We're taking a bath."

"You're making a mess."

"It's Trent's fault. He's a splasher."

"And who taught him how to splash?"

From the door of the bathroom Jenny smiled at her husband and son, who were both in the bathtub. Seven-month-old Trent was sitting in the crook of his father's lap, his back against Cage's thighs, his chubby feet on Cage's stomach.

"Is he getting clean?"

"Who, Trent? Sure. He's positively squeaky."

Jenny moved into the room and knelt down at the side of the bathtub. Trent, recognizing his mother, smiled droolingly, proudly showing off his two front teeth. He pointed at her and cooed.

"My sentiments exactly, son," Cage said. "She's a knockout, isn't she?"

"She's going to be knocking heads together if you don't get out and mop up this water." Jenny tried to sound stern, but she was laughing as she bent down and lifted Trent from the tub. When she raised him up, she saw the pinkish scar on Cage's abdomen. It never failed to sober her, at least long enough to wing a prayer of thanksgiving heavenward.

"Watch him, he's as slippery as an eel," Cage said, emerging from the bath. Water streamed down his hard, lean body. Jenny had come to learn that he was completely immodest, a trait she relished.

"How well I know." Jenny was trying to hold on to her squirming son while she wrapped a towel around him. She had given up on keeping herself dry. Trent's sturdy little body had already dampened the front of her robe.

She carried the baby into his nursery, which was across the wide hall from the master suite. She had converted one of the bedrooms of the old house into a picture-book nursery for him. Following her instructions, Cage had done most of the actual labor on weekends. They were well pleased with the results.

She was so adroit at handling her wriggling son that by the time Cage joined them, dried and wrapped in a terry robe, Trent was diaper and pajama clad.

"Tell Daddy good night." Jenny held Trent up to receive Cage's kiss. Cage took him from her, hugged him close, and kissed him soundly on the cheek.

"Good night, son. I love you." He hugged the baby to him while Jenny gazed on lovingly. Trent was tired. His head, with its cluster of dusty blond ringlets, dropped onto Cage's shoulder and he yawned broadly.

"He was ready for bed," Jenny said later as they crossed the hall into their own bedroom after seeing that Trent was safely tucked in. "And so am I." She spread her arms out to her sides and fell backward onto the bed. "The two of you wear me out."

"Oh, yeah?" Cage's eyes roamed over her reclining form, from the top of her head to the tips of her toes, which dangled just above the floor. Her robe had fallen open, revealing a beguiling length of smooth, tan thigh. Her breasts looked both wanton and vulnerable with her arms widespread. Without compunction he unknotted the belt of his robe, shrugged it off, let it slide soundlessly to the carpeted floor, and lay down on top of her. His knees wedged hers apart.

"You've got to overcome your shyness, Cage."

"Smart ass." He chuckled as his lips toyed with her ear. She had bathed just before him and Trent, and her skin was warm and fragrant. Beneath the robe she was wearing nothing but a rosy glow. "Why fool around with preliminaries? I believe in going after what I want."

"And you want me?"

"Hm." He pecked innnocent kisses on her neck. "I always have. The longest three months of my life were those after Trent was born."

"Don't forget the weeks before he was born."

"I haven't forgotten," he snarled. "I still say that doctor put the restriction on us earlier than necessary. He was getting back at me for something."

"What?"

"Nothing."

She threaded her fingers through his hair and pulled on it until he raised his head. "What?"

"Ouch!"

"Tell me."

"All right, all right. It's no big deal. Several years ago I dated one of his nurses. When I broke it off, she got upset and left town. He's still holding a grudge."

"How many women did you...romance?"

He became very still. His teasing manner ceased. His eyes probed into hers. "Does it matter, Jenny?"

Her eyes coasted down from his to stare at his throat. "Do you miss it? That carousing?"

"What do you think?" His body nudged apart her robe and she felt him virile and warm against her belly.

"I guess not."

"You guess right."

He kissed her with a passionate hunger that dispelled any lingering doubts. By the time he raised his lips from hers, her blood was pumping hotly through her veins. "I love you, Cage."

"I love you."

"Do you know what today is?"

He thought a moment. "The accident?"

"A year ago today."

"How did you remember that?"

She touched his lips. "Because that's the day I thought I'd lost you. I spent hours sitting in that hospital waiting room, wondering if you would live just long enough for me to tell you how much I love you and how important your life is to me. At first that was all I prayed for. Then, after you survived the surgery, I got greedy and prayed that you'd live to a ripe old age."

One corner of his mouth slanted up into a smile. "I hope God answers your second prayer."

"So do I. But I don't take a single day for granted. I thank Him for every one we have together." They kissed again. This kiss was a reconfirmation of their love.

When they pulled apart, he sank his fingers into her hair and spread it out on the bedspread behind her. "When I regained consciousness in that ICU, the first thing I saw was your face. I wasn't about to die and leave you."

"How much of those first few days do you remember?"

She thought it was strange that they'd never talked much about this. She had scolded and cajoled him through months of convalescence. He wasn't accustomed to being confined and having his activities limited. His psychological adjustment had been as difficult as the physical recovery.

But Jenny's patient diligence had paid off. Much to the doctors' surprise, within months of the accident Cage was back to normal. Better, in fact, the doctors teased him, because he was no longer smoking and wasn't drinking as much.

Then Trent had been born and they had settled into the routine of family life. Cage's business had continued to flourish, as he had been able to conduct it by telephone during his confinement. He now had two people on the payroll, a secretary who had taken over Jenny's position when Trent was born, and a geologist who took the core samples and analyzed them. But it was still Cage who speculated, who talked investors out of their money, who put the deals together, who found the oil.

The past year had been so busy that Jenny had put the harrowing hours and bleak days following the accident out of her mind. She had never really asked Cage about his impressions while he was in the hospital.

"I don't remember much, just that you were always there. One incident stands out. The first time I saw Mother and Dad. I remember trying to smile so they would know how glad I was to see them. Mother took my hand, leaned down, and kissed my cheek. Dad did the same. That might not sound like much, but it meant the world to me."

Jenny sniffed back her tears. "You would have been proud to see me standing up to them, telling them the baby I carried was yours."

The kiss that followed was considerably more heated than the one before. "Mother and Dad have come around," Cage said when they pulled apart. "They're crazy about Trent and think he's the most wonderful baby in the world."

"Wonder where they got the idea?" Teasingly she tweaked a clump of his chest hair. "Between them and Roxy and Gary, he'll be spoiled rotten if we don't keep a lid on their indulgence." She laughed. "You know when I first knew that your folks would accept us?"

"When Dad married us in the hospital room?"

"No," she said, automatically smiling at the memory. "Before that, when Gary called from El Paso, wondering why we weren't at the airport to pick them up when they got home from their honeymoon. I was upset and embarrassed. I had forgotten all about them while you were in intensive care. Bob volunteered to drive to El Paso and bring them home. I knew that if he could accept Roxy, he could accept us."

"You won a few points with them when you set up the Hal Hendren Fund to Aid Political Refugees."

"And you won even more when you made that hefty donation."

"Only because you insisted I match what I spent on your wedding ring."

"You would have anyway."

"I don't know," he hedged, glancing down at the diamond and emerald ring. "That was a damned expensive ring."

She pinched him on his bare bottom. They both laughed and when the laughter subsided, Cage stared down at her, his eyes alight with desire. "You're my darling, Jenny. I adore you. There was no light in my life until you loved me."

"Then that light will shine forever, because that's how long I'll love you."

"Cross your heart?"

"Cross my heart." She reached for his mouth with hers and when they met, their unquenchable desire was ignited. "But you're still a troublemaker," she whispered against his lips.

"I am?"

"Hm. Look what havoc you've wreaked on me." She opened her robe and carried his hand to her breast. He touched the warm fullness, the taut center.

"I did that?"

"Yes. And I used to be such a nice girl. I was led astray."

Lightly he pinched the aroused nipple between his fingers. "I'm a naughty boy, all right."

He lowered his head and rubbed his mouth against the hard, rosy peak. His tongue swept it. Again. "You still taste milky." He suckled her as his son had done until a month before.

Cage seemed to draw nurture from her, too. He got lost in her taste and texture. When he stroked his hand up her thigh, he found her dewy with anticipation. His caressing fingers and revolving thumb brought her to the edge of oblivion. Then his manhood claimed her.

"My God, Jenny, I love you so much."

Time was suspended until the universe split open and showered them with light. It took a long while for them to regain their breath. When they did, Cage eased up and smiled down into her shining face.

Her responding grin was slow and sexy and she all but purred when she said, "You're hell on wheels, Cage Hendren."

And it was good because they could laugh about it.

*   *   *   *   *

New York Times Bestselling Author

Sandra Brown

Tomorrow's Promise

**She cherished the memory
of love but was consumed
by a new passion too
fierce to ignore.**

For Keely Preston, the memory of her husband
Mark has been frozen in time since the day he was
listed as missing in action. And now, twelve years
later, twenty-six men listed as MIA have been
found.

Keely's torn between hope for Mark and despair
for herself. Because now, after all the years of
waiting, she has met another man!

**Don't miss TOMORROW'S PROMISE by
SANDRA BROWN.**

**Available in June wherever Harlequin
books are sold.**

TP

Silhouette Books
is proud to present
our best authors,
their best books...
and the best in
your reading pleasure!

Throughout 1993, look for exciting books
by these top names in contemporary
romance:

CATHERINE COULTER—
Aftershocks in February

FERN MICHAELS—
Nightstar in March

DIANA PALMER—
Heather's Song in March

ELIZABETH LOWELL
Love Song for a Raven in April

SANDRA BROWN
(previously published under
the pseudonym Erin St. Claire)—
Led Astray in April

LINDA HOWARD—
All That Glitters in May

When it comes to passion,
we wrote the book.

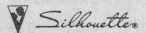

For all those readers who've been looking for something a little bit different, a little bit spooky, let Silhouette Books take you on a journey to the dark side of love with

SILHOUETTE Shadows™

If you like your romance mixed with a hint of danger, a taste of something eerie and wild, you'll love Shadows. This new line will send a shiver down your spine and make your heart beat faster. It's full of romance and more—and some of your favorite authors will be featured right from the start. Look for our four launch titles wherever books are sold, because you won't want to miss a single one.

THE LAST CAVALIER—Heather Graham Pozzessere
WHO IS DEBORAH?—Elise Title
STRANGER IN THE MIST—Lee Karr
SWAMP SECRETS—Carla Cassidy

After that, look for two books every month, and prepare to tremble with fear—and passion.

SILHOUETTE SHADOWS, coming your way in March.

Silhouette®

SHAD1

Sandra Brown

previously published under the
pseudonym Erin St. Claire

This September, look for another
of her great stories . . .

Honor Bound

Lucas Greywolf has taken a hostage—and
Aislinn is nothing if not intrigued by her captor.
In their trek to his Navajo reservation, she is
drawn closer to this unyielding man who drives
himself beyond human limits. And his potent
masculinity drives her to distraction!

Only from 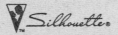 Silhouette®

where passion lives.